# THE STARRY RIFT

# THE STARRY RIFT

## JAMES TIPTREE, JR.

**TOR**

A TOM DOHERTY ASSOCIATES BOOK

THE STARRY RIFT

A TOR Book

Published by Tom Doherty Associates
49 West 24 Street
New York, N.Y. 10010

Cover art by Dave Archer
Cover design by Carol Russo


Printed in the United States

# THE STARRY RIFT

# In the Great Central Library of Deneb University _____

**M**oa Blue, Chief Assistant Librarian, snuffles his way back to the Historical Specialties carousel. His snuffling is partly constitutional—Moa is an amphibian—and partly directed at his current customers, two impossibly cheerful young Comenor. They are asking for a selection of Human fact/fiction from the early days of the Federation, "to get the ambience." A selection! In Moa's days as a student, you did the selecting yourself. The hard way. Now these two want to pick his brains.

Well, he can satisfy them. There've been a lot of similar requests this term—probably some ambitious instructor offering an "enriched" course. Moa sneezes definitively and punches up a readout.

When he comes back to the front, the young Comeno couple are leaning their upper arms on the counter, a sign of seriousness. Each also has an upper arm entwined with the other's, a likely sign of mating intent. Moa Blue's stern reptilian face softens; he has a tender spot for romance, if the truth be known. And also a soft spot for Comenor, who are known to like actual reading and learning alien psychology. In a student body full of engineering types briskly scanning tapes full of numbers, it's pleasant to encounter students who like the touch and feel of old books, and who know that the real problems lie in living hearts and brains.

"As you doubtless know," he tells them, "there's been a long Human vogue for what they call fact/fiction. That is, taking a crucial event or epoch with all its known details, and reconstructing it as a dramatic story. They claim it makes history more easily memorable; I daresay they're right. In any event, it gives you quite a hoard to choose from."

"That's why we need your help," smiles the taller Comeno, in richly accented Galactic. "We took one look at the inventory and got lost, even with the summaries."

"And you shall have help. Here's a nice little one I picked for you to start with. It's from way back before Humans had much FTL capability, and were just starting to explore the fringes of that great Rift that separates you from the Federation. In fact, I've chosen a group set in the Rift locale, both because you know it, and because it's about the same time-period as that well-known story about the explosion-front from the Murdered Star passing the planet Damiem, which you were probably assigned in class—but it's on the very opposite side of the Federation, so you'll get some interesting anomalies and contrasts. You *have* encountered Damiem and the Stars Tears business, haven't you? *Brightness* something, it's called."

"*Brightness Falls From the Air*—oh, yes, it was offered as an example of Human behavior toward other races. In fact, it started our interest in Humans. But it's so localized—something in a totally different sector is just what we need. Does this one have the Moom shipping lines, for instance?"

"No. You must realize that in pre-FTL days all cultural diffusion took place incredibly slowly. And this was well after the Ziellor and you were using it routinely."

"My goodness, you certainly have to know a lot of technological history!" says the smaller Comeno admiringly.

Moa smiles, a toothy effect that would have been intimidating in a different context. "Sometimes I think I should take every course in the syllabus, to serve our clients properly! . . . Now, I can't issue more than this one at a time, but it'll give you plenty to think over; it's from quite an unusual point of view."

"But is it all *true?*" the little Comeno asks anxiously.

"That's the remarkable part—the story is almost entirely taken from actual tapes dictated by the little Human herself. All that is extrapolated is a group of highly predictable subjective responses corroborated by other sources. And it involves one of the Humans' most extraordinary First Contacts, all in the alien's own words. . . . The Eeadron are well known now, of course—you may have come across the quarantine regs."

"I have," says the tall Comeno. "So this explains that, too! Well you *have* found a star for us, Myr Blue. We thank you more than I can say."

"Oh, yes!" chimes in his friend.

"And when you return I'll have one almost as good, and then there'll be a real treat for finale."

"Oh, thank you, thank you!" And with a resounding ceremonial tail-clap, they hurry toward the door, carefully clasping the ancient text.

# First Tale
# The Only Neat Thing
# to Do

Heroes of space! Explorers of the starfields!

Reader, here is your problem:

Given one kid, yellow-head, snub-nose-freckles, green-eyes-that-stare-at-you-level, rich-brat, girl-type fifteen-year-old. And all she's dreamed of, since she was old enough to push a hologram button, is heroes of First Contacts, explorers of far stars, the great names of Humanity's budding Star Age. She can name you the crew of every Discovery Mission; she can sketch you a pretty accurate map of Federation space and number the Frontier Bases; she can tell you who first contacted every one of the fifty-odd races known; and she knows by heart the last words of Han Lu Han, when, himself no more than sixteen, he ran through alien flame-weapons to drag his captain and pilot to safety, on Lyrae 91-Beta. She does a little math, too; it's easy for her. And she haunts the spaceport and makes friends with everybody who'll talk to her, and begs rides, and knows the controls of fourteen models of craft. She's a late bloomer, which means that the nubbins on her little chest could almost pass for a boy's; and love, great Love, to her is just something pointless that adults do, despite her physical instruction. But she can get into her junior space-suit in seventy seconds flat, including safety hooks.

So you take this girl, this Coati Cass—her full name is Coatillia Canada Cass, but everyone calls her Coati—

And you give her a sturdy little space-coupe for her sixteenth birthday.

Now, here is your problem:

Does she use it to jaunt around the star-crowded home sector, visiting her classmates and her family's friends, as her mother expects, and sometimes showing off by running a vortex beacon or two, as her father fears?

Does she? Really?

Or—does she head straight for the nearest ship-fitters and blow most of her credit balance loading extra fuel tanks and long-range sensors onto the coupe, fuel it to the nozzles, and then—before the family's accountant can raise questions—hightail for the nearest Federation Frontier, which is the Great North Rift beyond FedBase 900, where you can look right out at unknown space and stars?

That wasn't much of a problem, was it?

The Exec of FedBase 900 watches the yellow head bobbing down his main view corridor.

"We ought to signal her folks *c*-skip collect," he mutters. "I gather they're rich enough to stand it."

"On what basis?" his deputy inquires.

They both watch the little straight-backed figure marching away. A tall Patrol captain passes in the throng; they see the girl spin to stare at him, not with womanly appreciation but with the open-eyed unself-conscious adoration of a kid. Then she turns back to the dazzling splendor of the view beyond the port. The end of the Rift is just visible from this side of the asteroid Base 900 is dug into.

"On the basis that I have a hunch that that infant is trouble looking for a place to happen," Exec says mournfully. "On the basis that I don't believe her story, I guess. Oh, her ident's all in order, I've no doubt she owns that ship and knows how to run it, and knows the regs; and it's her right to get cleared for where she wants to go—by a couple of days. But I cannot believe her parents consented to her tooting out here just to take a look at unknown stars. . . . On the basis that if they did, they're certifiable imbeciles. If she were my daughter . . ."

His voice trails off. He knows he's overreacting emotionally; he has no adequate excuse for signaling her folks.

"They must have agreed," his deputy says soothingly. "Look at those extra fuel tanks and long-range mechs they gave her."

(Coati hadn't actually lied. She'd told him that her parents raised no objection to her coming out here—true, since they'd never dreamt of it —and added artlessly, "See the extra fuel tanks they put on my ship so

I'll be sure to get home from long trips? Oh, sir, I'm calling her the *CC-One;* will that sound too much like something official?"

Exec closes the subject with a pessimistic grunt, and they turn back into his office, where the Patrol captain is waiting. FedBase 900's best depot supply team is long overdue, and it is time to declare them officially missing and initiate and organize a search.

Coati Cass continues on through the surface sections of the base to the fueling port. She had to stop here to get clearance and the holocharts of the Frontier area, and she can top off her tanks. If it wasn't for those charts, she might have risked going straight on out, for fear they'd stop her. But now that she's cleared, she's enjoying her first glimpse of a glamorous Far FedBase—so long as it doesn't delay her start for her goal, her true goal, so long dreamed of: free, unexplored space and unknown, unnamed stars.

Far Bases *are* glamorous; the Federation had learned the hard way that they must be pleasant, sanity-promoting duty. So, the farther out a Base is, and the longer the tours, the more lavishly it is set up and maintained. Base 900 is built mostly inside a big, long-orbit airless rock, yet it has gardens and pools that would be the envy of a world's richest citizen. Coati sees displays for the tiny theater advertising first-run shows and music, all free to station personnel; and she passes half a dozen different exotic little places to eat. Inside the rock, the maps show sports and dance shells, spacious private quarters, and kilometers upon kilometers of winding corridors, all nicely planted and decorated, because it has been found that stress is greatly reduced if there are plenty of alternative, private routes for people to travel to their daily duties.

Building a Far Base is a full-scale Federation job. But it conserves the Federation's one irreplaceable resource—her people. Here at FedBase 900 the people are largely Human, since the other four space-faring races are concentrated to the Federation's south and east. This far north, Coati has glimpsed only one alien couple, both Swain; their greenish armor is familiar to her from the spaceport back home. She won't find really exotic aliens here.

But what, and who, lives out there on the fringes of the Rift—not to speak of its unknown farther shores? Coati pauses to take a last look before she turns in to Fuels and Supply. From this port she can really see the Rift, like a strange, irregular black cloud lying along the northern zenith.

The Rift isn't completely lightless, of course. It is merely an area that holds comparatively few stars. The scientists regard it as no great mystery; a standing wave or turbulence in the density-texture, a stray chunk

of the same gradients that create the Galactic arms with their interven-
ing gaps. Many other such rifts are seen in uninhabited reaches of the
starfield. This one just happens to form a useful northern border for the
irregular globe of Federation space.

Explorers have penetrated it here and there, enough to know that the
usual distribution of star-systems appears to begin again on the farther
side. A few probable planetary systems have been spotted out there; and
once or twice what might be alien transmissions have been picked up at
extreme range. But nothing and no one has come at them from the far
side, and meanwhile the Federation of Fifty Races, expanding slowly to
the south and east, has enough on its platter without hunting out new
contacts. Thus the Rift has been left almost undisturbed. It is the near
presence of the Rift that made it possible for Coati to get to a real
Frontier so fast, from her centrally located home star and her planet of
Cayman's Port.

Coati gives it all one last ardent look and ducks into the suiting-up
corridor, where her small suit hangs among the real Spacers'. From
here she issues onto a deck over the asteroid surface and finds *CC-One*
dwarfed by a new neighbor; a big Patrol cruiser has come in. She makes
her routine shell inspection with disciplined care, despite her excitement, and presently signals for the tug to slide her over to the fueling
stations. Here she will also get oxy, water, and food—standard rations
only. She's saved enough credits for a good supply if she avoids all
luxuries.

At Fuels she's outside again, personally checking every tank. The
Fuels chief, a big rosy woman whose high color glows through her
faceplate, grins at the kid's eagerness. A junior fuelsman is doing the
actual work, kidding Coati about her array of spares.

"You going to cross the Rift?"

"Maybe next trip. . . . Someday for sure." She grins back.

A news announcement breaks in. It's a pleasant voice, telling them
that DRS number 914 B-and-K is officially declared missing, and a
phase one search will start. All space personnel are to keep watch for a
standard supply tug, easily identifiable by its train of tanks, last seen in
the vicinity of Ace's Landing.

"No, correction, negative on Ace's Landing. Last depot established
was on a planet at seventeen-fifty north, fifteen-thirty west, RD eighteen." The voice repeats. "That's in Far Quadrant Nine B-Z, out of
commo range. They were proceeding to a new system at thirty-twenty
north, forty-two–twenty-eight West, RD three D.

"All ships within possible range of this course will maintain a listening watch for one minim on the hour. Anything heard warrants return to Base range. Meanwhile a recon ship will be dispatched to follow their route from Ace's Landing."

The announcer repeats all coordinates; Coati, finding no tablet handy, inscribes the system they're headed to on the inside of her bare arm with her stylus.

"If they were beyond commo range, how did they report?" she asks the Fuels chief.

"By message pipe. Like a teeny-weeny spaceship. They can make up to three $c$-skip jumps. When you work beyond range, you send back a pipe after every stop. There'll soon be a commo relay set up for that quadrant, is my guess."

"Depot Resupply nine fourteen BK," says the fuelsman. "That's Boney and Ko. The two boys who—who're—who aren't—I mean, they don't have all their rivets, right?"

"There's nothing wrong with Boney and Ko!" The Fuels chief's flush heightens. "They may not have the smarts of some people, but the things they do, they do one hundred percent perfect. And one of them, or both, maybe, have uncanny ability with holocharting. If you go through the charts of quadrants they've worked, you'll see how many BK corrections there are. That work will save lives! And they haven't a gram of meanness or pride between them, they do it all on supply pay, for loyalty to the Fed." She's running down, glancing at Coati to see if her message carried. "That's why Exec took them off the purely routine runs and let them go set up new depots up north. . . . The Rand twins have the nearby refill runs now, they can take the boredom because of their music."

"Sorry," the fuelsman says. "I didn't know. They never say a word."

"Yeah, they don't talk." The chief grins. "There, kid, I guess you're about topped up, unless you want to carry some in your ditty bag. Now, how about the food?"

When Coati gets back inside Base and goes to Charts for her final briefing, she sees what the Fuels chief meant. On all the holocharts that cover the fringes of 900's sector, feature after feature shows corrections marked with a tiny glowing "BK." She can almost follow the long, looping journeys of that pair—what was it? Boney and Ko?—by the areas of richer detail in the charts. Dust-clouds, gee-anomalies, asteroid swarms, extra primaries in multiple systems, all modestly BK's. The basic charts are composites of the work of early explorers—somebody called Ponz has scrawled in twenty or thirty star-systems with his big signature (BK have corrected six of them), and there's an "L," and a lot of "YBC" and more that Coati can't decipher. She'd love to know their names and adventures.

"Who's 'SS'?" she asks Charts.

"Oh, he was a rich old boy, a Last War vet, who tried to take a shortcut he remembered and jumped himself out of fuel way out there. He was stuck about forty-five Standard days before anybody could get to him, and after he calmed down, he and his pals kept themselves busy with a little charting. Not bad, too, for a static VP. See how the SSs all center around this point? That's where he sat. If you go near there, remember the error is probably on the radius. But you aren't thinking of heading out *that* far, are you, kid?"

"Oh, well," Coati temporizes. She's wondering if Charts would report her to the Exec. "Someday, maybe. I just like to have the charts to, you know, dream over."

Charts chuckles sympathetically and starts adding up her charges. "Lots of daydreaming you got here, girl."

"Yeah." To distract him she asks, "Who's 'Ponz'?"

"Before my time. He disappeared somewhere after messaging that he'd found a real terraform planet way out that way." Charts points to the northwest edge, where there's a string of GO-type stars. "Could be a number of good planets there. The farthest one out is where the Lost Colony was. And that you stay strictly away from, by the way, if you ever get that far. Thirty-five–twelve N. That's thirty minutes twelve seconds north, thirty-forty west. We omit the degrees; out here they're constants: eighty-nine degrees north by seventy west. Radial distance— that's from Base Nine hundred, they all are—thirty-two Bkm. Some sort of contagion wiped them out just after I came. We've posted warning satellites. . . . All right, now you have to declare your destination. You're entitled to free charts there, the rest you pay for."

"Where do you recommend? For my first trip?"

"For your first trip . . . I recommend you take the one beacon route we have, up to Ace's Landing. That's two beacons, three jumps. It's a neat place, hut, fresh-water lake, the works. Nobody lives there, but we have a rock-hound who takes all his long leaves there, with a couple of pals. You can take out your scopes and have a spree, everything you're looking at is unexplored. And it's just about in commo range if you hit it lucky."

"How can places be out of commo range? I keep hearing that."

"It's the Rift. Relativistic effects out here where the density changes. Oh, you can pick up the frequency, but the noise, the garble factor, is hopeless. Some people claim even electronic gear acts up as you really get into the Rift itself."

"How much do they charge to stay at the hut?"

"Nothing, if you bring your own chow and bag. Air and water's perfect."

"I might want to make an excursion farther on to look at something I've spotted in the scope."

"Green. We'll adjust the chart fee when you get back. But if you run around, watch out for this vortex situation here." Charts pokes his stylus into the holo, north of Ace's Landing. "Nobody's sure yet whether it's a bunch of little ones or a great big whopper of a gee-pit. And remember the holos don't fit together too well—" He edges a second chart into the first display; several stars are badly doubled.

"Right. And I'll keep my eyes open and run a listening watch for that lost ship, BK's."

"You do that. . . ." He tallies up an amount that has her credit balance scraping bottom. "I sure hope they turn up soon. It's not like them to go jazzing off somewhere. . . . Green, here you are."

She tenders her voucher chip. "It's go." She grins. "Barely."

Still suited, lugging her pouch of chart cassettes, Coati takes a last look through the great view-wall of the main corridor. She has a decision to make. Two decisions, really, but this one isn't fun—she has to send something to her parents, and without giving herself away to anybody who checks commo. Her parents must be signaling all over home sector by now. She winces mentally, then has an idea: Her sister on a planet near Cayman's has married enough credits to accept any number of collect 'skips, and it would be logical— Yes.

Commo is two doors down.

"You don't need to worry," she tells a lady named Pauna. "My brother-in-law is the planet banker. You can check him in that great big ephemeris there. Javelo, Hunter Javelo."

Cautiously, Pauna does so. What she finds on Port-of-Princes reassures her enough to accept this odd girl's message. Intermittently sucking her stylus, Coati writes:

*Dearest Sis, Surprise! I'm out at FedBase 900. It's wonderful. Will look around a bit and head home, stopping by you. Tell folks all okay, ship goes like dream, and million thanks. Love, Coati.*

There! That ought to do it without alerting anybody. By the time her father messages FedBase 900, if he does, she'll be long gone.

And now, she tells herself, heading out to the port, now for the big one. Where exactly should she go?

Well, she can always take Charts' advice and have a good time on
Ace's Landing, scanning the skies and planning her next trip. She's
become just a little impressed by the hugeness of space and the chill of
the unknown. Suppose she gets caught in an uncharted gravity vortex?
She's only been in one, and it was small, and a good pilot was flying.
(That was one of the flights she didn't tell her folks about.) And there's
always next time.

On the other hand, she's *here* now, all set. And her folks could raise
trouble next time she sets out. Isn't it better to do all she can while she
can do it?

Well, like what, for instance?

Her ears had pricked up at Charts' remark about those GO-type
suns. And one of them was where the poor lost team was headed for,
she has the coordinates on her wrist. What if she found them! Or—what
if she found a fine terraform planet, and got to name it!

The balance of decision, which had never really leveled, tilts deci-
sively toward a vision of yellow suns—as Coati all but runs into the
ramp edge leading out.

A last flicker of caution reminds her that, whatever her goal, her first
outward leg must be the beacon route to Ace's. At the first beacon turn
she'll have time to think it over and really make up her mind.

She finds that *CC-One* has been skidded out of Fuels and onto the
edge of the standard-thrust takeoff area. She hikes out and climbs in,
unaware that she's broadcasting a happy hum. This is *it!* She's really,
really, at last, on her way!

Strapping in, preparing to lift, she takes out a ration snack and bites
it open. She was too broke to eat at Base. Setting course and getting into
drive will give her time to digest it; she has a superstitious dislike of
going into cold-sleep with a full tummy. Absolutely nothing is supposed
to go on during cold-sleep, and she's been used to it since she was a
baby, but the thought of that foreign lump of food in there always
bothers her. What puts it in stasis before it's part of her? What if it
decided to throw itself up?

So she munches as she sets the holochart data in her computer, leaving FedBase 900 far below. She's delightedly aware that the realest part
of her life is about to begin. Amid the radiance of unfamiliar stars, the
dark Rift in her front view-ports, she completes the course to Beacon
900-One, AL, and listens to the big *c*-skip converters, the heart of her
ship, start the cooling-down process. The *c*-skip drive unit must be
supercooled to near absolute zero to work the half-understood miracle

by which reciprocal gravity fields will be perturbed, and *CC-One* and herself translated to the target at relativistic speed.

As the first clicks and clanks of cooling resound through the shell, she hangs up her suit, opens her small-size sleep-chest, gets in, and injects herself. Her feelings as she pulls the lid down are those of a child of antique Earth as it falls asleep to awake on Christmas morning. Thank the All for cold-sleep, she thinks drowsily. It gave us the stars. Imagine those first brave explorers who had to live and age, to stay awake through all the days, the months, the years . . .

She wakens in what at first glance appears to be about the same starfield, but when she's closed the chest, rubbing her behind where the antisleep injections hit, she sees that the Rift looks different.

It's larger, and—why, it's all around the ship! Tendrils of dark almost close behind her. She's in one of the fringy star-clumps that stick out into the Rift. And the starfield looks dull, apart from a few blazing suns —of course, there aren't any nearby stars! Or rather, there are a few very near, and then an emptiness where all the middle-distance suns should be. Only the far, faint star-tapestry lies beyond.

The ship is full of noise; as she comes fully awake, she understands that the beacon signal and her mass-proximity indicator are both tweeting and blasting away. She tunes them down, locates the beacon, and puts the ship into a slow orbit around it. This beacon, like FedBase, is set on a big asteroid, which gives her just enough gees to stabilize.

Very well. If she's going to Ace's Landing, she'll just set in the coordinates for Beacon 900-Two, AL, and go back to sleep. But if she's going to look at those yellow suns, she must get out her charts and work up a safe two- or three-leg course to one of them.

She can't simply set in their coordinates and fly straight there, even if there were no bodies actually in the way, because the 'skip drive is built to turn off and wake her if she threatens to get too deep in a strong gravity field or encounters an asteroid swarm or some other space hazard. So she has to work out corridors that pass really far away from any strong bodies or known problems.

Decide . . . But face it, hadn't she already decided when she stabilized here? She doesn't need that much time to punch in Beacon Two. . . . Yes. She *has* to go somewhere really wild. A hut on Ace's Landing is just not what she came out here for. Those unknown yellow suns *are* . . . and maybe she could do something useful, like finding the missing men; there's an off chance. The neat thing to do might be to go by small steps. Ace's Landing first—but the *really* neat course is to take advantage of all she's learned and not to risk being forbidden to come back, green, go!

She's been busy all this while, threading cassettes and getting them lined up for those GO suns. As Charts had warned her, edges don't fit well. She's working at forcing two holos into a cheap frame made for one, when her mass-proximity tweeter goes off.

She glances up, ready to duck or deflect a sky-rock. Amazed, she sees something unmistakably artificial ahead. A ship? It grows larger—but not large enough, not at the rate it's coming. It'll pass her clean. Whatever can it be? Visions of the mythical tiny ship full of tiny aliens jump to her mind.

It's so small—why, she could pick it up! Without really thinking, she spins *CC-One*'s attitude and comes parallel, alongside the object. She's good at tricky little accelerations. The thing seems to put on speed as she idles up. Touched by chase fever, she mutters, "Oh, no you don't!" and extrudes the rather inadequate manipulator-arm.

As she does so, she realizes what it is. But she's too excited to think; she plucks it neatly out of space and, after a bit of trying, twists it into her cargo-lock, shuts the port behind it, and refills with air.

She's caught herself a message pipe! Bound from the gods know where to FedBase. It was changing course at Beacon One, like herself, hence moving slowly. Has she committed an official wrong? Is there some penalty for interfering with official commo?

Well, she's put her spoon in the soup, she might as well drink it. It'll take a while for the pipe to warm to touchability. So she goes on working her charts, intending merely to take a peak at the message and then send the little thing on its way. Surely such a small pause won't harm anything—pipes are used because the sender's out of range, not because they're fast.

She hasn't a doubt she can start it going again. She's seen it's covered with instructions. Like all Federation space-gear, it's fixed to be usable by amateurs in an emergency.

Impatiently, she completes a chart and goes to fish the thing out of the port while it's still so cold she has to put on gloves. When she undoes its little hatch, a cloud of golden motes drifts out, distracting her so that she brushes her bare wrist against the metal when she reaches for the cassette inside. Ouch!

She glances at her arm, hoping she hasn't given herself a nasty cold-burn. Nothing to be seen but an odd dusty scratch. No redness. But she can feel the nerves twitch deep in her forearm. Funny! She brushes at it and takes out the cassette with more care. It's standard record, she soon has it threaded in her voder.

The voice that speaks is so thick and blurry that she backs up and restarts, to hear better.

"Supply and Recon Team number nine fourteen BK reporting," she makes out. Excitedly she recognizes the designation. Why, that's the missing ship! This *is* important. She should relay it to Base at once. But surely it won't hurt to listen to the rest?

The voice is saying that a new depot has been established at thirty-twenty north, forty-two–twenty-eight west, RD twenty-seven. That's one of the yellow suns' planets; and the coordinates Coati has on her wrist. "Ninety-five percent terraform." The voice has cleared a little.

It goes on to say that they will work back to FedBase, stopping to check a highly terraform planet they've spotted at eighteen-ten north, twenty-eight–thirty west, RD twenty-seven, in the same group of suns. "But—uh . . ." The voice stops, then resumes.

"Some things happened at thirty-twenty. There're people there. I guess we have to report a, uh, First Contact. They—"

A second voice interrupts abruptly.

"We did just like the manual! The manual for First Contacts."

"Yeah," resumes the first voice. "It worked fine. They were really friendly. They even had a few words from Galactic, and the signals. But they—"

"The wreck. The wreck! Tell them," says the other voice.

"Oh. Well, yeah. There's a wreck there, an old RB. Real old. You can't see the rescue flag, it has big stuff growing on it. We think it's Ponz. So maybe it's his First Contact." The voice sounds unmistakably downcast. "Boss can decide . . . Anyway, they have some kind of treatment they give you, like a pill to make you smart. It takes two days, you sleep a lot. Then they let you out and you can understand everything. I mean—everything! It was—we never had anything like that before. Everybody talking and understanding everybody! See how we can talk now? But it's funny . . . Anyway, they helped us find a place with a level site and we fixed up a fuel dump really nice. We—"

"What they looked like!" the other voice butts in. "Never mind us. Tell about them, what they looked like and how they did."

"Oh, sure. Well. Big white bodies with fur all over. And six legs, they mostly walk on the back four, the top two are like arms. They have like long bodies, long white cats, big; when they rear up to look, they're over our heads. And they have . . ." Here the voice stammers, as if finding it hard to speak. "They have like two, uh, private parts. Two sets, I

mean. Some of them. And their faces"—the voice runs on, relieved—
"their faces are *fierce.* Some teeth! When they came and looked in first,
we were pretty nervous. And big eyes, sort of like mixed-up people and
animals. Cats. But they acted friendly, they gave back the signals, so we
came out. That was when they grabbed us and pushed their heads onto
ours. Then they let us go, and acted like something was wrong. I heard
one say, 'Ponz,' and like 'Lashley' or 'Leslie.' "

"Leslie was with Ponz, I told you," says the second.

"Yeah. So then they grabbed us again and held on, that was when
they gave the treatment. I think something went into me, I can still hear
like a voice. Ko says him, too. . . . Oh, and there were young ones and
some others running around on an island, they said they're not like
them until they get the treatment. 'Drons' they called the young ones.
And afterwards they're 'Ee-ah-drons.' The ones we talked to. It's sort of
confusing. Like the Ee-ah are people, too. But you don't see them." His
voice—it must be Boney—runs down. "Is that all?" Coati hears him
ask aside.

"Yeah, I guess so," the other voice—Ko—replies. "We better get
started, we got one more stop . . . and I don't feel so good anymore. I
wish we was home."

"Me too. Funny, we felt so great. Well, DRS nine fourteen BK signing off. . . . I guess this is the longest report we ever sent, huh? Oh, we
have some corrections to send. Stand by."

After a long drone of coordinate corrections, the record ends.

Coati sits pensive, trying to sort out the account. It's clear that a new
race has been contacted, and they seem friendly. Yet something about it
affects her negatively—she has no desire to rush off and meet the big
white six-legs and be given the "smart treatment." Boney and Ko were
supposed to be a little—innocent. Maybe they were fooled in some way,
taken advantage of? But she can't think why, or what. It's beyond
her. . . .

The other thing that's clear is that this should go to Base, fastest.
Wasn't there a ship going to follow Boney and Ko's route? Which
would take them to the cat-planet, that's at—she consults her wrist—
yes, thirty-twenty north, et cetera. Oh, dear, must she go back? Turn
back, abort her trip, to deliver this? Why had she been so smart, pulling
in other people's business?

But wait—maybe she's still in commo range. In fact—why, if it's
urgent, she could speed it by calling Base and reading the message, thus
bypassing the last leg. Then surely they wouldn't crack her for interfering!

She powers up the transponder and starts calling FedBase 900. Finally a voice responds, barely discernible through the noise. She fiddles with the suppressors, gets it a bit clearer.

"FedBase Nine hundred, this is *CC-One* at AL Beacon One. Do you read me? I have intercepted a message pipe from Supply Ship DRS nine fourteen BK, the missing ship. Boney and Ko." She repeats. "Do you read that?"

"Affirmative, *CC-One*. Message from nine fourteen B-and-K intercepted. What is the message?"

"It's too long to read. But listen—important. They are on their way to a planet at—wait a minim—" She rolls the record back and gets the coordinates. "And before that they stayed at that planet thirty-twenty north, you have the specs. There are people there! It's a First Contact, I think. But listen, they say something's funny. I don't think you should go there until you get the whole message. I'm sending it right on."

"*CC-One*, I lost part of that. Is planet at thirty-twenty north a First Contact?"

Garble is breaking up Commo's voice. Coati shouts as clearly as she can, "Yes! Affirmative! But don't, repeat do—not—go—there—until you get B-and-K's original message. I—will—send—pipe—at once. Did you get that?"

"Repeating . . . Do not proceed to planet thirty-twenty north forty-two–twenty-eight west until BK message received. Pipe coming soonest. Green, *CC-One?*"

"Go. If I can't make the pipe work I'll bring it. *CC-One* signing off." She finishes in a swirl of loud static and turns her attention to getting the pipe back on its way.

But before she takes the cassette out of the voder, she rechecks the designation of the planet BK are headed for. Eighteen-ten north, twenty-eight–thirty west, RD twenty-seven. That's closer than the First Contact planet; that's right, they said they'd stop there on their way home. She copies the first coordinates off her work-pad and replaces those on her wrist with the new ones. If she wants to help look for Boney and Ko, she could go straight there—but of course she hasn't really made up her mind. As she rolls back her sleeve, she notices that her arm still feels odd, but she can't see any trace of a cold-burn. She rubs the arm a couple of times and it goes away.

"Getting goosey from excitement," she mutters. She has a childish habit of talking aloud to herself when she's alone. She figures it's because she was alone so much as a child, happily playing with her space toys and 'grams.

Putting the message pipe back on course proves to be absurdly simple. She blows it clean of the yellow powdery stuff, reinserts the cassette, and ejects it beside the view-ports. Fascinated, she watches the little ship spin slowly, orienting to its homing frequency broadcast from Base 900. Then, as if satisfied, it begins to glide away, faster and faster. Sure enough, as well as she can judge, it's headed down the last leg from Beacon One to Far Base. Neat! She's never heard of pipes before; there must be all kinds of marvelous Frontier gadgets that'll be new to her.

She has a guilty twinge as she sees it go. Isn't it her duty to go nearer back to Base and read the whole thing? Could the men be in some kind of trouble where every minim counts? But they sounded green, only maybe a little tired. And she understands it's their routine to send a pipe after every stop. If some of those corrections are important, she could never read them straight, her voice would give out. Better they have Boney's own report.

She turns back to figuring out her course and finds she was fibbing; she has indeed made up her mind. She'll just go to the planet BK were headed for and see if she can find them there. Maybe they got too sick to move on, maybe they found another alien race they got involved with. Maybe their ship's in trouble. . . . Any number of reasons they could be late, and she *might* be helpful. And now she knows enough about the pipes to know that they can't be sent from a planet's surface. Only from above atmosphere. So if Boney and Ko can't lift, they can't message for help—by pipe, at least.

She's half talking this line of reasoning out to herself as she works on the holocharts. Defining and marking in a brand-new course for the computer is far more work than she'd realized; the school problems she had done must have been chosen for easy natural corridors. "Oh, gods . . . I've got to erase again, there's an asteroid path there. Help! I'll never get off this beacon at this rate—explorers must have spent half their time mapping!"

As she mutters, she becomes aware of something like an odd little echo in the ship. She looks around; the cabin is tightly packed with shiny cases of supplies. "Got my acoustics all buggered up," she mutters. That must be it. But there seems to be a peculiar delay; for example, she hears the word "Help!" so tiny clear that she actually spends a few minim searching the nearby racks. Could a talking animal pet or something have got in at Far Base? Oh, the poor creature. Unless she can somehow get it in cold-sleep it'll die.

But nothing more happens, and she decides it's just the new acoustical reflections. And at last she achieves a good, safe three-leg course to that system at eighteen-ten north. She's pretty sure an expert could pick out a shorter, elegant, two-leg line, but she doesn't want to risk being waked up by some unforeseen obstacle. So she picks routes lined by well-corrected red dwarfs and other barely visible sky-features. These charts are living history, she thinks. Not like the anonymous holos back home, where everything is checked a hundred times a year, and they only give you trip-strips. In those charts she can read the actual hands of the old explorers. That man Ponz, for instance, he must have spent a lot of time working around the route to the yellow suns, before he landed on thirty-twenty and crashed and died. . . . But she's dawdling now. She stacks the marked cassettes in order in her computer take-up and clicks the first one in. To the unknown, at last!

She readies her sleep-chest and hops in. As she relaxes, she notices she still has a strange sensation of being accompanied by something or someone. "Maybe because I'm sort of one of the company of space, now," she tells herself romantically, and visualizes a future chart with a small "CC" correction. Hah! She laughs aloud, drowsily, in the darkness, feeling great. An almost physical rosy glow envelops her as she sinks to dreamless statis.

She can take off thus unconscious amid pathless space with no real fear of getting lost and being unable to return, because of a marvelously simple little gadget carried by all jump-ships—a time-lapse recorder in the vessel's tail, which clicks on unceasingly, recording the star-scene behind. It's accelerated by motion in the field, and slows to resting state when the field is static. So, whenever the pilot wishes to retrace his route, he has only to take out the appropriate cassette and put it up front in his guidance computer. The computer will hunt until it duplicates the starfield sequences of the outward path, thus bringing the ship infallibly, if somewhat slowly, back along the course it came.

She wakes and jumps out to see a really new star-scene—a great sprawl of radiant golden suns against a very dark arm of Rift. The closest star of the group, she finds, is eighteen-ten north, just as she's calculated! The drive has cut off at the margin of its near gravity field; it will be a long thrust-drive in.

Excitement like a sunrise is flooding her. She's made it! Her first solo jump!

And with the mental joy is still that physical glow, so strong it puzzles her for a minim. Physical, definitely; it's kind of like the buzz of self-stimulation, but without the stickly-sickly feeling that usually gives her. Their phys. ed. teacher, who'd showed them how to relieve sex tension, said that the negative quality would go away, but Coati hasn't bothered with all that very much. Now she thinks that this shows that sheer excitement can activate sex, as the teacher said. "Ah, go away," she mutters impatiently. She's got to start thrust-drive and run on in to where the planets could be.

As soon as she's started, she turns to the scope to check. Planets—yes! One—two—four—and there it is! Blue green and white even at this distance! Boney and Ko had said it tested highly terraform. It looks it all right, thinks Coati, who had seen only holos of antique Earth. She wonders briefly what the missing nonterraform part could be; irregularities of climate, absence of some major life-forms? It doesn't matter—anything over 75 percent means livable without protective gear, air and water present and good. She'll be able to get out and explore in the greatest comfort—on a *new* world! But are Boney and Ko already there?

When she gets into orbital distance from the planet, she must run a standard search pattern around it. All Federation ships have radar-responsive gear to help locate them. But her little ship doesn't have a real Federation search-scope. She'll have to use her eyes and fly much too narrow a course. This could be tedious; she sighs.

She finds herself crossing her legs and wiggling and scratching herself idly. Really, this sex overflow is too much! The mental part is fairly calm, though, almost like real happiness. Nice. Only distracting. . . . And, as she leans back to start waiting out the run in, she feels again that sense of *presence* in the ship. Company, companionship. Is she going a little nutters? "Calm down," she tells herself firmly.

A minim of dead silence . . . into which a tiny, tiny voice says distinctly:

"Hello . . . hello? Please don't be frightened. Hello?"

It's coming from somewhere behind and above her.

Coati whirls, peers up and around, everywhere, seeing nothing new.

"Wh-where are you?" she demands. "Who are you, in here?"

"I am a very small being. You saved my life. Please don't be frightened of me. Hello?"

"Hello," Coati replies slowly, peering around hard. Still she sees nothing. And the voice is still behind her when she turns. She doesn't feel frightened at all, just intensely excited and curious.

"What do you mean, I saved your life?"

"I was clinging to the outside of that artifact you call a message. I would have died soon."

"Well, good." But now Coati *is* a bit frightened. When the voice spoke, she definitely detected movement in her own larynx and tongue —as if she's speaking the words herself. Gods—she *is* going nutters, she's hallucinating! "I'm talking to myself!"

"No, no," the voice—her voice—reassures her. "You are correct—I am using your speech apparatus. Please forgive me, I have none of my own that you could hear."

Coati digests this dubiously. If this is an hallucination, it's really complex. She's never done anything like this before. Could it be real, some kind of alien telekinesis?

"But where are you? Why don't you come out and show yourself?"

"I can't. I will explain. Please promise me you won't be frightened. I have damaged nothing and I will leave any time you desire."

Coati suddenly gets an idea and eyes the computer sharply. In fantasy shows she's seen holos about alien minds taking over computers. So far as she knows, it's never happened in reality. But maybe—

"Are you in my computer?"

"Your computer?" Incredibly, the voice gives what might almost be a giggle. "In a way, yes. I told you I am very, very small. I am in, in empty places, in your head." Quickly, it adds, "You aren't frightened, please? I can go out any time. But then we can't speak."

"In my head!" Coati exclaims. For some reason she, too, feels like laughing, she knows she should be making some more serious response, but all she can think of is that this is why her sinuses feel stuffy. "How did you get in my head?"

"When you rescued me. I was incapable of thought. We have a primitive tropism to enter a body and make our way to the head. When I came to myself, I was here. You see, on my home, we live in the brains of our host-animals. In fact, we are their brains."

"You went through my body? Oh—from that place on my arm?"

"Yes, I must have done. I have only vague, primitive memories. You see, we are really so small. We live in what I think you call intermolecular, maybe interatomic spaces. Our passage doesn't injure anything. To me, your body is as open and porous as your landscape is to you. I didn't realize there was so much large-scale solidity around until I saw it through your eyes! Then when you went cold, I came to myself and learned my way around, and deciphered the speech centers. I had a long, long, time. It was . . . lonely. I didn't know if you would ever awaken. . . ."

"Yeah. . . ." Coati thinks this over. She's pretty sure she couldn't imagine all this. It must be *real!* But all she can think of to say is, "You're using my eyes, too?"

"I've tapped into the optic nerve, at the second juncture. *Very* delicately, I assure you. And to your auditory channels. It's one of the first things we do, a primitive program. And we make the host feel happy, to keep from frightening. You do feel happy, don't you?"

"Happy? . . . Hey, are *you* doing that? Listen, if that's you, you're overdoing it! I don't want to feel quite so 'happy,' as you call it. Can you turn it down?"

"You don't? Oh, I *am* sorry. Please wait—my movements are slow."

Coati waits, thinking so furiously about everything at once that her mind is a chaos. Presently there comes a marked decrease in the distracting physical glow. More than all the rest, this serves to convince her of the reality of her new inhabitant.

"Can you read my mind?" she asks slowly.

"Only when you form words," her own voice replies. "Subvocalizing, I think you call it. I used all that long cold time tracing out your vocabulary and language. We have a primitive drive to communication. Perhaps all life-forms have."

"Acquiring a whole language from a static, sleeping brain is quite a feat," says Coati thoughtfully. She is beginning to feel a distinct difference in her voice when the alien is using it; it seems higher, tighter— and she hears herself using words that she knows only from reading, not habitual use.

"Yes. Luckily I had so much time. But I was so dismayed and depressed when it seemed you'd never awaken. All that work would be for nothing. I am so happy to find you alive! Not just for the work, but for —for life. . . . Oh, and I have had one chance to practice with your species before. But your brain is quite different."

However flustered and overwhelmed by the novelty of all this, Coati isn't stupid. The words about "home" and "hosts" are making a connection with Boney and Ko's report.

"Did the two men who sent that message you were riding on visit your home planet? They were two Humans—that's what I am—in a ship bigger than this."

"Oh, yes! I was one of those who took turns being with them! And I was visiting one of them when they left. . . ." The voice seems to check itself. "Your brain is really very different."

"Thanks," says Coati inanely. "I've heard those two men—those two Humans—weren't regarded as exactly bright."

" 'Bright'? Ah, yes. . . . We performed some repairs, but we couldn't do much."

Coati's chaotic thoughts coalesce. What she's sitting here chatting with is an alien—an *alien* who is possibly deadly, very likely dangerous, who has invaded her head.

"You're a *brain parasite!*" she cries loudly. "You're an intelligent brain parasite, using my eyes to see with and my ears to hear with, and talking through my mouth as if I were a zombie—and for all I know you're taking over my whole brain!"

"Oh, please! P-please!" She hears her own voice tremble. "I can leave at any moment—is that what you wish? And I damage nothing—nothing at all. I use very little energy. In fact, I have cleared away some debris in your main blood supply tube, so there is more than ample for us both. I only need a few components from time to time. But I can withdraw right now. It would be a slow process, because I've become more deeply enmeshed and my mentor isn't here to direct me. But if that's what you want, I shall start at once, leaving just as I came. . . . Maybe—n-now that I'm refreshed, I could survive longer, clinging to your ship."

The pathos affects Coati; the timbre of the voice calls up the image of a tiny, sad, frightened creature shivering in the cold prison of space.

"We'll decide about that later," she says somewhat gruffly. "Meanwhile, I have your word of honor you aren't messing up my brain?"

"Indeed not," her own voice whispers back indignantly. "It is a beautiful brain."

"But what do you want? Where are you trying to go?"

"Now I want only to go home. I thought, if I could reach some central Human place, we could find someone who would carry me back to my home planet Nolian, and my proper host."

"But why did you leave Boney and Ko and go with that message pipe in the first place?"

"Oh—I had then no idea how *big* the empty spaces are, I thought it would be like a long trip out-of-body at home. Brrr-rr! There's so much I don't know. Can you tell that I am a quite young being? I have not at all finished my instructions. My mentors tell me I am foolish, or foolhardy. I—I wanted adventure!" The little voice sounds suddenly quite strong and positive. "I still do, but I see I must be better prepared."

"Hmm. Hey, can you tell I'm young, too? I guess that makes two of us. I guess I'm out here looking for adventure, too."

"You do understand!"

"Yeah." Coati grins, sighs. "Well, I can carry you back to FedBase, and I'm sure they'll be sending parties to your planet soon. It's a First Contact for us, you know; that's what we call meeting a new non-

Human race. We know about fifty so far, but no one just like you. So
I'm certain people will be going."

"Oh, thank you! Thank you so much."

Coati feels a surge of physical pleasure, an urge—

"Hey! You're doing *that* again! Stop it."

"Oh, I am sorry." The glow fades. "It's a primitive response to gratitude. To give pleasure. You see, our normal hosts are quite mindless,
they can be thanked only by physical sensation."

"I see." Pondering this, Coati sees something else, too.

"I suppose you could make them feel pain, too, to punish them, if
they did something you didn't like?"

"I suppose so. . . . But we don't like pain, it churns up the delicate
brain. That's some of the lessons I haven't had yet. I only had to once,
when my host was playing too near a dangerous cliff. And then I
soothed it with pleasure right after it moved back. We use it only in
emergencies, if the host threatens to harm itself, rare things like that.
. . . Or, wait, I remember, if the host gets into what you call a *fight*.
. . . You can see it's complicated."

"I see," Coati repeats. Uneasily, she realizes that this young alien
passenger might have more control over her than was exactly neat. But
it seems to be so well meaning, to have no intent at all to harm her. She
relaxes, unable to suppress a twinge of wonder whether her easy emo-
tional acceptance of its presence in—whew! her *brain*—might not be a
feeling partly engineered by the alien. Maybe the *really* neat thing to do
would be to ask her passenger to withdraw, right now. Could she fix
some comfortable place for it to stay outside her? Maybe she'll do that,
when they get a bit closer to FedBase.

Meanwhile, what about her plan for visiting the planet Boney and Ko
were headed for? If she could pick up a trace of them, it would be a real
help to FedBase. And wouldn't it be a shame to come all this way out
without taking a look?

That argument with herself is soon over. And her young appetite is
making itself felt. She picks out a ration snack and starts to set the drive
course for the planets, explaining between munches what she plans to
do before return to FedBase. Her passenger raises no objection to this
delay.

"I am so grateful, so grateful you would think to deliver me," her
voice says with some difficulty around the cheese bites.

As Coati opens the cold-keeper, a flash of gold attracts her attention.
It's more of that gold dust, clinging to the chilly surface. She bats it
away, and some floats to her face.

"By the way, what is this stuff? It came in the message pipe, with you. Can you see it? Hey, it's on my legs, too." She extends one.

"Yes," her "different" voice replies. "They are seeds."

She's getting used to this weird dialogue with herself. It reminds her of a show she saw, where a ventriloquist animated a dummy. I'm a ventriloquist's dummy, she chuckles to herself. Only I'm the ventriloquist, too.

"What kind of seeds, of what?" she asks aloud.

"Ours." There's a sound, or feeling, like a sigh, as if a troubling thought had passed. Then her voice says more briskly, "Wait, I forgot. I should release a chemical to keep them off you. They are attracted to— to the pheromones of life."

"I didn't know I knew those words," Coati tells her invisible companion. "I guess you were really into my vocabulary while I slept."

"Oh, yes. I labored."

A moment later Coati feels a slight flush prickling her skin. Is this the "chemical"? Before she can feel alarmed, it passes. And she sees that the floating dust, or seeds, have fallen away from her as if repelled by a charge.

"Good-o." She eats a bit more, finishing the course set. "That reminds me, what do you call your race? And you, you must have a name. We should get better acquainted!" She laughs for two; all sense of trouble has gone.

"I am of the Eea, or Eeadron. Personally I'm called Syllobene."

"Hello, Syllobene! I'm Coati Cass. Coati."

"Hello, Coati Cass Coati."

"No, I meant, just Coati. Cass is my family name."

"Ah, 'family.' We wondered about that, with the other Humans."

"Sure, I'll be glad to explain. But later—" Coati cuts herself off. "I mean, there'll be plenty of time to explain everything, while we slowly approach the planet orbiting that star. And I think I'm entitled to your story first, Syllobene, since I'm providing the body. Don't you agree that's fair?"

"Oh, yes. I must take care not to be selfish, when you do so much."

Somehow this speech, for the first time, conveys to Coati that her passenger really is a young, almost childish being. The big words it had found in her mind had kept misleading her. But now Syllobene sounds so much like herself reminding herself of her manners. She chuckles again, benignly. Could it be that they are two kids—even two females— together, out looking for adventure in the starfields? And it's nice to have this unexpected companion; much as Coati loves to read and view, she's beginning to get the idea that a lot of space voyaging consists of lonely sitting and waiting, when you aren't in cold-sleep. Of course, she guiltily reminds herself, she could be checking the charts to see if all the coordinates of the relatively few stars out here are straight. But Boney and Ko have undoubtedly done all that—after all, this was their second trip to this sun; on the first one they merely spotted planets. And learning about an alien race is surely important.

She leans back comfortably, and asks, "Now, what about your planet? What does it look like? And your hosts—how does that work? How did such a system ever evolve in the first place? Hey, I know—can you make me see an image, a vision of your home?"

"Alas, no. Such a feat is beyond my powers. Making speech is the utmost I can do."

"Well, tell me about it all."

"I will. But first I must say, we have no such—no such material equipment, no such *technology* as you have. What techniques we have are of the mind. I am filled with amazement at all you do. Your race has achieved marvels! I saw a distant world when I looked through your device—a world! And you speak of visiting it as casually as we would go to a lake or a tree farm. A wonder!"

"Yes, we have a lot of technology. So do some other races, like the Swain and the Moom. But I want *yours*, Syllobene! To start with, what's this business of Eea and Eeadron?"

"Ah. Yes, of course. Well, I personally, just myself, am an Eea. But when I am in my proper host, which is a Dron, I am an Eeadron. An Eea by itself is almost nothing. It can do nothing but wait, depending on its primitive tropisms, until a host comes by. It is very rare for Eea to become detached as you found me—except when we are visiting another Eeadron for news or instruction. And then we leave much of ourselves in place, in our personal Dron, to which we return. I, being young, was able to detach myself almost completely to go with the Humans as one of their visitors."

"Oh—were there other Eeas inside Boney and Ko when they took off?"

"Yes—one each, at least."

"What would you call that—Eeahumans?" Coati laughs.

But her companion does not seem to join in. "They were very old," she hears herself mutter softly. And then something that sounds like, "No idea of the length of the trip . . ."

"So you came away when they messaged. Whew—wild act! Oh, Syllobene, I'm so glad I intercepted it and saved you."

"I, too, dear Coati Cass."

"But now we've got to get serious about this crazy system of yours. Are you the only people on your planet that have their brains in separate bodies? Oh, wait. I just realized we should record all this, we'll never be able to go over it twice. Hold while I put in a new cassette."

She gets set up and bethinks herself to make it sound professional with an introduction.

"This is Coati Cass recording, on board the *CC-One*, approaching unnamed planet at—" She gives all the coordinates, the standard date and time, and the fact that Boney and Ko were last reported to be headed toward this planet.

"Before that, they landed on a planet at thirty-twenty north and reported a First Contact with life-forms there. Their report is in a message forwarded to Base before I came here. Now it seems that when they left that planet, some of the life-forms came with them, specifically two at least of the almost invisible Eea, in their heads. And some seeds, and another Eea, a very young one, who came along, she says, for the adventure. This young Eea moved to the message pipe, not realizing how long the trip would be, and was almost dead when I opened the pipe. She—I call it she because we haven't got sexes, if any, straightened out yet—she moved over to me when I opened the pipe, and is right now residing in my head, where she can see and hear through my senses, and speak with my voice. I am interviewing her about her planet, Nolian. Now, remember all the voice you hear will be mine—but I myself am the one asking the questions. I think you will be soon able to tell when Syllobene—that's her name—is speaking with my voice; it's higher and sort of constricted, and she uses words I didn't know I knew. She learned all that while I was in cold-sleep coming here. Now, Syllobene, would you please repeat what you've told me so far, about the Eea and the Eeadron?"

Coati has learned to relax a little while her own voice goes on, and she hears Syllobene start with a nice little preface: "Greetings to my Human hearers!" and go on to recite the Eea-Eeadron system.

"Now," says Coati, "I was just asking whether the Eea are the only life-forms on their planet to have their brains in separate animals, so to speak."

"Oh, no," says her Syllobene voice, "it is general in our, ah, animal world. In fact we are still amazed that there is another way. But always in other animals the two are very closely attached. For instance, in the Enquaalons, the En is born with the Quaalon, mates when it mates, gives birth when it does, and dies when it dies. The same for all the En

—that is what we call the brain-animal, except for ourselves, the Eea. Only the Eea are so separate from the Dron, and do not die when their Dron dies. . . . But we have seen aged Endalamines—that is the nearest animal to the Eeadron—holding their heads against newborn Dalamines, as though the En was striving to pass to a new body, while the seed-Ens proper to that newborn hovered about in frustration. We think in some cases they succeed."

"So you Eea can pass to a new body when yours is old! Does that make you immortal?"

"Ah, no, Eea too age and die. But very slowly. They may use many Dron in a lifetime."

"I see. But tell about your society, your government, and how you get whatever you eat, and so on. Are there rich and poor, or servants and master Eeadron?"

"No, if I understand those words. But we have farms—"

And so by random stages and probings, Coati pieces together a picture of the green-and-golden planet that Syllobene calls Nolian, with its sun, Anella, all ruled over by the big white Eeadron, who have no wars and only the most rudimentary monetary system. The climate is so benign that housing is largely decorative, except for shelter from the nightly mists and drizzles. It seems a paradise. Their ferocious teeth, which had so alarmed Boney and Ko, derive from a forgotten, presumably carnivorous past; they now eat plant products and fruits. (Here Coati recollects that certain herbivorous primates of antique Earth also had fierce-looking canines.)

As to material technology, the Eeadron have the wheel, which they use for transporting farm crops and what few building materials they employ. And long ago they learned to control fire, which they regard almost as a toy except for some use in cooking. Their big interest now appears to be the development of a written code for their language; they picked up the idea from Ponz and Leslie. It's a source of great pleasure and excitement, although some of the older Eea, who serve as the racial memory, grumble a bit at this innovation.

Midway through this account, Coati has an idea, and when Syllobene runs down she bursts out, "Listen! Oh—this is Coati speaking—you said you cleaned out my arteries, my blood tubes. And you cure other hosts. Would you—I mean, your race—be interested in being healers to other races like mine, who can't heal themselves? We call such healers *doctors*. But our doctors can't get inside and really fix what's wrong, without cutting the sick person up. Why, you could travel all over the Federation, visiting sick people and curing them—or, wait, you could set up a big clinic, and people, Humans and others, would come from everywhere to have the Eea go into them and fix their blood vessels, or their kidneys, or whatever was wrong. Oh, hey—and they'd *pay* you—you're going to need Federation credits—and everybody would love you! You'd be the most famous, valuable race in the Federation!"

"Oh, oh—" replies the Syllobene voice, sounding breathless, "I don't know your exclamations! We would say:" She gives an untranslatable trill of excitement. "How amazing, if I understand you—"

"Well, we can talk about that later. Now, you learned about Humans from what you call visiting, in the brains of Boney or Ko, is that right?"

"Yes. But if I had not had the experience of visiting my mentor and a few other Eeadron, I would not have known how to enter and live there without causing damage. You see, the brains of the Dron are just un-formed matter; one can go anywhere and eat anything without ill effect in the host's brain. In fact, it is up to the Eea to form them. . . . And, I almost forgot, my mentor was old; and was one of those who had known the living Humans, Ponz and Leslie. The two who landed vio-lently and died. They were beyond our powers to cure them, but we could abolish their pain. I believe they mated before they died, but no seeds came. My mentor told me how your brains are, with everything developed and functioning. We are still amazed."

"Why do you visit other Eeadron?"

"To learn many facts about some subject in a short time. We send out tendrils—I think you have a word, for your fungus plants—mycelium. Very frail threads and knots, permeating the other brain—I believe that is what I look like in your brain now—and by making a shadow-pattern in a certain way, we acquire all sorts of information, like history, or the form of the landscapes, and keep it intact when we withdraw."

"Look, couldn't you learn all about Humans and the Federation by doing that in my head?"

"Oh, I would not dare. Your speech centers alone frightened me with their complexity. I proceeded with infinite care. It was lucky I had so much time while you slept. I wouldn't dare try anything more delicate and extensive and emotion-connected."

"Well, thanks for your consideration. . . ." Coati doesn't want to stall the interview there, so she asks at random, "Do you have any social problems? Troubles or dilemmas which concern your whole race?"

This seems to puzzle the Eea. "Well, if I understand you, I don't think so. Oh, there is a heated disagreement among two groups of Eeadron as to how much interest we should take in aliens, but that has been going on ever since Ponz. A panel of senior councillors—is that the word for old wise ones?—are judging it."

"And will the factions abide by their judgment?"

"Oh, naturally. It will be wiped from memory."

"Whew!"

"And . . . and there is the problem of a shortage of *faleth* fruit trees. But that is being solved. Oh—I believe I know one social problem, as you put it. Since the Eea are becoming personally so long-lived, there is arising a reluctance to mate and start young. Mating is very, ah, disruptive, especially to the Dron body. So people like to go along as they are. The elders have learned how to suppress the mating urge. For example, I and my siblings were the only young born during one whole season. There are still plenty of seeds about, you saw them, but they are becoming just wasted. Wasted . . . I think I perceive something applicable in your verbal sayings, about nature."

"Huh? Oh—'Nature's notorious wastefulness,' right?"

"Yes. But our seeds are very long-lived. Very. And that golden coat, which is what you see, is impervious to most everything. So maybe all will be well."

Her informant seems to want to say no more on this topic, so Coati seizes the pause to say, "Look, our throat—*my* throat—is about to close up or break into flames. Water!" She seizes the flask and drinks. "I always thought that business of getting a sore throat from talking too much was a joke. It isn't. Can't you *do* something, Doctor Syllobene?"

"I can only block off some of the inflamed channels, and help time do its work. I could abolish the pain, but if we used it, it would quickly grow much worse."

"You sound like a doctor already," Coati grumbles hoarsely. "Well, we'll just cut this off here—oh, I wish I had one of those message pipes! Ouch . . . Then we'll have some refreshments—I got some honey, thank the gods—and take a nap. Cold-sleep doesn't rest us, you know. Could you take a sleep, too, Syllobene?"

"Excellent idea." That hurts.

"Look, couldn't you learn just to nod my head like this for 'yes' or like this for 'no'?"

Nothing happens for a moment, then Coati feels her head nod gently as if elfin fingers were brushing her chin and brow, yes.

"Fantastic," she rasps. "Ouch."

She flicks off the recorder, takes a last look through the scope at the blue-green-white planet—still far, far ahead—sets an alarm, and curls up comfortably in the pilot couch.

"Sleep well, Syllobene," she whispers painfully. The answer is breathed back, "You, too, dear Coati Cass."

Excitement wakes her before the alarm. The planet is just coming into good bare-eye view. But when she starts to speak to Syllobene, she finds she has no voice at all. She hunts up the med-aid kit and takes out some throat lozenges.

"Syllobene," she whispers. "Hello?"

"Wha—er, what? Hello?" Syllobene discovers whispering.

"We've lost our voice. That happens sometimes. It'll wear off. But if it's still like this when we get on the planet, you'll *have* to do something so we can record. You can, can't you?"

"Yes, I believe so. But you must understand it will make it worse later."

"Green."

"What?"

"Green . . . means I understand, too. Listen, I'm sorry about your turn to ask questions. That'll be later. For now we'll just shut up."

"I wait."

"Go."

"What?"

"Oh, green, go—that means, understood and we will proceed on that course." Coati can scarcely force out the words.

"Ah, informal speech . . . most difficult . . ."

"Syl, this is killing me. We shut up *now*, green?"

A painful giggle. "Go."

Some hot tea from the snack pack proves soothing. Meanwhile, the enforced silence gives Coati a chance to think things over, for the first time. She is, of course, entranced by the novelty of it all and seriously stirred by the idea that Syllobene's race could provide the most astounding, hitherto inconceivable type of medical help to the others. If they want to. And if a terrible crowd jam doesn't ensue. But that's for the big minds to wrestle out.

And, like the kid she is, she relishes the sensation she fancies her return will provoke—with a real live new alien carried in her head! But gods, they won't be able to *see* Syllobene—suppose they jump to the obvious conclusion that Coati's gone nutters and hustle her off to the hospital? She and Syl better talk that over before they get home; Syllobene has to be able to think of some way to prove she exists.

Funny how firmly she's taken to thinking of Syllobene as "she," Coati muses. Is that just sheer projection? Or—after all, they're in pretty intimate contact—is this some deep instinctive perception, like one of Syl's "primitive tropisms"? Whatever, when they get it unscrambled, it'll be a bit of a shock if Syl's a young "he" . . . or, gods forbid, an "it" or a "them." What was that Boney had said about the Dron, that some of them had two sets of "private parts"? That'd be his modest term for sex organs; he must have meant they were like hermaphrodites. Whew. Well, that still doesn't necessarily mean anything about the Eea.

When they can talk, she must get things straightened out. And until then, not get too romantically fixated on the idea that they're two girls together.

All this brings her to a sobering sense of how little she really knows about the entity she's letting stay in her head—in her very brain. If indeed Syl was serious about being able to leave. . . . With this sobriety comes, or rather, surfaces, a slight, undefined sense of *trouble.* She's had it all along, she realizes. A peculiar feeling that there's more. That all isn't quite being told her. Funny, she doesn't suspect Syl herself of some bad intent, of being secretly evil. No. Syllobene is *good,* as good as she can be; all Coati's radar and perceptions seem to assure her of that. But nevertheless this feeling persists—it's coming clearer as she concentrates—that something was making the alien a little sad and wary now and then—that something troubling to Syl had been touched on but not explored.

The lords know, she and Syl had literally talked all they could, Syl had answered every question until their voice gave out. But Coati's sense of incompleteness lingers. Let's see, when had it been strongest? . . . Around that business of the seeds in the message pipe, for one. Maybe every time they touched on seeds. Well, seeds were being wasted. That meant *dying.* And a seed is a living thing; an encysted, complete beginning of a new life. Not just a gamete, like pollen, say. Maybe they're like embryos, or even living babies, to Syllobene. The thought of hundreds of doomed babies surely wouldn't be a very cheerful one for Coati herself.

Could that be it? That Syl didn't want to go into the sadness? Seems plausible. Or, wait—what about Syl herself? By any chance did she want to mate, and now she can't—or, *had* she—and that's the mystery of where those seeds in the message pipe had come from? Whew! Is Syl old enough, is she sexually mature? Somehow Coati doesn't think so, but again, she knows so little—not even that Syl's a she.

As she ruminates, her eyes have been on the front view-ports, where the planet is rapidly growing bigger and bigger. She must put her wonderments aside, with the mental note to question Syl at the first oppor-

tunity. In a few minim it'll be time to kill the torches and go on antigrav
for the maneuvers that will bring her into a close-orbit search pattern.
She will have to fly a lot of extra orbits, doing the best she can by eye
and with her narrow little civilian radarscope. It'll be tedious; not for
the first time, she deplores the unsuitability of a little sports coupe for
serious exploration work.

The planet still looks remarkably like holos of Terra. It has two big
ice caps, but only three large landmasses set in blue ocean. It looks cold,
too. Cloud-cover is thin, wispy cirrus. And for many degrees south of
the northern ice, the land is a flat gray green, featureless except for an
intricate shallow lake system, which changes from silver to black as her
angle of reflection changes. Like some exotic silken fabric, Coati thinks.
The technical name for such a plain is tundra, or maybe muskeg.

No straight lines or curves, no dams, no signs of artificial works,
appear. The place appears devoid of intelligent life.

Hullo, what's this ahead? A twinkling light is rounding the shadowed
curve of the planet, far enough out to catch the sun. That's reflected
light; the thing is tumbling slowly. Coati slows and turns to the scope.
Big sausage tanks! Such tanks must belong to a DRS, a depot resupply
ship. Boney and Ko must have left them in orbit before they landed.
And they wouldn't omit to pick them up when they left; that means the
men are here. Oh, good. That'll give her the enthusiasm to sit out a
long, boring search.

She tunes up every sensor on *CC-One* and starts the pattern while
she's still, really, too far out. This is going to be a long chore, unless
some really wild luck strikes.

And luck does strike! On her second figure-eight orbit, she sees an
immense blackened swath just south of the northern ice cap. A burn.
Can it have been caused by lightning or vulcanism? Or even a natural
meteorite?

No . . . on the next pass she can see a central line of scorch, growing as it leads north, with a perceptible zigzag such as no incoming
natural object could make. She clicks on the recorder and whisperingly
reports the burn and the tanks in orbit.

On the third pass she's sure. There's a gleam at the north end of the
burn-scar.

"Oh, the poor men! They must have been sick, they had to correct
course with rockets. . . . Syl! Syllobene! Are you awake?"

"Uh—hello?" her voice mumbles. Funny to hear herself sounding
sleepy.

"Look, you have to do something to our throat so I can report; I think I've found the men."

"Oh. Yes. Wait . . . I fear I need nourishment. . . ."

"Go right ahead. Be my guest."

For an instant Coati pictures Syl sipping blood, like a vampire; but no, Syl is too small. It'll be more like the little being snagging a red-blood corpuscle or two as they rush by. Weird. Coati doesn't feel the least bit nervous about this. Syl had said she's increased the blood flow overall. And in fact Coati herself feels great, very alert and well. They *would* make wonderful healers, she thinks.

The gleam at the end of the burn is definitely a ship; the scope shows her a big Federation supply tug. Her calls on Fed frequencies bring no response. She kills the search pattern and prepares to land on antigrav. The plain beside the strange ship looks good. But maybe there was another reason for their use of torches, she thinks; those two men were superexperienced planetary pilots. Maybe this place has weird mascons or something that had to be corrected for. She'd better keep alert and be ready to torch if she finds her course going unsteady.

When she calls the supply ship again, her voice is back and her throat suddenly feels great.

"Hey, thanks, Syl."

"Coati, why are we landing?"

"The Humans you left are down somewhere on the planet. They were never heard of after you left them, they're officially missing. That means, everybody search. Now I've found their ship, but they don't answer. I have to land and find out what's happened to them. So you'll get to see a strange planet."

The news doesn't seem to cheer her little passenger, who only repeats, "We must land?"

"Oh, yes. Among other things, they may need help."

"Help. . . ." Syllobene's voice repeats, with an odd, almost bitter inflection.

But Coati is too busy to brood over this. "What condition were they in when you left them, Syl?"

"Ohhh . . ." Her throat sighs. "I do not know your race well enough to tell what is normal. They were speaking of going to cold-sleep when I withdrew and left them. I was trying to hurry because I understood that the message device would soon be sent out. As I said, it's a slow process. As soon as I was dependent on my Eea senses, the men were too large to perceive—for example, I could no longer discern the sound waves of their voices."

Coati thinks this over as she gentles the ship down through thick atmosphere. Her ablation-shielding isn't all that good.

"Syl, you have just as much technology in your way as we do. Imagine going back and forth from the molecular to the molar scales!"

"Yes. It *is* a big learning. Very frightening the first time, when we're taught to visit."

"You said there were other Eea in Boney and Ko?"

"Yes . . . but I couldn't establish good contact, and they controlled everything. That's why I slipped away, when I understood about the message device."

Coati grins. "I can understand that, Syl. But you took an awful chance."

She feels the elfin hands nod her head emphatically. "You are my savior."

"Oh, well. I didn't know it. But if I had known it, I would have got you off there, Syllobene. I *couldn't* have let you die in space."

A feeling of indefinable warmth and real happiness glows within her. Coati understands. There is genuine friendship between her and her tiny alien passenger.

The recorder has been clicking away as they talked. But of course it won't show her feelings. Pity.

"Just for the record," she says formally, "I have, uh, subjective reasons to believe that this alien has sincere feelings of friendship for me. I mean for me, not just as a convenience. I think that's important. I feel the same toward Syl."

It's time to set *CC-One* down. With all care, Coati jockeys her little ship in above the big supply tug and comes down neatly beside it. Nothing untoward shows up. That must mean that Boney and/or Ko were really in wobbly condition when they came in.

The atmosphere tests out green, but still she suits up for her first trip out. As her ports open she gets her first good look at the DRS.

"Their ramp's down," she tells the 'corder. "And, hey, the port's ajar! Not good. I'm going in. . . . Hello! Hello in there! . . . . Oh!"

Her voice breaks off. Sounds of footsteps, squeak of ports being pulled.

"Oh, my. What a mess. There were gloves on the ramp—and the inside looks like they didn't clean anything up for a long time. I see food dishes and cassettes and a suit—wait, two suits—in a heap on the deck, as if they'd just jumped out of them. Oh, dear, this looks like trouble. . . . I think somebody threw up here. . . . There's a lot of those goldy seeds around everywhere, too."

She prowls the cabin, reporting as she checks the sleep-chests and any place a man-sized body could be. Nothing. And the big cargo-hold is empty too, except for a carton of supplies bound somewhere.

She comes outside, saying, "I think I should try to find them. The ground here is soft, like peat, with low vegetation or whatever, and I can see trampled places. There's one big place that looks like a trail leading"—she checks her bearings—"leading north, of all things. The atmosphere is highly Human-compatible, lots of oxy. I have my helmet off. So I'm going to try to follow their trail. But just in case I get into trouble, I think I better send this record off first. It has all about Syl's planet on it. Lords, I wish I could send it from the surface. I guess I'll have to lift above atmosphere. I'm taking some of their message pipes over to my ship. So here goes. It's the only neat way to do."

She sighs, clicks off, and gets back into her ship.

Preparing to lift off, she says, "You're very quiet, Syllobene. Are you all right?"

"Oh, yes. But I am—I am afraid."

"Afraid of what? Walking around on a strange planet? Listen, I do have a hand weapon in case we run into big wild vicious beasts. But I don't think there's anything like that around here. Nothing for a carnivore to eat."

"No . . . I am not afraid of the planet. I fear . . . what you will find."

Coati is maneuvering her ship up for a fast single orbit and return. "What do you mean, Syl?" she asks a trifle absently.

"Coati, my friend"—it sounds weird to hear her name in her own voice—"I wish to wait until you search. Perhaps I am wrong. I hope so."

"Well-ll, green, if you must." Coati is preoccupied with opening a message pipe. "Oh, bother, there's some of those little yellow dust-seeds in here. How do I clear them out? I don't want to kill them—you say they can live in space, like you—but I don't think they should get loose in FedBase, do you?"

"No! No!"

"Look, I'm sorry about your seeds. I just want to make them get out of this pipe. How do I do that?"

"Heat. High heat."

"Huh . . . Oh, I know." She clicks the recorder on and tells it what she's doing. "I'm going to put it in my food heater, and run it to one twenty C. That won't hurt the cassette. . . . All right, I'm taking it out with tongs. By the gods, there's a couple of those seeds coming out of the 'corder as it gets near heat. All out, you. I will now end this record as I remove the cassette to send. *CC-One* signing off, before returning to planet to search for B-and-K.

"Good thing we did that," she tells Syl as she closes the pipe and puts it in the lock to be blown out. "Here goes the air. And there goes the pipe! I hope the Base frequency reaches this far. . . . Yes, it does. Neat, how the little thing knows where to go. Bye-bye, you. . . . Funny, I'm getting a feeling like we're a long, long way from anywhere. Being a space adventurer can be a trifle spooky." She noses the ship over into landing mode, thinking, I'm going down to hike over a strange planet looking for two people who, face it, may be very dead. . . .

"Syllobene?"

"Yes?"

"I'm really glad I have you for a friend here. Hey, maybe there's another thing your people could do, I mean, for credits: going with lonely space people on long trips!"

"Ah . . ."

"I was just joking. . . . Or was I?"

Soon they are back on the planet, beside the abandoned DRS. Coati puts on planetary weather gear and tramping shoes. It's sunny but bleak, outside. She packs a week's rations and some water, although the ground is spongy wet. Then she clips the recorder to her shoulder and carefully loads it with a fresh cassette.

A long time later, after Coati has been officially declared missing, the same fresh cassette, its shine somewhat dimmed, is in the hands of the deputy to the Exec of FedBase 900. It is about to be listened to by a group of people in the Exec's conference room.

Weeks before, the message that Coati had lifted off-planet to send had arrived at FedBase. The staff has heard all about Syllobene and the Eea, and the Eeadron, and the Drons and all the other features of Syllobene's planet, Nolian, and her short trip with Boney and Ko; they have left Coati and her brain-passenger about to go back down to the unnamed planet on which sits Boney and Ko's empty ship.

One of the group of listeners now is not of FedBase.

When that first message had come in, the Exec had signaled the Cass family, and Coati's father is now in the room. He looks haggard; he has worn out his vocabulary of anger—particularly when he found that no rescue mission was being planned.

"Very convenient for you, Commander," he had sneered. "Letting a teenage girl do your dirty work. I say it's your responsibility to look for your own missing men, and to go get my daughter out of there and free her from that damn brain parasite. You should never have let her go way out there in the first place! If you think I'm not going to report this—"

"How do you suggest I could have stopped her, Myr Cass? She injected herself of her own free will into an ongoing search, without consulting anyone. If anyone is to blame for her being out here, it's you. It was your responsibility to have some control over your daughter's travels in that ship you gave her. Meanwhile my responsibility is to my people, and I'm not justified in risking another ship pursuing a Federation citizen on her voluntary travels."

"But that cursed alien in her—"

"Yes. To be blunt about it, Myr Cass, your daughter is already infected, if that's the word, and she has given us evidence of the great mobility and potential for contagion of these small beings. We have probably already lost the men who first visited them. Now I suggest we quiet down and listen to what your daughter has to say. It may be that your concerns are baseless."

Grumblingly, Cass senior subsides.

"This message pipe has been heated, too," says the deputy. "The plastic shows it. From which we can infer that she was compos mentis and probably in her own ship when she sent it."

The recording starts with a few miscellaneous bangs and squeaks.

"I've decided to take another look at BK's ship before I start," Coati's voice says. "Maybe they left a message or something."

The 'corder clicks off and on again.

"I've been hunting around in here," says Coati. "No message I can see. There's a holocam focused on the cabin, but it's been turned off. Hey, I bet the Feds like to keep an eye on things, for cases like this. I'll root around by the shell."

Clicks—off, on.

"I've spotted what I think is another holocam up in the bow, I heard it click. . . . How can I get at it? Oh, wait, maybe from outside." Off —on. "Yo-ho! I got it. It's in time-lapse mode; I think it caught the terrain around the ship. We'll just take it over to my ship and run it."

Click, off.

Exec shifts uneasily. "I believe she's discovered the planetary recorder. I'm not sure the two men knew it was there."

"That must be the additional small cassette in this pipe," the deputy says.

The recorder has come on. "It's really small," Coati is saying. "Hey, it's full of your seeds, Syllobene. Those things must like cassettes. I'm threading it—here we go. "Oh, my, oh, my— Syllobene!"

"This is my home," says Coati in what they have come to recognize as the voice of the alien speaking through Coati's throat. "Oh, my beautiful home! . . . But what a marvel, how do you—"

"Later," Coati cuts herself off. "Later we'll look at it all you want. Right now we have to run it ahead to where it shows this planet and maybe the two men we're looking for."

"Yes— Oh, that was my mentor—"

"Oh, gods, I'd love to look. But I'm speeding up now." Sounds of fast clicking, incoherent small sounds from Coati's Syllobene-voice.

"See, now they've taken off. It'll be stars for a long time, nothing but the starfield." Furious clicks. "Gods, I hope it doesn't run out."

"No fear," says the deputy. "These things are activated by rapid action in the field. When the action is as slow as a passing starfield, it reverts to its resting rate of about a frame an hour—maybe a frame a day, I forget. Only a passing rock or whatnot will speed them up briefly."

"Here we are," says Coati's voice. "I see that great string of GO suns. . . . Yes, they seem to be heading in to the planet now, I'd need a scope to tell—ah! It's getting bigger. That's it all right. . . . Closer, closer . . . they're going into orbit. But Syl, look at that frame wobble. I tell you, whoever's flying is not all right. . . . Oo-oops—that could be changing pilots, or maybe switching over to the rockets. Oh, dear . . . yes, they're coming in like a load of gravel, I'm glad I know they made it. . . . Smoke now, nothing but smoke. Their torches have hit. Down —I see flames. This must be action-activated; there'll be a pause now, but we can't tell how long. I know this doesn't mean much to you, Syl, wait till the smoke clears—ah! Look, there's the landscape we saw around the ship, right?"

The alien voice makes a small murmur.

"Action again—that's the edge of the ramp. Here comes one of the men—now the other—which is which? I'll call the tall thin one Boney. Oh, dear gods, they're staggering. See, they dropped those gloves. And look, the begetation around the ship outside the burn is all untrampled. This is their first exit, of course— Oh, the Boney one fell down! Could the cold-sleep have done that, have they come out too soon? I don't think so, I think they're sick. Look, there's a funny place on Ko's face, over the nose, he keeps scratching. They're not stopping to look around, or anything. This isn't good, Syl. . . . Now they're both down on their hands and knees, in the burn. Oh, I wish I could help them. Look, do you see that goldy cloud, like your spores, by the ramp?"

A pause, with small "ohs" and murmurs.

"They're up now, I hope they're not burned—why, they're running, or trying to run! Away from the ship. Toward that trampled place we saw, only it isn't trampled now. Oh. Boney is—and Ko—they're *stripping!* What are they trying to do, take a bath? But there's no— Oh! Oh, wait, *what?* Oh, no! Oh! Oh, dear gods, I don't like this much. I thought all Spacers operated under the Code, I didn't know recon teams did sex!"

"They don't," growls Exec, startling everybody.

General stirrings in the room as Coati's voice goes on haltingly, "Well, this is weird . . . I don't much want to look at it, it's not happy-looking like our demo teams back at school. Huh . . . I don't think they know what to do, exactly . . . their faces look crazy, why, one of them has his mouth open like he was yelling or screaming. They look terrible. . . . Whoever's listening to this, I'm sorry, I hope I'm not saying anything bad. But this is weird, it's like *ugly*. . . . They have to stop soon, I hope. Oh, *no*—" Her voice is shaking, on the verge of some kind of outcry.

"Oh, oh, oh—" But it's the other voice that begins sobbing frankly now. The record blurs in a confusion of, "Syl! What's the matter? What's wrong?" and, "Oh, I was afraid, oh, I'm afraid, oh, Coati, it's terrible—"

"Yeah, it's ugly. That's not the way Humans really mate, Syl."

"No," says Syl's tones, "I don't mean that, I mean we—oh, oh—" and she's sobbing again.

"Listen, Syl!" Coati gulps back alien tears, cuts her off. "I think you know something you aren't telling me! You tell me what's frightening you this instant, or I'll—I'll bash my own brains so hard it'll shake you loose. See?"

There's the sound of a hard slap on flesh and then a sudden sharp outcry.

"Hey—what— *You hurt me,* Syl. I th-thought you never—"

"Oh, I'm sorry," the alien voice moans. "I p-panicked when you said you would harm yourself—"

"Or harm *you,* huh? Look, I can stand a lot of pain if I have to. You tell me right now what's got into those men. Look, they've collapsed again. *Tell* me!"

"It—it's the young ones."

"The young what?"

"The young Eea—from s-seeds in th-the ship."

"But you said there were grown-up Eea in each of the men. Didn't they keep the seeds off, like you did for me?"

"They— Oh, Coati, I told you, they were very old. They must have died, and the seeds went in the men. I saw them getting feeble. That's when I got frightened and l-left. Before the Humans went in cold-sleep. . . . Oh, Coati, it's so horrible—I feel so bad—"

"Hush up now, Syl, and let me understand. What could seeds do?"

"Seeds hatch, when they're in—they hatched into young ones. With no mentors, no one to train them. They're like wild animals. They grow. They eat—they eat anything. And then in the cold-sleep some of them must have matured. No teachers, no one to teach them discipline. Oh, the others should have known the seeds and spores would seek hosts, they should have seen those visitors who went with them were too old. B-but nobody knew how long, how far. . . . When I began to understand how long a time it was going to be, I knew something bad would happen. And I c-couldn't *do* anything, they wouldn't listen to me. So I-I ran away. . . ." The alien is convulsing Coati with sobs.

"Well-ll . . ." Long sigh from Coati. "Oh, dear gods, the poor men. You mean the young ones just ate their brains out?"

"Y-yes, I fear so. As if they were Dron. Worse, because no teachers."

"And that sex stuff—that was the mature ones making them do it?"

"Yes! Oh, yes! Like wild animals. We're taught strictly to control it, we're shown. It takes much training to be fully Eea. Even I am not fully trained. . . . Oh, I wish I'd died there in space, instead of seeing this—"

"Oh, no. Brace up, Syl. It's not your fault. Nobody who isn't used to space could grasp how long the distances are. They probably thought it would be like a long trip in your country . . . Oh, look—the men have gotten up. Gods, they're holding each other up, their legs keep going out of control. Motor centers gone, maybe. They're going—they went up that path north, only it wasn't a path then. They're making the path, trampling. . . . That's where we go, Syl, unless this shows them coming back. It'll have to be soon, we're almost at where the camera stopped. I wish I knew how long ago this was. The sun looks kind of different, and the colors of the vegetation, but that could be the camera. I'm going to speed up. Syl, stop crying, honey, it's *not your fault.*"

Rapid clicking from the record.

"Nothing, nothing," Coati's voice says. "Still nothing. I doubt they came back. Nothing— Wait, what's that? Oh, my goodness, it's the

wake—it's our ship landing. Well! I don't think I want to see us, do
you? Let's go."

Click.

In the Executive office, the deputy stops the recorder for a moment.
"Is all that clear to everyone?"

Grunts of assent answer him.

"I think this casts a new light on the potentials of Coati's little
friend's race," the medical officer says. "I suggest that we all keep a
sharp eye open for anything that looks like grains of yellow powder, in
case the young woman's heat treatment did not completely clean out
this pipe. Or the preceding one. Her initial precautions were very wise."

Before he's finished speaking, Exec had turned on stronger lights.
There is a subdued shuffling as people look themselves over, brushing at
imaginary golden spots.

"Gods, if a pipeful of that stuff had got loose in here, and nobody
warned!" Xenology mutters. "Hmm . . . Boney and Ko."

"Yes." Exec understands Xenology's shorthand. "If we get any indi-
cation that their ship lifted off, we have some hard decisions to make. I
gather the seeds can affix themselves to the *outside* of space vessels, too.
Well, we'd best continue and see what our problem is."

"Right." The deputy douses the top light, restarts the 'corder.

"We are now proceeding north on the trail left by Boney and Ko,"
says Coati's voice. "We've come about five kiloms. The trail is very
plain, because the vegetation, or whatever this is, is very delicate and
frail. I don't think it's built to have animals walk over it or graze. But
the trail isn't all that fresh because there're little tips of new growth. We
haven't seen any animals or birds, only plantlike things and an occasional insect going by fast, like a bullet. It's a pretty cold, quiet, weird
place. The ground is almost level, but I think we're headed roughly for
one of those lakes we saw from above.

"Syllobene is so shook up by what happened to the men that she
won't talk much. I keep trying to tell her it's not her fault. One thing
she said shows you—she said the grown-up Eea must have assumed
that we could make ourselves immune to the seeds, just as they can,
since we're so *complete*. They can't get used to the idea of whole, single
animals born that way. And the ship, we had so many wild, powerful
things. It never occurred to them that the men would be as vulnerable
as Drons. . . . Syl, do you hear what I'm telling my people? Nobody's
going to think for a minim that you're at fault. Please brace up, honey,
it's awfully lonesome here on this primordial tundra or whatever it is."

"After you saved my life," murmurs the Syllobene voice sadly.

"Oh-h-h! Listen, hey—Syl, you saved my life, too, for the lords' sake. Don't you realize?"

"I? How?"

"By being on that message pipe, dopus. It was full of seeds, remember? If you hadn't been there, at the risk of your life, if you hadn't been there to keep them off me, I'd have gone just like Boney and Ko. They'd have eaten my brains out. *Now* will you cheer up? You've personally saved my life, too. Hey, Syl, how about that? Hello!"

"Hello . . . Oh, dear Coati Cass—"

"That's my Syl. Listen, I've about had the hiking for today; these boots aren't the greatest. I see a little hummock ahead, maybe it's drier. I'll tramp down a flat place and lay out my bag and screen—I don't want one of those bullet-bugs to hit me. I don't think this sun is going to set, either; it must be summer up here, with a big axial tilt." She chuckles. "I've heard of the lands of the midnight sun! Now I've seen one. This is Coati Cass, en route to I don't know where, signing off."

"Your daughter is a remarkable young woman, Myr Cass," Exec says thoughtfully. Cass grunts. Looking more carefully at him, Exec sees his eyes are wet.

The record continues with a few words by Coati on awakening. Apparently she—they—had slept undisturbed.

"Green, on we go. Now, Syl, I hope you feel better. Think of me, having to lug a Weeping Willie—that means a sad lump of a person—all over the face of this godlost planet. Hey, don't you know any songs? I'd really like that."

"Songs?"

"Oh, for the gods' sake. Well, explaining and demonstrating will give me something to do. But I don't think our audience needs it."

Click.

In an instant her voice is back again, sounding tired.

"We've been walking eighteen hours total," she says. "My pedometer says we're sixty-one kiloms from the ship. The trail is still visible. We're nearing an arm of one of the glaciers that extend south from the ice cap. I can see a line of low clouds—yes, with rainbows in them!—like a miniature weather front. The men seem to have been making straight towards it. Syl says the seeds have a primitive tropism to cold. That they can live a very, very long time if it's cold enough. I don't think anybody should come near this planet for a very, *very* long time. All right, onward."

Click, off. Click, on.

"The glacier edge and a snowbank are right ahead. I think I see them

—I mean, their bodies. . . . There's a cold wind from under the glacier, it smells bad."

Click. . . . Click.

"We found them. It's pretty bad." The voice sounds drained. "I did what I could. They're like frozen, they crawled under the edge of the ice, it stands off the ground and makes a cave there, with deep green light cracks. Nothing had been at them that I could tell, but they both have big, nasty-looking holes above their noses, where the sinuses are.

"I don't know their last names, so I just scratched 'Boney and Ko, brave Spacers for the Federation, FedBase Nine hundred' on a slatey piece.

"Oh—they left a message, on the same sort of rock. It says, 'Danger. We are Infetked. Fatel,' all misspelled, like a kid. I guess the . . . things . . . kept eating their brains out.

"And there are seeds all over around here, like gold dust on the snow. They rise up in a cloud when a shadow falls on them. Syllobene says these are new seeds and spores that the young Eea formed, they mated when the men did and the seeds grew while the men walked here. Anyway, those holes in their faces are where the new seeds spouted out in a big clump or stream.

"I got out my glass and looked at a group of seeds. That gold color is their coat or sheath. Syl says it is just about impermeable from outside. There's a big difference in the seeds, too—some are much, much larger and solid-looking, others are more like empty husks. Syl says the big ones beat out the others, when competing for a host, and the earliest big one takes all." A sigh.

"Let's see, have I said everything? Oh, maybe I should add that I don't think those holes were bad enough to cause the men's deaths. It must have been what went on inside. I didn't see any other wounds, except scratches and bruises from falling down, I think. They . . . they were holding each other by the hand. I fixed them up, but I didn't change that.

"Now I guess that's all. I don't want to sleep here, I'm going to get as far back toward the ships as I can tonight. It may not be night, I told you the sun doesn't set, but it makes some pretty reddish-glow colors. Syl is so sad she'll hardly talk at all. . . . Signing off now, unless something drastic happens."

The deputy clicked the 'corder off.

"Is that all?" someone asks.

"Oh, no. I merely wanted to know if everyone is satisfied that they're hearing clearly so far. Did everyone get enough on the men's conditions, or would Doc like me to run back over that?"

"Not at present, thanks," says Medical. "I would assume that the action of forming a large number of embryos requires extra energy, and consequently, during the men's last walk, their parasites were consuming nutrients—brain tissue and blood—at an ever-increasing rate. As to the exact cause of death, it could be a combination of trauma, hypothermia, malnutrition, and loss of blood, or perhaps the parasites attacked brain structures essential to life. We won't know until we can— I guess we won't know, period."

"Anyone else?" says the deputy in his "briefing session" manner.

Coati's father makes an ambiguous throat-clearing noise but says nothing. No one else speaks, despite the sense of large unuttered questions growing in the room.

"Oh, get on with it, Fred," Exec says.

"Right."

"We're back at the ship resting up," says Coati's voice. "Syl, you've been very quiet for a long time. Are you all right? Are you still shook from seeing what the young ones did?"

"Oh, yes."

"Well, push it aside, honey. If I can, you can. Try."

"Yes . . ."

"You don't sound like you're trying. Listen, I can't carry a melancholy, dismal person *in my head* all the way back to FedBase. I'll go nutters, even in cold-sleep. Don't you think you could cheer up a little? Wasn't it fun when we tried singing? . . . After all, the men all happened a long time back, it's all over. There's nothing you can do."

In the room at Far Base, Coati's father recognizes a piece of his own advice to his daughter in long-ago days, and blinks back a tear.

"And we've done something useful—actually invaluable, because only you and I are safe on this planet. Right? So maybe we've saved the lives of whoever might have come to look."

"Umm . . ."

"She's right," says Exec.

"Of course, it's only Human lives, but it was the Human men made you sad, wasn't it, Syl. So really it's all even. And those two had a really nice time on your planet first. Hey, think how good you'll feel when you get home. Would it make you feel better if I showed you the scenes from Nolian when we get going?"

"Yes . . . Oh, I don't know."

"Syl, you're hopeless. Or is something else bothering you? I'm getting hunches. . . . Anyway, we've done everything we can here, I'm taking *CC-One* up. I collected Boney and Ko's last charting cassettes, I'll put them in a pipe with this, and with the little cassette from the bow camera. I don't think they have left anything else of v-value. I closed the door and wrote a sign on the port to stay out. If you at the Fed want to salvage that ship, you're going to have to go in with flamers. Or get an Eea to go in with you. Personally I'd think it wasn't worth the danger, some seeds could be on the outside, and get left wherever you went with it. Hey, something I've been thinking—I wonder if possibly this could be the plague that wiped out the Lost Colony? Seeds drifting in from space. This whole great group of suns could be dangerous. Oh, lords. What a blow. . . . Hey, that's something that Syl and I could check someday! Syl, after you get home and have a nice rest-up, how would you like to come with me on another trip? If they'd let me—I'm sure they would, because we'd be their only seed-proof scouts! Only, my poor folks. That reminds me, my father may have messaged Far Base, it'd be great if somebody could message him and Mother collect that all's well and I'm coming back. Thanks a million. My address at Cayman's Port and all is on record there. Syl, there's another thing we could do—how'd you like to meet my folks? You could learn all about families, and go back and be a big mentor on Nolian. They'd love to meet you, I know . . . I guess. Green, I'm taking the ship up now."

Click. Click.

"We're up, and I'm setting in course for the first leg back to Far Base. Whew, these yellow suns are really beautiful. But Syl is still in a funk. It *can't* be because of what we saw on the planet. I keep feeling sure there's something you aren't telling me, Syl. What is it?"

"Oh, no, I—"

"Syl! Listen, you're thinking with *my* brain, and I can *sense* something! Like every time I suggested something we could do, I got drenched in some kind of sadness. And there's a feeling like a big thing tickling when you won't talk. You've got to tell me, Syl. What *is* it?"

"I . . . Oh, I am so ashamed!"

"See, there *is* something you're hiding! Ashamed of what? Go on, Syl, tell me or I'll—I'll bash us both. *Tell me!*"

"Ashamed," repeats the small voice. "I'm afraid, I'm afraid. My training. . . . Maybe I'm not so completely developed as I thought. I don't know how to stop— Ohhh," Coati's voice wails, "I wish my mentor was here!"

"Huh?"

"I have this feeling. Oh, dear Coati Cass, it is increasing, I can't suppress it!"

"What? . . . Don't tell me you're about to have some kind of primitive fit? Did that mating business—?"

"No. Well, maybe, yes. Oh, I *can't*—"

"Syl, you must."

"No. All will be well. I will recollect all my training and recover myself."

"Syl, this sounds terrible . . . But, face it, you're all alone—*we*'re all alone. You can't mate, if that's what's coming over you."

"I know. But—"

"Then that's it. The sooner we get going, the sooner we'll be at FedBase and you can start home. I was going to take a nice nap first, but if you've got troubles, maybe I better just go right into the chest. Couldn't you try to sleep, too? You might wake up feeling better."

"Oh, no! Oh, no! Not the cold! It stimulates us."

"Yes, I forgot. But look, I can't live through all those light-years awake!"

"No—not the cold-sleep!"

"Syl. Myr Syllobene. Maybe you better confess the whole thing *right now*. Just what are you afraid of?"

"But I'm not sure—"

"You're sure enough to be glooming for days. Now you tell Coati exactly what you're afraid of. Take a deep breath—here, I'll do it for you—and start. Now!"

"Perhaps I must," the alien voice says, small but newly resolute. "I don't remember if I told you: If the mating cycle overtakes us when an Eea is alone, we can still . . . reproduce. By—I know your word—spores. Just like seeds, only they are all identical with the parent. And the Eea grows them and gives birth like seeds, as you s-saw. Then the Eea comes back to itself." Syl's words are coming in a rush now, as from relief at speaking out. "It's very rare, because of course we are taught to stop it when the feeling begins. I—I never had it before. I'm supposed to seek out my mentor at once, to be instructed how to stop it, or the mentor will visit the young one and make it stop. But my mentor is far away! I keep hoping this is not really the feeling that begins all that, but it won't go away, it's getting stronger. Oh, Coati, my friend, I am so afraid—so fearful—" The voice trails off in great sobs.

The Coati-voice says, slowly, "Oh, whew. You mean, you're afraid you're going to be grabbed by this mating thing and make spores in my head? And they'll bore a hole?"

"Y-yes." The alien is in obvious misery.

"Wait a minute. Will it make you go crazy and stop being you, like a Human who gets intoxicated? Oh, you couldn't know about that. But you'll act like those untrained young ones? I mean, what will you do?"

"I may—eat blindly. Oh-h-h . . . Don't leave me alone in your cold-sleep!"

"Well. Well. I have to think."

Click—the deputy has halted the machine.

"I thought we should take a minim to appreciate this young woman's dilemma, and the dilemma of the alien."

The xenobiologist sighs. "This urge, or cycle, is evidently not so very rare, since instructions are given to the young to combat it. Instructions which unfortunately depend on the mentor being available. But it doesn't appear to be a normal part or stage of maturing—more like an accidental episode. I suggest that here it was precipitated by the experience with the two Humans infected by untrained young. That awakened what the Eea seem to regard as part of their primitive system."

"How fast can they get back to that Eea planet, ah, Nolian?" someone asks.

"Not fast enough, I gather," Exec says. "Even if she took the heroic measure of traveling without cold-sleep."

"She's got to get rid of that thing!" Coati's father bursts out. "Cut into her own head and pull it out if she has to! Can't somebody get to her and operate?"

He is met by the silence of negation. The moments they are hearing passed, for good or ill, long back.

"The alien said it could leave," the deputy observes. "We will see if that solution occurs to them." He clicks on.

As if echoing him, Coati's voice comes in. "I asked Syl if she could pull out, and park somewhere comfortable until the fit passed. But she says—tell them, Syl."

"I have been trying to withdraw for some time. Early on, I could have done so easily. But now the strands of my physical being have been penetrating so very deeply into Coati's brain, into the molecular and—is 'atomic' the word?—structure. So I have attempted to cut loose from portions of myself, but whenever I succeed in freeing one part, I find that the part I freed before has rejoined. I—I have not had much instruction in this technique, not since I was much smaller. I seem to have grown greatly while with Coati. Nothing I try works. Oh, oh, if only another Eea was here to help! I would do anything, I'd cut myself in half—"

"It's a gods-cursed cancer," Coati's father growls. He perceives no empathetic young alien, but only the threat to his child.

"But dear Coati Cass, I cannot. And there is no mistake now, the primitive part of myself that contains this dreadful urge is growing, growing, although I am fighting it as well as I can. I fear it will soon overwhelm me. Is there not something you can do?"

"Not for you, Syl. How could I? But tell me—after it's all passed, and you've, well, eaten my brains out, will you come back to yourself and be all right?"

"Oh—I could never be all right, knowing I had murdered you! Killed my friend! My life would be a horrible thing. Even if my people accepted me, I could not. I mean this, Coati Cass."

"Hmm. Well. Let me think." The record clicks, off-on. Coati's voice comes back. "Well, the position is, if we carry out our plan to go back to FedBase, I'll be a zombie, or dead, when I get there, and you'll be miserable. And the ship'll be full of spores. I wouldn't be able to land it, but somebody'd probably manage to intercept us. And the people who opened it would get infected with your spores, and by the time things got cleared up a lot of Humans would have died, and maybe nobody would feel like taking you back to your planet. Ugh."

The alien voice echoes her.

"On the other hand, if we cut straight for Nolian, even at the best, you'd have made spores and they'd have chewed up my brains, and it'd be impossible for me to bring the ship down and let you out. So you'd be locked up with a dead Human and a lot of spores, flying on to gods know where, forever. Unless somebody intercepted us, in which case the other scenario would take over. . . . Syl, I don't see any out. What I do see is that this ship will soon be a flying time bomb, just waiting for some non-Eea life to get near it."

"Yes. That is well put, Coati-my-friend," the small voice says sadly. "Oh!"

"What?"

"I felt a strong urge to—to hurt you. I barely stopped it. Oh, Coati! Help! I don't want to become a wild beast!"

"Syl, honey . . . It's not your fault. I wonder, shouldn't we sort of say our good-byes while we can?"

"I see. . . . I see."

"Syllobene, my dear, whatever happens, remember we were great friends, and had adventures together, and saved each other's lives. And if you do something bad to me, remember I know it isn't really you, it's just an accident because we're so different. I . . . I've never had a friend I loved more, Syl. So good-bye, and remember it all with joy if you can."

A sound of sobbing. "G-good-bye, dear Coati Cass. I am sad with all my being that it is through me that badness has come. Being friends with you has lifted my life to lightness I never dreamed of. If I survive, I will tell my people how good and true Humans are. But I don't think I will have that chance. One way or another, I will end my life with yours, Coati Cass. Above all I do not wish to bring more trouble on Humans."

"Syl . . ." Coati says thoughtfully. "If you mean that about going together, there's a way. Do you mean it?"

"Y-yes. Yes."

"The thing is, in addition to what happens to us, our ship will be a menace to anybody, Human or whatever, who gets at it. It's sort of our duty not to do a thing like that, you know? And I really don't want to go on as a zombie. And I see that beautiful yellow sun out there, the sun we saw all those days and nights down on the planet . . . like it's waiting for us. . . . Syl?"

"Coati, I understand you."

"Of course, there're a lot of things I wanted to do, you d-did, too—maybe this is the b-big one—"

The record lapses to a fuzzy sound.

"Something has been erased," the deputy says.

It comes back in a minim or two with Coati's voice saying, "—didn't need to hear all that. The point is, we've decided. So—ow! Oh-h-h-*ow!* What?"

"Coati!" The small voice seems to be screaming. "Coati, I'm losing—I'm losing myself! Something wants to hurt you, to stop you—to make you go in cold-sleep—I'm fighting it— Oh, forgive me, forgive me—"

"OW! Hey, I forgive you, but— Oh, *ouch!* Wait, hold it, baby, I just have to set our course, and then I'll hop right into the chest. I *have* to set the computer; try to understand."

Undecipherable noise from the alien. Then, to everyone's surprise, the unmistakable sound of a young Human voice humming fills the room.

"I know that tune," the computer chief says suddenly. "It's old—wait—yes. It's 'Into the Heart of the Sun.' She's trying to tell us what she's doing without alerting that maniacal parasite."

"We better listen closely," the deputy observes superfluously.

A moment later the humming gives place to a softly sung bar of

words—yes, it's "Into the Heart of the Sun." It ends in a sharp yelp.
"Hey, Syl, try not to, *please*—"

"I try! I try!"

"We'll get into cold-sleep just as soon as I possibly can. Don't hurt
me, you doppelgänger, or I'll make a mistake and you'll end up as fried
spores— Owwwww! For an amateur, you're a little d-devil, Syl." The
voice seems to be trying to conceal the wail of real agony. Exec is
reminded of the wounded Patrolmen he tended as a young med-aid long
ago, during the Last War.

"I just have to regoogolate the fribiliser that keeps us from penetrating high gee-fields," says Coati. "You wouldn't want *that* to happen,
would you?"

Her own throat growls at her. "Hurry."

"That's an old nonsense phrase," Computer speaks up. " 'Googolat-
ing the fribiliser'—she's trying to tell us she's killing the automatic
drive-override. Oh, good girl."

"And now I *must* send this message pipe off. It's in your interests,
Syl, it shows you doing all those useful things. And I have to heat it first
—oh, ow—please let me, Syl, please try to let m-me—"

Sounds that might be a heat oven, roughly handled, punctuated by
yelps from Coati. Her father is gripping his chair arms so hard they
creak.

"Yes, I know that big yellow sun ahead is getting pretty hot and
bright. Don't let it worry you. If we go close by it, we'll save a whole leg
of our trip. It's the only neat way to do. Han Lu Han, anybody there?
Here, I'll pull the bow blinds.

"And now the cassettes from Boney and Ko go in the pipe—*ow!*—
and where's that little one from their bow camera? Syl, try to tell your
primitive self you're just slowing me down with those jabs. Please,
please— Ah, here it is. And out come the spores, I mean, the seeds that
were in there, that pipe is *hot!*

"And now it's time to say good-bye, put this in the pipe, and climb
into the chest. I really hope the pipe's frequency can pull it through
these gees. On second thought, maybe I'd like to see where we're going
while it lasts. As long as I can stand the pain, I think I'll stay out and
watch."

Loud sounds of the cassette being handled.

"Good-bye, all. To my folks . . . Oh, I do love you, Dad and Mum.
Maybe somebody at FedBase can explain—*ow!!* Oh . . . Oh . . . I
can't . . . Hey, Syl, is there anybody you want to say good-bye to?
Your mentor?"

A confused vocalization, then, faintly, "Yes . . ."

"Remember Syl. She's the real stuff, she's doing this for Humans. For an alien race. She could have stopped me, believe it. Bye, all."

A crash, and the record goes to silence.

"Han Lu Han," says the xenobiologist quietly into the silence. "He was that boy on the Lyra mission. 'It's the only really neat thing to do.' He said that before he took the rescue-run that killed him."

Exec clears his throat. "Myr Cass, we will send a reconnaissance mission to check the area. But I fear there is no reason to believe, or hope, that Myr Coati failed in her plan to eliminate the contagious menace of herself, her passenger, and the ship, by flying into a sun. By the end of the message she was close enough to feel its heat, and it was doubtless the effect of its gravity which delayed this message pipe so much longer than the preceding one, which was sent only a few days earlier. She had moreover carefully undone the precautions which prevent a ship on automatic drive from colliding with a star. Myr Cass, when confronted by a terrifying and painful dilemma capable of causing great harm to others, your daughter took the brave and honorable course, and we must be grateful to her."

Silence, as all contemplate the sudden ending of a bright young life. Two bright young lives.

"But you said she was alive and well when the message was sent." Coati's father makes a last, confused protest.

"Sir, I said that she was compos mentis and probably in her ship," the deputy reminds him.

"Thank the gods her mother didn't come here. . . ."

"You can pinpoint the star she was headed for?" Exec asks Charts.

"Oh, yes. The BK coordinates are good."

"Then if nobody has a different idea, I suggest that it be appropriately named in the new ephemeris."

"Coati's Star," says Commo. People are rising to leave.

"And Syllobene," a quiet voice says. "Have we forgotten already?"

"Myr Cass, I think you may perhaps prefer to be alone for a moment," Exec tells him. "Any time you wish to see me, I'll be at your service in my office."

"Thank you."

Exec leads his deputy out and opts for a quiet lunch in their private small dining room. Added to the list of things that were on his mind before he entered the conference chamber to hear Coati's message are now the problem of when and how to contact the Eea, how to determine the degree of danger from their seeds, or spores, in space near the promising GO suns, the Lost Colony question, whether to quarantine the area, and whether there is any chance of any seeds in FedBase itself from the earlier messages. Also, a sample of the chemical that Syllobene had immunized Coati with would seem to be a rather high priority.

But behind all these practical thoughts, an image floats in his mind's eye, accompanied by the sound of a light young voice humming. It's the image in silhouette of two children, one Human, the other not, advancing steadfastly, hand in hand, toward an inferno of alien solar fire.

# At the Library _____

**M**oa Blue smiles as he sees the two young Comenor approaching; the old text is carefully wrapped in a broidered packing.

"Well? Did you like it? And did it meet your needs?" Moa inquires.

"Fascinating!" the Comeno girl breathes. "And we had no idea so young a Human female could, could, well—"

"Pull off such an exploit!" Her friend finishes for her. Their interlocked upper arms tighten tenderly. "But so sad, at the end."

"And did they really name the star after her?"

"They did. I should have emphasized, whatever is given as fact in these dramatized accounts really *is* fact. You'll run across a similar naming in my third tale—all true." Moa unwraps the documents and sets them carefully aside before he produces another, slightly thicker one.

"Now here's your next. Also set in the fringes of the Rift, but quite, quite different. Purely Human interaction, and much more of the dialogue had to be extrapolated from interviews with the participants. It was written up quickly because one—no, two—of the actors achieved considerable celebrity later. You do know what their Gridworld was?"

Two Comeno brows wrinkle. "Ah . . . the planet where their entertainment broadcasts originated?" the little female ventures.

"Right you are. And more, almost a culture of its own. Its name became an adjective for things showy, sensational, slightly meretricious, perhaps. The grid covered the whole Federation and really helped hold it together, by means of shared language, gossip, celebrities, jokes, scandals—we haven't anything quite like it . . . yet. At the date of this story, FTL communication was virtually unknown, and FTL transport was used only for emergency; it wasn't the same system we now use at all. Of course it's hard to set exact dates on these things, in relation, say, to the Damiem story taking place hundreds of light-years away, because you must remember that Humans for a time borrowed or rented some technology from other races like the Swain, or from the Dhaldiggern, before they so tragically blew themselves up. At any rate, you'll find here some unusual Human motivations—rather like one of their old grid-shows. And you'll get your first taste of the Black Worlders.''

"Oh, yes, we've been curious about those. Our texts just say bland things like 'In those times the Humans from the so-called Black Worlds gave trouble,' but what does that tell you?''

"Exactly. Oh, and another thing, if I recall my Comeno biology—you might have to ask a Human specialist exactly why the hero's choice was so emotionally wrenching. The interviewers and writers, in their haste, have been a bit chauvinistic and perhaps not made things clear enough for races with other reproductive arrangements.''

The taller Comeno says reflectively, "Professor Imgrenno has already given us a little tutoring on Human reproductive responses. I expect he'd help us. The main thing seems to be the intensity.''

"Poor things,'' the little female puts in. "I *know* it's chauvinistic of me, but I always feel so sorry for the two-gender races. . . . Oh, I do hope I don't offend your species mores, Myr Blue? Terribly rude of me.''

"Not at all, not at all,'' says Moa genially. "True, my race is bipolar, but we spend ninety percent of our time in neuter mode, in which all the passions of coupling, tripling, or what you will, seem quite remote and feverish. You couldn't possibly give offense.''

The red-furred girl sends him what even Moa can recognize as a melting smile, and her future mate pats her upper hand. "Great are the wonders of the All,'' she murmurs.

A rumbling noise is coming from their other side, where a big Moom student is impatiently awaiting his turn. The rumble is his multiplex gullet working in displeasure. The Comeno boy hastens to transfer the rainproof wrapper to the new text, nodding civilly to the Moom—who as usual makes no reply. Moa and the Comeno couple exchange amused glances; Moom bad manners are known all over the Galaxy and tolerated only because they so rarely mingle with others—and are such eminently reliable drive-ship engineers.

"I do hope this one lives up to your hopes," Moa tells them. "Remember, if it seems a little specialized on their love and mating habits—the third one is my special selection for you."

They thank him above the Moom's renewed rumblings and depart, eagerly hugging their next treasure.

# Second Tale
# Good Night,
# Sweethearts

*Blat-blat-blat beeep blat—*

Far, far out, where Raven lies dreamless in his cold-chest, as near to death as living man may come, a hypo-needle jabs him in his unconscious arse. Then, gently, the chest tumbles him out onto its padding. Raven sits up, the last films of cold-sleep draining quickly from his mind.

How long is it since he left FedBase 900?

His panel tells him that while he was in cold-sleep, *Blackbird*, his salvage tug ship, has carried him the long trip out to Rift-edge and taken up her precomputed patrol toward the five colony planets that are newly on her holocharts, in the fringes of the Rift.

The *Blat-beep* turns out to be two signals.

One is a loud out-of-fuel call from an unknown ship.

The other is FedBase 900, almost beyond useful commo range out here. Raven tunes down the O.O.F. to catch the whispery voice.

"It's all yours, *Blackbird*," says FedBase through the space jazz. "If they're not an ell-dee, tell 'em we can't make it under thirty days. Good pickings!"

"Right. Thanks." Raven signs off, wondering what "pickings" they expect from an out-of-fuel call. Somebody really has a loud ship, though.

When Raven figures the distance to the calling ship, he sees it isn't worth going back into cold-sleep for. Good. He can use some time checking where to refuel *Blackbird* after he's filled up the dry ship's tanks.

Too bad he hasn't also a wreck to work on and restore, as he often does. "Raven's Wrecks" are well known and sought after.

The nearest fuel depot turns out to be on one of those new colony planets; it's now called Cambria. There's a scrawled notation that FedBase 900 lost contact with Cambria about a hundred days ago. That could mean anything or nothing. Colonists are notoriously poor on commo equipment maintenance.

On the other hand, last sleep Raven has three times been awakened by vanishers, which could mean that a nest of Black Worlders or trashheads left over from the great Rare Asteroid Rush, or lords knew what, are operating in his sector. They won't have meddled with the fuel dump, though, Raven decides; the Federation's explosive tamper-proofing is widely respected.

But colonies are innocent and vulnerable, and overly preoccupied with planting and irrigating and drainage and climate and domesticating local fauna—until somebody lands and surprises them. Human renegades can also be bad news for a sleeping man in a ship, but Raven's special alarm programs protect him there. He has twice had the pleasure of grappling, sealing, and delivering to FedBase a shipload of pirates out to take him.

Thinking of this, he grins and throws back his shock of dark hair and turns up the gees for a few warm-up exercises to subdue the rich diet he ate at his birthday celebration on FedBase 900. He isn't stiff from coldsleep—cold-sleep doesn't make you stiff, or anything else. In fact, absolutely nothing goes on, biologically speaking, in that chest in which he's spent, now, close to seven decades. You don't age. You don't ever rest—if you go down tired, you wake up tired, too, which is why Raven always has a nap before he goes under.

He catches his toes under the chest to do some sit-ups, thinking, Seventy Standard years. And thirty more awake; it was his hundredth birthday, by the little Terra-Timer on the corner of his panel—one of Humanity's last links with the planet that bore it—that he was celebrating at FedBase 900. And yet he's a young man, with the bounce and the bones and the unwrinkled hide of a man of thirty. Living years, that is.

He knows this disconcerts some people. Back at FedBase, where he is something of an historical celebrity, he was aware of an occasional curious, troubled look. This usually happened when he forgot and spoke of the Last War as if it had ended the day before yesterday, which, to him, it had. And after that there are the blank years in his mind, which represent the stretch in Compassionate Rehab they'd put him through.

Rehab had been the Federation's answer to war memories too traumatic to live with. Raven appreciates this. He's careful not to try any deep remembering; he gave away the medal somebody awarded him for the gods knew what. And he's always been very wary about mixing with people or places that give him strange cold little pricklings of déjà vu.

Hence he took up his excellent trade of salvage and rescue, out here in the high and hairy, where the northern edge of Federation space frays into the Rift and the times and distances between jobs are very great. The Patrol is delighted to have him here; Raven and his tough little high-thrust, versatile grappler tug are known as a pair that can be relied on to cope with all things copable, and some that aren't. The credits he accrues go usually into newer, fancier hard- and software for *Blackbird*. And out here he is in no danger—particularly *now*—of running into anything that will undo Rehab's work.

Business had fallen off after the great Rare Rock Rush, as expected. But Sector 900 still attracts enough misjumpers and O.O.F.s and would-be explorers in busted colony ships, and active idiots who can manage to hit the only other ship or rock in a cubic light-year, to keep Raven nicely supplied with excess credits.

A good life, Raven thinks, snapping back his exerciser grips, a very good life. And a great birthday party, too. He's made a lot of new friends; they may be gray-haired when he sees them next, but he's used to that. In fact he likes everything, just as it is, for him.

His mass-proximity indicator chimes: the calling ship is in scope range.

The "pickings" joke is clear at once: she is a whopping private luxury yacht, bearing among her golden scroll-work the name *Mira II*. Raven checks her over visually with care. No sign of anything amiss, save that she's dead in space. Some power left—lights show inside. He then tries out his most recent extravagance, a Janes' program, and finds that the owner of *Mira II* is one Myr-and-Ser Pavel bar Palladine. Looks, sounds, smells rich.

He's all but on her now, using impellor power, and he makes one slow pass around her gold-tinted ports. There's an orange-clad man apparently asleep in the pilot's couch, and a girl's figure in copilot. Back in the lounge area he can glimpse two or three dim forms in the armchairs.

The girl has seen him; she waves languidly.

Raven spots *Mira*'s mag grapplers; shortly he has his extension tunnel lapped over their main air lock and is suited up.

By the lock is more gold-work, containing a speaker grille.

"All green! Open up!" he calls. "Your fuel is here."

No reply, no audible action.

He calls again with no result. What's wrong with them?

Then he sees, of all things, an obvious arrival holocam, also in gold. It looks as if these characters spend most of their time ship-hopping in social marinas. What are they doing out here?

He punches the holocam with his gloved hand and says formally. *"Mira Two?* Salvage and Rescue Officer Raven here, come to fill up your fuel."

Still no action.

He yells a couple of times less formally. Then he ungloves and whips down his stethoscope, a gadget indispensable for exploring wrecks; the earpieces are incorporated in his helmet. Taking care not to touch *Mira*'s icy shell with bare skin, he locates two—no, three—voices. They're droning on in unmistakable loud monotones. Not a conversation.

Uh, oh. Talkers.

He puts the steth back up his sleeve, considering. The Talkers' chairs are right by the port, drowning out any noise he can raise. And they sound high as space.

Raven has never tried Talkee, or Taraka-Talaka, to give it its right name; solo Spacers take extreme care of their heads. He knows only that Talkee is supposed to make words—any words—indescribably enchanting, sexy, mystic. A few Talkee users just sit and listen to their inner voices. But most of them *talk*—an unstoppable flow of gibberish, with no attention to anything else. And they talk loudly, because Talkee makes you slightly deaf, among other things. Drive you mad to be around one.

Well, the girl looked reasonably alert, and the commo has to be right by her.

Raven ducks back into *Blackbird*. His receiver was tuned down to cut out *Mira*'s help call, still blasting away. He turns up the gain, making a face.

*"Mira! Mira Two!* Your fuel is here, I've been banging on your port. Cut off that godlost signal and open up. This is Officer Raven, Salvage and Rescue."

In a minim the signal stops. The speaker gives a soft, female sound between a sigh and a giggle. Then Raven sees *Mira*'s port slide silently aside, revealing a mirrored air lock carpeted in cream, with a big gold monogram. Raven glances at his own boots and reluctantly gives them a swipe.

He steps into their lock; the port closes behind him, to the usual accompaniment of a *whuck* in ears and stomach due to gravity change. Their air is quick; in a minim the inner port slides open and Raven is assaulted by the Talkers' loud drones. *Mira* is gee'd light, and the spacious lounge is almost unlit, letting the starfields blaze in. A gorgeous hydroponics display of plants lights one side. Dreamy—except for the hoarse, braying voices coming from the huge lounge chairs. Raven makes out the figures of two trim, well-dressed older men, who are Talking, and one much younger, plump—no, frankly fat—a man clad in some sort of embroidered robes, who is staring druggishly into space. None of them appears to notice his entry.

Raven throws back his helmet, getting a breath of deliciously fresh, springlike air, and step-floats forward toward the pilots' area. As he passes beyond the lounge, he brushes through what feels almost like a palpable, cobweb curtain where nothing is—and the noise behind cuts off abruptly. A privacy shield; he hadn't known they were in civilian hands yet. It's a fine relief.

When he reaches the observers' bench behind the pilots' seats, the man he saw asleep is just waking, stretching long, orange-ruffled arms. Raven sees only thick, silvery-gray hair until the man turns to face him, revealing a hawk-sharp countenance with hooded eyes. The effect is of impatience, imperious vigor as yet unweakened by some considerable age.

The girl has turned to watch his approach. Raven can see only a small, pale face under a great cloud of silver-gilt hair. But something about her bothers him immediately. He keeps his eyes strictly off her, addresses himself to the man.

"Myr—ah, Myr-and-Ser bar Palladine?"

"Yes?" The voice is weary, and clearly used to command.

Somehow Raven doesn't see any point in demanding proof that he is *Mira II*'s legal owner, or is bar Palladine. Part of his mind reproaches him; it would be easy enough for a gang of Black Worlders to take over *Mira*, drug the occupants, and act out this part, to get fuel. Too far-fetched, he tells his mind—and in his experience the Black Worlds don't produce types like these. Still, a little caution wouldn't be amiss.

"I'm Salvage and Rescue Officer Raven. I understand you're out of fuel."

The girl's glittering head nods vigorously; bar Palladine gives a faintly scornful grunt.

"Now, before I fill you up, if you so decide"—bar Palladine's eyebrows flicker in surprise—"there's a couple of matters to straighten out. First, the possibility of a leak or a pump malfunction. May I ask, did it seem reasonable to you when you ran out, or were you at all surprised by the rate of use?"

Bar Palladine actually seems to give this his attention.

"Reasonable. We refueled last at Base One oh five."

Raven whistles. "And jumped all the way out here? It's none of my business, but may I inquire why you didn't use the beacon routes?"

A flash of anger on the hawk face, quickly abandoned. "That *is* none of your business. But . . . things have changed . . . more than I estimated, since my time."

"Pavel knew a shortcut," the girl says in that seductive, breathy whisper. Not a giggle, no way. Raven can no longer wonder about imposters.

"As you say, very reasonable," Raven agrees. "Now, if I may just exchange places with the young lady, so I can check out a few functions? This is regulation, by the way; out here they frown on our risking the waste of a milliliter of fuel."

"Go ahead, honey."

The girl rises. But Raven, reluctantly watching her, senses discrepancy; her movement isn't a girl's quick jump-up, it shows a woman's flowing grace. And in the bright pilot light he sees something else—a faint white line—no, several white hairlines, running from her chin up into her hair and down across one shoulder. Almost imperceptible. The scars of some dire accident, he guesses; no cosmetic surgery he knows of. She settles on the bench behind him, a very delicate fragrance wafting to his unwilling nose.

"Do you want me to call off what I'm testing?" he asks bar Palladine.

"No. Just get on with it. I've made myself late."

Behind him the girl gives a disappointed murmur. It comes to Raven, as he sends a reverse bypass around the main fuel pump, that perhaps she also is a pilot; or learning to be one.

He runs carefully down his checklist. *Mira II* is well equipped, including refinements that permit him to blow air through possible leaky hoses and a reverse pouch for flushing the pumps. But she isn't a new ship.

"Would I be guessing wrong to say that this is one of the first long trips you've made in quite a while?"

"Right." Despite the older man's disclaimer, he's following the procedure closely. The technicalities seem to have soothed him.

"I did some . . . space work toward the end of the Last War," he says in a low voice. Raven restrains himself from turning to look at him; this man has to be a lot older than he'd guessed. A lot.

"Did you serve out in these sectors?" Raven is waiting for the pressure indicator to show movement.

"Nearby. It so happened that I and my friends back there"—his mouth twists wryly—"my two friends, all experienced the Goulart System. You've heard of it?"

"Seen it. Unbelievable."

They are referring to one of the marvels of Federation space; a stupendous tight-orbit dance of multicolored suns that has unexplained subjective effects on the Human psyche.

"Well, in an incautious moment I volunteered to fly us all out for one last, nostalgic look. Glad I did. It—it lived up to memory. Few things do, young man."

*Mira*'s pressure readouts hold unchanging; good. Raven is smiling to himself at that "young man," but sobers—after all, bar Palladine had *lived* all or most of those years, while Raven slept.

"I'm glad," he says sincerely. "Now, everything shows green here. I believe we're ready to fill you up. But first there's a business aspect you must know about me."

All reflectiveness vanishes from the hawk face.

"Everything I've done so far, including the trip over here, is reimbursed to me by the Federation. But I'm not Patrol, I'm what's called an Assimilated Independent. The 'Officer' title is genuine. There's a number of independents working the Frontier sections, some licensed, some not. You're out in the cold, high empty here, Myr-and-Ser. The force is spread vacuum-thin. They get around to everything eventually, but it takes time. FedBase Nine hundred—that's this sector—told me to tell you it'd be about thirty Standard days before they could get fuel out to you."

"So?" says bar Palladine icily; the girl murmurs disgustedly, "Thirty days!"

"Two points. First, you have only my word for this, or for who I am. Here's some ident. But I'd strongly advise—in fact, I insist, that you try your caller and verify my story. If you can't reach them from here, I want your word that you'll check on it when you get in closer. It'll take me off the hook—if you report a contact like this and it doesn't check out, they come for the imposter with a tractor beam. And it'll keep you from looking a shade—well, naive. I could be filling you with H-two-O."

At that, the hooded eyes glint, and bar Palladine gestures the girl to the commo station. As he goes on, Raven can hear her low voice, apparently getting through the static.

"Secondly, the Force can reach you much earlier if it's a matter of life or death. They'll gear up a *c*-jumper and get right out. But it has to be real; the last false claimer is still in the squadron brig. . . . He cut his girl's neck," Raven adds aside to bar Palladine—but the girl hears and glances at him with those smoky eyes he doesn't want to meet.

"So—you can get filled up right now by me, if you're willing to pay approximately double FedBase's price. The taxpayer doesn't support me. Mine is eighty per, delivered right now. Or you can wait for FedBase and get it at thirty-nine."

During this long speech, bar Palladine seems at first faintly amused, but as Raven plows doggedly on, a gleam of interest comes into the cold features and once or twice he blinks. Raven guesses the man, by old habit, focuses on any business new to him and has by now probably figured Raven's annual take, costs, and net worth.

Now bar Palladine glances at the port, where *Blackbird*'s needlenose can be seen in slight to-and-fro motion, the effect of vibration from *Mira*. "We'll take yours, of course. But my ship has big tanks and I'll need every bit of it to reach home. I certainly don't propose to wait while you take that thing back for more to finish the job."

Raven grins. "That thing, as you call it, is a flying fuel depot, Myr-and-Ser. Everything hollow has fuel in it, pressurized. And it's fresh from a top-off at Base. Going to make a great bonfire one day."

"Oh, no," whispers the girl.

"Tell you what: If I fail to top you off complete, everything you get is free. I'll punch-print on that."

The older man waves that away. "Good enough. Just get at it."

"Right. I'm going for some tools. Now you two check over that confirmation, remembering that my ident *could* be stolen. So could *Blackbird*, too—over my dead body."

He goes jauntily aft to the port, wincing as the Talk hits him.

"Analog, avatar, ambergris, avalanche, attribute, alcohol, arquebus," rises from the lounge chair occupied by a thin bald man in a blue lounge suit, echoed by, "Mirth . . . earth . . . girth . . . dearth . . . worth . . ." from a chair whose occupant Raven can't see. The robed fat man is still silent. He is much younger, certainly no Last War veteran. Bar Palladine hasn't explained his presence. Curious.

As Raven enters the lock, he catches a gleam of direct vision from the fat face, so brief he may have imagined it. The face is drug-vacant again as the port slides closed.

Back in *Blackbird,* tying on his fueling belt loaded with gauges, wrenches, lubricants, pressure-funnels, he finds himself a trifle shaky. What in the hells is wrong with him? An ordinary fueling job, and a lucrative one? . . . But he knows what it is. That godlost girl. Surely she can't be connected—

*Don't think of it.*

But she draws his mind like a shining magnet, a magnet whose field is drifting cold wisps across his back and loins . . . a magnet luring him to a vortex where all direction, all reason, will be lost in a hurting chaos of past and present . . . Stop this!

He slaps his helmet hard and stamps back into *Mira* to inquire whether there's anything special he should know about her tanks.

"No, I don't think so," bar Palladine says. "The combinations." He hands over a slim ivory sliver with a suit-hook.

Combination locks on your fuel tanks? Marina life all right!

"Then I'll just pop out your emergency hatch here." Raven swivels and tips the copilot's couch to reveal a circular crawl-through on the side opposite the main port and *Blackbird.* "It'll save uncoupling. You don't mind a short draft?"

"So long as it's short."

"I never knew that was there!" the girl exclaims.

Raven shakes his head. *"And* it needs grease something fierce." He unhooks a container and starts working on the hatch.

"I'm going out there!" the girl announces suddenly. "Please, Myr Raven, I won't get in your way, truly." She moves pleadingly to bar Palladine. "Pavel, oh, please—I have cabin fever so badly, so badly—I *need* to be out in space—" The murmur ends in something inaudible to Raven.

Bar Palladine looks thunderous, but all he says is, "Wear your tether. And *keep it fastened."*

"Oh, I will, I will, I promise! Thank you, Pavel—" She kisses him lightly behind one ear and snaps open a privacy-cocoon fastened against the hull at one end of the bench. In an instant she's hidden in it.

Raven is cursing his gods. This is the last thing he wants. He has a wild impulse to pull out of there and leave them dry—thirty days is nothing. . . . But he knows he won't, for two reasons. One is his conscience, and the other comes out of the privacy-cocoon in a kind of suit he's never seen before.

It's heavy, ultraclear plastic, with glossy silvery designs over strategic spots. As far as he can see, that's all she has on.

"Where's your air?" he blurts.

"Here." Smiling, she taps a tiny canister at her tiny waist.

"That sprays a special strain of oxygenating bacteria under the helmet," bar Palladine explains. "Good for twenty-four hours. Then you refresh the can."

"My, my." Raven knows his voice doesn't sound quite right.

"I won't charge you with her safety, because she's virtually uncontrollable," bar Palladine says. "Let's just say that if she doesn't come back in good shape, you'll have that fire."

"Not to worry too much," Raven tells him. "I've had good friends who got space-happy. . . . And I know a few fancy knots," he adds privately to the older man, grinning.

"What did you say?" the girl demands.

"Time to close up and go. Here, let me fasten this." Gloved, helmeted, he secures her tether to his belt, feeling as if her waist might snap, feeling as if he were tying fire to himself. He double-checks her almost invisible helmet-clamps against all that hair, which seems to be trying to writhe out.

"Test commo," he says through his suit radio.

"Testing," he hears her say to his ears alone, and then suddenly she sings a bar or two from an old, old song. Raven staggers backward, saves himself on the bench. Her speaker doesn't have the usual tinny sound, but conveys a voice delicate and sweet and rich.

"All right, all right," Raven snaps, and bends to complete unscrewing the emergency hatch, cautious because it must be a long time since the outer bag was used.

The cabin air jolts; outside, the bag snaps open solid and true. No leaks he can detect. "Now follow me and do exactly what I do."

He crawls out into the bag, grasping a hand-hold on one side, and motions her to the other. Then he slides the temporary hatch-cover over the opening from outside; when it's secure, he turns and unzips the bag. Air exits with a *whoosh*. He reels it in around them one-handed. An awkward job; she helps him timidly. When he has it stowed away in its circular slot, ready for reentry use, he pulls his legs in and lets his mag soles engage. She does the same, but he continues to hang on to a hand-hold until she is solidly on her feet. Then he rises beside her, with her tether looped under the hold.

They are free, standing among the stars.

It's glorious, the alien suns bright and close enough to touch. He wants to stand there peacefully a minim or two, the mag soles holding him lightly, his soul refreshed by space. But he has—has this ship to fuel. This girl to tend. She's standing very close to him now, looking up. Stop staring at me, stranger woman. . . . That suit must be warmer than it looks, he observes neutrally. Even more neutrally, he registers that she is really very beautiful.

"All right now, let's take a minim to see how you do in space. Myr, uh—"

"I'm Illyera," she says absently. "Illya."

A memory bell chimes faintly. He frowns. "I don't see many grid-shows . . . but I seem to recall—"

She makes a moue. "Oh, devils take it! You'd think, way out here—please can't I be just me?"

He has it now, and a great relief it is. Of course, Illyera. One of the immortals, one of the Galaxy's great grid-queens, the queen of all men's hearts—and women's, too. That mysterious, supernatural beauty, that smile that seemed to promise the secret of secrets—Illyera. Her face, a shot of her leaning on her naked elbows, had been plastered everywhere in FedBase 900, a few of his long sleeps ago. No elbows had ever looked so naked, so vulnerable . . . He had cut short that visit, he recalls. He supposes half the Federation would change places with him now.

As for Raven, he has to fill up *Mira*'s tanks. No more need for his cold-backbone tremors.

"Very well, Myr Illyera. If you don't mind, would you go over to that hold there and circle around me? Take it slow, any way you like."

A trill of real laughter comes in his ears as he gathers the tether in his hand. "I feel like a pet *poonta!*"

She's grinning like a girl now, first shuffling carefully in her mag soles, then more and more freely, until at last she takes off, dives for a farther hold, and completes the circle walking on her hands, her feet prettily pointed.

"Green, green," he says. "Wait there, we'll cross over the top of the hull and get *Blackbird*'s hose."

"Is that your ship—*Blackbird?* Raven—and *Blackbird!*" She's panting more than she ought to be. Heart?

"Yes, but no more jumping around. I'll get roasted alive, your friend promised."

"Oh, Pavel. He's sweet. He keeps them all off me." They're shuffling sedately, he has her arm. But every time he glances down at her, she's staring straight up into his eyes, with an odd, expectant look. What gives? Does she think she has some strange hypnotic effect? Is she waiting for him to throw himself at her feet? It'll be a long wait, he thinks, his eyes refusing hers, going instead to *Blackbird* nestled by the fat yacht. When they reach the ship he finds himself giving it an odd pat, as though he'd deserted a living creature.

"Oh, I wish I could see in," the girl says. Raven has tied her tether not to *Blackbird,* but to *Mira*'s elaborate rails, and is busy unreeling fuel hose to reach the first of *Mira*'s loading caps. Illyera looks incandescent, lit by the rays of two close blue-green suns.

"Nothing much to see," Raven tells her. "Come over here and look in if you want."

And then, as she bends close beside him in the dazzling starlight, he sees—not only two on her neck and shoulders, but on nearly every decimeter of exposed skin, flanks, thighs, upper arms to the elbows, and elbows to the wrists—everywhere is a network of fine scar-lines, planned, symmetrical, invisible save for this trick of the light. And he knows, though he can't believe it, what accident has struck her so cruelly.

The most drastic, irrevocable, supreme blow:

Old age.

He is looking at a masterpiece of cosmetic surgery such as he's never imagined; the woman before him is not merely an older woman, but a very old woman indeed. How long ago was it really that he'd seen her face about? Forty, fifty years?

Raven would be staggering were they in gravity; as it is, his hands have been working by themselves, connecting *Blackbird*'s hose to *Mira II*'s intake valves. He shakes himself, checks his work. It seems green. Meanwhile Illyera has been looking into *Blackbird,* exclaiming something—oh, yes, about the absence of a copilot's couch. He answers something, seeing, when he dares to look back at her, that the trick of lighting has gone. The lines have disappeared again.

But they were there—and with them, undoubtedly, is all the most elaborate inner work of replacement, regeneration, restoration. A total and ferocious holding-on to youth, a total refusal of age. And he sees, too, now that he dares look more coolly, that all the exquisite tucks and tightenings have been—ever so slightly—*wrong.* A shade too much here, a tiny lump or curve there, so that the result, while a beautiful woman, is not the same woman.

Not the same as what?

He almost cries it in terror, pushing the words away from him, slamming shut the tank valve as if he could crush the thought he *will not* think. And at the same time hearing her ask:

"Look. Are you a clone?"

It would have seemed as reasonable to him if she had asked if he were a hippogriff. From the whirl of his thought he says, "No. . . ."

"But I've got to know! What *is* it? Why don't you recognize me, Raven? Am I that changed? You saw my hair bleached. You *can't be* the Raven I—"

And then the only answer he can make is really to throw himself at her feet, one arm clenching her legs, the other on a hold-bar, weeping in his helmet, crying incoherently, "Oh—oh—oh—oh— No! Stop! Oh!— Illya, my darling, my girl Illya—"

And she crouches over him, sobbing "Oh, my gods," over and over, until his storm passes. And then, "But how, Raven? How? . . . That's why I asked if you were a clone."

Slowly, he answers, "I've been asleep . . . a lot. I've been asleep all my life, since." Then, still incredulous, insanely: "Look—you *are,* you *were* at FedTech, on Fairhaven? At Fairhaven U?"

"I was at FedTech on Fairhaven," she says gravely. "With you—you were a couple of classes behind me."

"And you left—"

She nods, sadly.

" 'The night has a thousand eyes, and the day but one; yet the light of a whole life died when—you—were gone.' You went to the grid-shows. . . ."

A shrill alarm has been in his ears; it's the fuel-up alarm ringing. With a start Raven comes partially to himself and transfers the nozzle to an auxiliary input. But his eyes won't stay away from her, they're so dilated that she sees their dark blue almost black. The light has changed again, he's seeing a girl now, the right girl; her eyes that had held his soul glowing up at him in their great smudge of lashes, the long lush lips with their secret smile, the perfect throat and shoulders, and the impossibly high, full, wide-pointing breasts, the hand-span waist rising like a stem from her sumptuous hips and thighs. Even her hair is back smoky black again, in this instant of shadow.

"Rehab must have wiped part of you out . . . anything painful." He remembers now; the war seemed the most respectable way of getting himself killed fast. Evidently it didn't work.

"I hurt you. . . . Oh, Raven—"

Without knowing how he got there, he's holding her right now, terribly tight through his awkward suit, caressing the soft curves of hers. Rehab stole the details, but not the pain. "You're the first, I think you're the only woman I ever loved." She's holding him, too, he can feel her tenderness, as if he were a hurt child.

But across the hull another fuel alarm is going; it brings back the bleak impossibility of everything.

"Oh, gods, the tanks. Look, I better carry you." He swoops her up by the waist, goes loping over the hull like some kind of animal.

"My looks," she says when he sets her on her feet and turns to the valves. "My cursed godlost looks. They ruined everything. . . . That's why my girl, I mean, my clone, why she—"

"You had yourself cloned?"

"Yes. A thousand years ago. She wanted to go, go out to a colony. I got her out before Gridworld ever saw her."

"What colony?"

"Fleetdown. But she's moved since, something happened."

Fleetdown is in the next sector. Out there someplace is a middle-aged woman, the pearly skin tanned, the long fingers work worn. Sending home a hologram of herself on a tractor. . . . He doesn't care.

Somewhere in those moments, Raven has become two men.

One is the superficially normal Raven, who completes the topping-off of *Mira*'s tanks and finally leads Illyera back to the emergency lock, brings the bag up around them, and zips it. Then he unscrews the temporary port, feeling the rush of *Mira*'s air filling the bag. He slides the emergency cover away and turns to help her through to where bar Palladine must be getting impatient.

The other is a Raven who knows his whole life has changed, who cannot take his eyes off her between every task, who feels Rehab-blotted scenes of memory wheeling and shifting inside his head, becoming almost—but not quite—clear. It's this Raven who can't help asking her, at the port, "Do you remember the roses?"

And this Raven who bleeds a little when she answers, frowning delicately, "Oh, yes . . ." so that he knows she doesn't. So many, many men must have given her roses. But it was *his* quarterly stipend that went, on that extravagant blanket of real Terran roses for their last lovemaking . . . *His* hands clasping her silken haunches, *his* body weighting hers down on the flowers. The pink tips of her young breasts matching the rosebuds, the great black curly bush on her belly around the brighter pink of her sex, the feel of her . . .

The Raven who recalls these things bends at the last moment, whispering, "I'll come to you . . . somehow."

"I'll be waiting," she breathes back with that dazzling smile—he remembers now that it was always as if she knew something, came from some secret place of strange experience. . . .

They crawl in backward, she first. He hears her exclaiming to bar Palladine about how beautiful it was, and, "What do you think? Myr Raven and I were at the same university!"

"Quite a few years back," says the "normal" Raven. "Here're your combinations," handing over the ivory chip.

"She's old enough to be your grandmother," bar Palladine grunts as Illyera gets into the cocoon to unsuit. "Now, can we get out of here?"

Just then Raven hears an instrument giving out the jitter that means it's just about to chime. But the jitter fades again. He frowns.

"Has your mass-proximity indicator been doing that much lately?"

"Ah . . . yes. Rocks?"

"Maybe. Also, maybe a ship hanging around just off range."

"Oh?"

"It's probably nothing. But you're a long way from Fed Central here, and there are a few bad actors out on the Frontier sectors."

"How exciting," sighs Illyera mockingly. She has stepped from the cocoon wearing a fluffy little short-suit that makes Raven's heart shiver, it looks so like the things she once wore. But the rational Raven bats down the quiver; that sportsuit is made of pelts of *rava*-down; it would cost his whole account.

"Don't be an idiot," he tells her lovingly.

"All the more reason to get going," says bar Palladine.

"Exactly. And don't, repeat, do not let any strangers in here, or let anybody get a beam on you. You represent a godlost bunch of credits flapping around with no protection."

Bar Palladine scowls at that but says civilly enough, "Thanks for the warning. And now I think we'll settle up and be on our way."

"Right." Raven gives him the figures—*Mira II* was, as he'd been warned, a fuel hog—and bar Palladine produces his credit chips for registry in both their credit computers. Raven gathers up his stuff and is back in his ship fast; he has no wish to watch them leave. His heart has not been able to resist one last look at Illyera; he figures bar Palladine must be used to that. And it effectively insulates him from the Talkers on his route out, aside from the impression that they are running down.

He boosts out of there before the other ship's engines start.

But once at the limit of standard-proximity indicators, he slows and halts, and tunes in his special high-range finder. Yes, there's the fat echo of *Mira II,* accelerating away—and there, by gods, is a second echo, large and slick—a sizable strange ship, on an interception course!

Raven curses. And then curses again, louder. Against his warnings, *Mira* is slowing, slowing. Slowing to a stop. He watches angrily as the two echoes merge. What in the hells has bar Palladine got himself and Illyera into?

It could be perfectly all right, Raven tells himself—a Lost Colony ship, for instance. But if so, why hadn't it signaled? Power too weak? Maybe. . . . What was it doing, nosing around until he left? Well, maybe they were frightened of intercepting two strange ships. Maybe. But odd that they'd go so unerringly to the yacht. . . . None of his business, really, what bar Palladine wants to do.

But it is his heart's business. And even as he reasons with himself, his hands have played across the controls, jockeying *Blackbird* into position to return. And then his reason comes up with a congruent point— here is the ideal opportunity to try out a nice new piece of *Blackbird*'s equipment he's acquired and not yet tested—a radar-shield for unobserved approach. Excellent. . . .

He's already on course, coming into their range. Now he slows to impellor power and turns on the shield. To use it properly means a dead-center approach: the area of shielding is small. As he purrs toward the linked ships, he steadies *Blackbird* carefully behind the small circumference of undetectability. He is concentrating so hard that at first he doesn't hear an odd thing—a high, steady hum from his transceiver. When he finally notices it he sees that it's mostly beyond audible range. A malfunction of some sort?

Holding position carefully, he puts the analyzer on it, finds it's a complex chord of frequencies, absolutely steady. And coming from the ships.

If Raven hadn't been as old as he was, he wouldn't have understood the nasty implications of that sustained EM chord. But he'd been fighting men who knew it well. And although it's now outlawed, he knows that some unpleasant Last War gadgetry is still around.

He opens his caller's coils and, with the utmost care, sets himself to duplicate that frequency. If this is what he fears, his duplication must be perfect, or people will die hideously.

When he has it to his satisfaction, he gets up and rummages out two more loud EM transmitters from *Blackbird*'s ample stores. He opens them up and lays in his best copy of that multiple frequency. Perfect; it has to be perfect. He gets them operating to his specs, pushes the master copy under his couch, pulls out a can of Sticktite, and loosens his extrusion grapple, to be ready for fast work.

Meanwhile he is desperately keeping *Blackbird* hidden behind that ultrasuperabsorptive field. This is no game of trying out equipment, now.

He is almost on the connected ships, flying by visual guidance. Incredible that they haven't sensed him. But the EM transmission must be jamming their sensors, and they're probably busy.

He had a good look at the strange ship. It might have been a colony ship once—half-hidden under burns and smears he can see her name: *New Hope.* But she isn't one now. Colony ships have an unmistakable look—so clean, and scribbled with messages of good luck and bravado. This ship is dark with dirt and ill maintained; a work beast in uncaring hands.

And Raven sees he's been given a stroke of good luck; the *New Hope* has closed with *Mira* along her bows and locked on so that they drift head to tail. Tied together, neither would get away. And that's just what *Blackbird* is built to accomplish. He's about to float over them; time to act.

He fires up the torque and sends *Blackbird* rolling around the linked ships, whipping out her wreck-securing cable. His sensors show EM peaks—alarms must be going off within both ships, but they're no help to them now. In one circuit he has the pair lashed together with the twin-strand cable that could pull a liner out of a thousand gees. And as he goes around them, he has accomplished the vital task—with his extruded grapples he has slapped and stuck a sending transmitter onto each hull. That will take care of them for a while—gods send he's set them right!

Now, with the speed of long practice, he reverses to a stop above *Mira*'s emergency port and slams the lip of his work-dock tunnel around it. His big magnetic grapple lays hold of the port and spins it in, tearing the plastic bag, as he had often spun-in the ports of burnt, corroded wrecks. He drops it inside, where voices can be heard crying out and cursing in panic. He takes no notice but snatches up his projector gun, already loaded with sleep-gas, and fires a canister straight in. Then he edges closer to the port and fires another into *Mira* in the direction of the main lock, where she is joined to *New Hope.*

In a minim the sounds within *Mira* have quieted.

He snaps shut his faceplate and draws a work curtain across the tunnel behind him—no need to saturate *Blackbird*—and waits till the last few stirrings from beyond the tunnel cease.

Now everyone should be asleep—unless somebody was suited up. So far only instants have passed; he has another three minim before the situation of any captives would become lethal, if he has misduplicated those frequencies.

He whips down a large sack, blows it up, and sticks it on the gun. Then he makes a few approach noises and edges the bag into sight beyond the inner port.

Bang—clash! A ballistic weapon fires into the bag, and a blade chops through it to the gun barrel. Damnation—one of the raiders *is* suited up and is waiting for him alongside the port.

Well, Raven still has a trick left, if that's a standard suit. Salvage operations often require fishing things out of inaccessible holes. The bastard who fired and slashed must be tight up against the hull.

Raven reaches back for his fishing equipment—actually a whippy metal rod bearing a reel wound with superwire, tipped with a vicious automatic minigrapple. With one skillful cast he sends the triple-barbed hook spinning through the port, then checks it hard right-handed so it sweeps around the inside of *Mira*'s hull, where the slash came from; the action is almost too fast to see. On his second sweep he connects with something. He braces and jerks hard, sets the rod in its stanchion, and commences reeling in. The reel is geared heavy enough to pull an asteroid out of orbit. In a few spins he succeeds in dragging part of a resisting, suited leg into sight across the port. Fabric starts to tear. A hand appears, sawing futilely at the wire with the bayonet.

Raven doesn't bother trying to parley. He has armed himself with a small aerosol canister stuck on the end of his projector. This is not salvage equipment, but a choice item one of his friends in the Patrol gave to him. Its formal name is Suit-Off, but it is usually referred to as "Balls-Off."

As the tear in the suit widens, Raven gets the aerosol nozzle aimed and shoots in a couple of healthy puffs before the knife bangs him away. Then he waits.

A heartbeat later comes a torrent of high-volume curses, and the knife clatters to the tunnel side. The hand ungloves and dives into the tear in the suit leg, tearing it farther. The leg convulses, the hand scratches violently, and another hand appears briefly as the owner rips open his crotch hooks. In a moment the stranger will be free of his suit; but the grapple and line are obstructing him. To save time, Raven wrangles the grapple loose and reels the line in.

The stranger falls back from the port in a tangle of limbs and suit; he is trying to scratch and unsuit at once. With difficulty, he forces his helmeted head to the port opening. Raven can see his mouth opening and closing but can hear no words. Behind the mouth is space-burned black skin and dirty pale hair. Raven shrugs.

The stranger tears open his faceplate to yell, "Give me the drench, you bastard, or I'll kill 'em all!" The "drench" is the closely guarded antidote to the ferocious itching power of Suit-Off. Raven shrugs again. He is more interested in a transmitter clamped to the man's wrist. He had been right. They were collar-slavers. And hence, desperate. The Federation's penalty for collar-slavery is death.

Slave collars are made of an alien alloy sensitive to radio waves. So long as the collar receives its frequency it stays loose. If the frequency is cut off, the collar constricts abruptly, shutting off the victim's air and blood supply. Attempts to loosen one by force also make it contract. The slave-controller carries an EM transmitter with a spring-loaded switch, which closes if he relaxes his grip, thus making him impossible to attack. The vicious things surfaced in enemy prisons during the Last War and are thought to have all been destroyed. But these raiders must be in possession of more. It vaguely occurs to Raven that there is quite a large Federation reward out for any; but he doesn't think about that.

Is Raven's duplication of the loosening frequency working, or are the raiders' captives strangling to death?

He can wait no longer. That yell had cost the raider a lungful of gas, he's crumpling into sleep. Raven vaults over him, whirling to check that no other suited men are in ambush for him, and then stops to yank the transmitter off the slaver's sleeve. It's as he expected, the transmitter has a pressure switch now released to "off." Raven squeezes it on and locks it—that'll relieve the emergency, if it isn't too late—and stands up, breathing hard, to look around *Mira*.

A line of bodies lie sprawled on the big lounge couch—Raven sees the orange suit of bar Palladine, the shower of pale hair that hides Illyera, and the mounds of the other three. Asleep or dead? He goes to them.

They haven't collared her—the white throat lies sweetly pulsing, unblemished. But bar Palladine's ruffled collar is cruelly compressed under a slender metallic circlet. He seems to be breathing normally, no signs of recent crushing. Raven cautiously releases the transmitter in his hand, leaving control up to his duplicate on the hull. Bar Palladine's collar doesn't move. So Raven's duplication is green! And it's sending with sufficient strength to keep the collars loose. Now he has all the time he needs.

Two other raiders in addition to his assailant lie sprawled nearby. All of them wear dingy black shirts, like some kind of uniform.

Before releasing the captives—Raven is a cautious man—he makes himself take the time to snatch out his pack of syrettes and shoot each of the raiders a dose that will keep them out of trouble. No need to waste drench on the blond who had attacked him; the itching would wear off in his slumbers. He arranges the man's clothing decently— Raven is also a man of the Spacers' Code.

As he runs from body to body, it occurs to him that there's every legal and practical reason for him to kill them then and there. It would save air, water, and trouble. But some old scruple makes him pass over the black syrettes and use the red knock-out instead. . . . Besides, these beasts may be wanted alive by Fed, for questioning on the source of the collars.

As he works, he keeps an eye on the open lock connecting with the pirates' ship; anything could be in there. Just to be on the safe side, he lobs another canister of sleep-gas into *New Hope* before turning to the captives.

He has thought that he'd have to go for his molecular disrupter kit. But first he bethinks himself to try an old rumor about the later imitation collars. He pulls bar Palladine into sitting position and brings the radio's transmitter into contact with the thin circlet around his throat. In a moment the thing sags loose, looser yet—until he can actually pull it off over the man's head. Good! So these *are* later Human-manufactured collars, not the alien originals. The Federation has located and demolished a Human manufacturing plant on one of the Black Worlds. The process is difficult and requires a rare catalyst; maybe these are part of its original make, not a new source. But that'll be for the Feds to settle.

Raven has been untangling the other bodies and arranging them decorously on the couch, including that slim, luscious sleeper he scarcely dares to touch. She is not quite inert and makes a tiny protesting sound that means she will soon awaken. Raven finds her translucent scarf up in the pilot's area and wraps it around her sitting figure.

"It's all right, Illya," he opens his faceplate long enough to whisper to her. "I'm here, it's all right now, my girl."

The two ex-Talkers turn out to be what Raven thinks of as typical Fed-Central rich old boys; their skins glow with expensive health, their now limp muscles are expensively exercised; faint marks show where wattles have been discreetly clipped and eye-pouches tightened. One has a full head of white hair, the other is stylishly bald. Only the bald man is wearing a collar; the raiders might be short. Raven brings up the transmitter and eases him out of it.

The man Raven thinks of as the Fat Boy is at the end of the line, his embroidered robe askew and a collar murderously tight on his plump neck. He must have struggled, from fear or pain, Raven judges, squeezing him free. As he does so, he notices an odd tonsure shaved in the man's hair and guesses that he might be some sort of priest or cult healer attached to one of the older men.

When he has them all free, he pockets the collars and turns to tackle his next job—*New Hope*'s contents.

No sounds have come from the pirates' ship that he could detect while he was occupied. Raven edges silently into *Mira*'s lock and from there into a short, dirty tunnel leading into *New Hope*. Her lighting is dim and gravity weak; Raven guesses she's short of power. He uses his extension mirror to check that no one has been waiting for him and emerges into a long, empty chamber with the pilot chairs to his left and a pile of some sort of pads aft and at the end. A few sleep-chests are by the hull. A man could be hiding there or in the crude waste cubicle; Raven wrinkles his nose as organic stink penetrates his filters. The slavers must have been living in here some time.

He peers at the pilots' chairs and makes out a black-sleeved arm dangling from one. As he watches, it stirs aimlessly. Raven cracks another canister of sleep-gas and hurls it forward. The arm jerks once and is still.

He then leaps to the side, applies his stethoscope to the hull, low down, and settles silently to wait. Is he hunter or hunted? He doesn't know, but either demands patience.

The minims pass. Nothing. Silence, except for one rattling snore from the limp pilot.

Just as Raven is about to give up, it comes—something slithers against the hull down by the heap of pads. He freezes, listening hard. The soft dragging sound comes again, followed by a click against the hull.

All right.

Raven hangs the steth in his belt to serve as an in-air receiver, takes out his welding-pistol, and gives the pads a burst that starts a smudge.

"I'm going to flame this pile," he tells his invisible listener. "If you don't want to get burnt, come out crawling. I want to see both hands flat empty."

The pile heaves, and a slender black-shirted figure wiggles out from under, reaching out for the floor with one hand. The other is occupied, Raven sees, holding up the hose of an emergency nose-mask. As the figure wriggles free, it shows as a woman, with an air tank slung over one shoulder.

If that tank had been oxy, she'd have been dead, Raven thinks belatedly. He unhooks an extinguisher can from the hull and works the long-unused nozzle to foam the smudge.

"I think you'll be better off asleep for a while," he tells the girl. "I'm not going to hurt you while you're asleep, I give you my word. Put down that mask and breathe."

She turns big glinty eyes on him above the mask, looks him over for a few blinks. Then she takes a deep breath of canned air, lowers the mask, and cries out fiercely, "I'm not one of them! I'm a prisoner! Help! Don't let them get at me—" But she has to breathe in. Her head bows under its shock of black hair, and she crumples down, asleep.

A new puzzle. Raven bends over her, feeling his backbone twitch, but can see no collar, no weapons. He puts back the welder and picks her up, by her slim waist, in the light gravity and hangs her over his shoulder, fighting the mop of dirty hair from his faceplate.

The pilot still hasn't moved as far as he can see. Raven dumps his captive in the lock and goes forward. The figure on the pilot couch is wearing a black shirt, but he has a collar on. Puzzle number two. Is this man a raider or a prisoner? No matter, no man should wear one of the diabolical things. Raven takes out his transmitter and loosens it. Then he sits down in the other seat and makes a careful space check to be sure the linked ships aren't drifting into trouble, and a quick check of *New Hope*'s readouts. As he suspected, they're low on fuel. Everything else seems normal.

He starts to pick up the pilot, then slaps his own helmet.

"Slowing down!" he mutters, and turns back to the controls. In an instant he locates their trail recorder, extracts and pockets the cassette. This will tell where the raiders came from.

The pilot, if that's what he is, is lightly built, but by the time Raven has lugged both captives into *Mira* and tied them up in armchairs where they can't see each other, he is tired from long work in a suit. Bar Palladine and his guests are beginning to open their eyes and stir. *Mira*'s air system is good. Raven knocks back his helmet and takes a chair facing everybody.

The two older men and Fat Boy emit waking-up grunts, but bar Palladine's hooded eyes come steadily awake, eyeing Raven, then glancing around the lounge at the recumbent pirates and, finally, at Illyera. One hand steals to his throat and his eyes go back to Raven. Raven nods. "I came back. I thought you'd be better off without that. Now, do you see what I meant about not stopping for strangers?"

Bar Palladine's face clouds, but he only says controlledly, "Thank you. . . . They had a girl, a girl did all the talking. Illya insisted—Hell, it's my ship. I stopped. And I was godlost sorry I did."

"Well said." Raven nods at the girl, who is murmuring with oncoming wakefulness. "I assume that was the girl? Did you have any reason to think she was a prisoner, or one of them?"

"A prisoner, I'd say. She was crying, and she begged our pardon, until one of them knocked her down."

"Oh," the girl cries weakly. "Oh, yes—they were torturing Bobby. With the collar . . . I couldn't stand it. And we *were* out of fuel, I don't know what they would have done if you hadn't stopped. But Jango said it was only for the fuel—"

"Jango?" Raven asks her.

"Jangoman, that one. He's the leader. . . . Oh! They aren't tied up!"

"As good as," Raven tells her. "They'll be well wired before they come to."

But the girl keeps staring so fearfully that Raven gets up and wires the pirates' ankles and wrists behind them to *Mira*'s hull holds. Meanwhile bar Palladine has risen and is riffling through *Mira*'s fancy-looking aid cabinet. Raven sees that his left shin has a nasty laser burn through the orange silk. One of his companions, the bald man in the blue lounge suit, is with him, holding his forearm. The raiders must have used that laser before they got the collars on them. Raven does a quick search of the raiders' pockets, finds a nasty-looking little laser pistol. He puts it with the collars in his work-pocket.

Bar Palladine is slathering tannic acid in gel on both of them. Raven approves. It turns you black, but it's the only efficient burn medication. Somebody with sense had packed the aid kit.

Raven stands tall and stretches. He's used to long hours in a suit, but playing war-games is something else. His condensers are sweated through.

"All right, Myr-and-Ser. First I suggest this girl tells us her story. Your true story this time, please."

"I haven't lied," the girl protests. "They made me say we were out of fuel—and we are."

Bar Palladine snorts. "Giving me to understand you were a colony ship full of women and children."

"Th-that was Jangoman."

"All right, the story," Raven repeats impatiently. He can't quite look at her. "Where are you from?"

"From Cambria. Both Bobby and I are. They—Jangoman and his men—landed, oh, I haven't been able to keep track, but a long time back, and th-they killed several people and took us. Cambria has a lode of gemstones, see. They made them promise to dig a lot to ransom us, or they'd come back and kill some more. And they wrecked our transmitter so we couldn't call for help."

"Is that your ship? The *New Hope?*"

"Um-hmm—" She was weeping. "We—we were the hope of, of another colony. Fleetdown, the L-Lost Colony. Everybody got a terrible brain parasite, but they sent away us children with a few adults who weren't affected. . . . Those older people were the ones they killed. They just shot them down like—like—"

"All right. I'm sorry." Raven was thanking his luck he hadn't gone to Cambria to refuel and perhaps been caught by the pirates coming back. "Where's their base? Where did they keep you?"

"They don't really have a base in air. They're staying on a weird thing, a big kind of junk-pile, orbiting some star, way out. It's all old ships and satellites, smooshed together. Some of the bodies hold air, see. They have hydroponics. But it's awful and dirty."

Raven's ears have been tingling at what he heard. Unless he was much mistaken, Jangoman and his godlost crew had run across one of the fabled treasures of space, more mythical than real. A salvageman's dream. The story is that there are gravity-null points in space, in which millennia of junk have been slowly accreting. Now he's apparently hearing of a real one! Pity the Feds'll probably get to it first, when this story comes out. . . . He shakes himself.

"How many pirates are there?"

"Just Jangoman and Steer and Mickey there is all we've seen. And maybe one left on Cambria, to—to oversee work. We were supposed to harvest for winter, see, but the pirates made them dig gems."

"And Bobby here?"

"They made him run the ship, so they could be free to—to fight here. . . . Is he all right?" Her face is so dirty the features can be anything.

"As far as I can tell," says Raven. But Bobby speaks up groggily:

"I'm all right, Laine, are you? Did someone rescue us?"

"Yes, I think so," the girl says doubtfully. "I hope so."

"If your story checks out, you have nothing more to worry about, Myr Laine . . . That's your name?"

"It's Illaine, really, but everyone calls me Laine. Oh, please, could you take us back to Cambria?"

"In due course, Myr Laine. First the Feds'll be right over to Cambria to see if there are more of those characters. It's no use trying to message them first."

"N-no . . ."

"Raven, don't be so cold-hearted," Illyera exclaims suddenly. "Let me help this poor girl, she's been through all hells. Let me untie her and Bobby."

"Right." Raven is a shade reluctant. "Now we have a set of facts, I hope. Conference time."

Illyera has moved to the girl and is picking at Raven's knots. Unwillingly, he gets up and helps her release the girl and the pilot. He is nagged by the notion that he has forgotten something . . . dangerous . . . And the girl bothers him. He is delighted when she vanishes with Illyera into her cubicle.

"I see no need for any conference," bar Palladine says when Raven rejoins them. "If you'll kindly get these thugs off my ship, and submit your bill, I can start for home as soon as possible. I'm overdue already."

"Wrong on both counts, Myr-and-Ser," says Raven. "I don't charge for my duty as a Federation citizen to rescue other citizens in peril; and if I charged for endangering myself in the process, you couldn't pay it. Next, *your* duty as a citizen is to report this to the nearest FedBase. That's Nine hundred. They won't keep you long, and you have to go back that way to pick up your beacons. But you must check in. And I may have to take back some of your fuel to get these ships to FedBase Nine hundred. Moreover, my *Blackbird* only sleeps one; we may need some of your cold-chests. And I could charge you with endangering citizens' lives by failing to heed official warnings, but I'll charge that off to crass inexperience."

Bar Palladine blazes. "Absolutely no—"

"Pavel! Pavel!" Illyera pokes her head out. "Don't you think we should thank Myr Raven for coming back and saving us? Those collars—"

The other men, silent till now, speak up. "You're right, Illyera," the bald man says, rubbing his neck. "Illyera is right, Pavel. We've forgotten the decencies. I fear the shock affected us. Myr Raven, please accept my apologies and my gratitude. I'd very much enjoy hearing how you did it! And permit me to introduce myself: I'm Cameron di Connor."

The two others chime in. "Well done, indeed," says the fat younger man in an admiring tone. He turns out to be called Roy. The other older man gives the single name Danta.

Bar Palladine, assuming a more courteous demeanor, adds his thanks. "But I still do have to get home."

"Right. I'll put in my word to see they hurry things at FedBase," Raven tells him.

And so matters are decided, not without further talk and work, until two shocks make it all come unglued again.

The first is minor—the discovery that two of *Mira*'s sleep-chests have been hit by projectiles fired by Jangoman's gun. One is right behind the emergency port. When they open up the chests they see the damage is so extensive that the chests are unusable.

"They must have been explosive pellets," Cameron di Connor says thoughtfully. "I hate to think what would have happened to anyone in them."

"Never wake up," says Raven. "Why sleep-chests, Jangoman? What have you got against them?"

The white-blond pirate is now awake, watching them out of his space-blackened face and sleepy eyes. To their surprise, he replies, in a curious high-pitched drawl that Raven recognizes as a Black World specialty.

"As any fool would know, bullets are dangerous in a ship." His tone is more educated than Raven had expected. "The chests make good bunkers."

"Hmm," says Raven. "Remind me not to be asleep next time I'm—" And he has to close his mouth because the second shock has arrived.

It's Illyera, pulling a reluctant Laine out of the cubicle, where she's been helping the girl clean herself and don fresh clothes.

"Look, everybody!" She pushes her forward.

And Raven sees.

Two Illyeras—rather, Illyera and a blond counterfeit.

Oh, gods . . .

Raven, clutching a chair back, looks thunderstruck at his old love—exactly his girl, Illya, mint-fresh, black-haired, and perfect. He shakes his head like a wounded beast, unable to comprehend how this can be, unable to grasp what Illyera is saying so excitedly.

"My clone!—I mean, my grandclone! My clone's clone! My clone was Illandra, who went to that colony; she had herself cloned before the tragedy that wiped them out. And this is her—my—Illaine! Oh, Raven, isn't she sweet?"

"Sweet" is not the adjective, Raven thinks—though, looking closer, he sees she is sweet, too—fresh, new-made, a genuinely *young* girl, his young Illyera all over again.

But this Illyera does not remember Fairhaven U. This Illyera never loved and left young Raven. This Illyera has never seen a rose.

Beside her, Illyera looks—looks different. But she is the Illyera Raven loved. . . . Loves . . . He is staggered, dumbfounded by double love. So beautiful, so young, so young, so beloved— He realizes he is about to become unstuck, longs to be back in *Blackbird.*

And yet, for all the surrounding eyes and ears, he must contrive to say feebly, "Yes . . . amazing."

"This changes things," says Illyera.

And so it is decided all over again. There are five functional, if unappetizing, sleep-chests on *New Hope,* and five left on *Mira,* in addition to the one in *Blackbird,* which is Raven's own.

"I'll hitch *Blackbird* to *New Hope,* and pilot the big ship till her tanks run dry. Then I'll turn around and pull her on in to FedBase with *Blackbird.* I'll take Jangoman, and Bobby, and the—the girl. But I think you should take these two henchmen, Myr-and-Ser. And if you can, spare a couple of volunteers to come with me. We'll have to stay awake a while until the switch-over. If we put everybody asleep, the out-of-fuel alarm will wake us and we can't get back to sleep for the safety period."

"I'll come!" Illyera exclaims. "I insist on it, Pavel, this is my only chance to talk with my own dear clone! My own flesh and blood. Oh, I'm so happy!"

"And I will," unexpectedly says the fat man, Roy.

"Oh, but our card games," says Cameron. "What'll we do for a fourth?"

"I'd have preferred to take the two women," says bar Palladine icily.

"But Rama Roy—" says the full-haired older man, Danta, who, Raven has learned, had brought Roy along as a spiritual adviser and fourth at play.

"You must remember," says the fat Roy, quietly, "that these men are headed toward certain death at the hands of the Federation. I cannot forgo a chance to talk with their leader. If I have any healing powers—"

"Oh, you do, Rama Roy, you do," puts in Danta.

"It's my duty to do what I can, in that interval of grace, to change his heart."

This is said with so much solemn conviction, the fat face looking momentarily quite different, that the others fall silent. Raven remembers that during the talks Roy had found occasion to give the raiders some water.

"I'd have preferred you to take the women," says Raven grimly to bar Palladine. "But frankly I've got to get some sleep, and I don't feel prepared to have those three animals aboard and awake with me during the first hours of the run." Danta and Cameron make understanding noises. "If you wouldn't mind? I'll see your two safely in their chests before we separate."

"No need, no need," says bar Palladine stiffly, but the other two add: "Thanks, Raven. We'd be grateful!"

One of the pirates, Steer, speaks up hopefully: "I play a pretty good game, Myrrin."

Nobody answers him, then. Raven wonders if dedicated card players will forever resist the bait, even if the proffer comes from, technically, a dead man.

"Right," says Raven. "Now I've got to go out and get these boats apart."

And thus, presently, they set out for FedBase, with *Mira II,* freed from the larger ship, in the lead and drawing away. Her pirates are already locked in cold-sleep, their wrists and ankles fettered. She's following her own trail record back to a star configuration where she can pick up a FedBase beacon. A copy has been made for the other crew, who are following in the bulky shape of *New Hope* with *Blackbird* mated to its stern.

In *New Hope*'s pilot area, the two women are curled together in one of the big pilot couches. Behind them Raven sits on a cold-chest that has been put there as an observer's bench. On the other end of the bench sits Bobby, looking disconsolate despite a clean-up and a fresh shirt with a Bohemian Club logo donated by Danta. Back in the big cargo-space, Rama Roy is talking with Jangoman; only a faint murmur can be heard up here.

The women are chatting.

"—and you haven't lived until you've seen Fed Central," Illyera is telling her grandclone. "The hub of the whole great Federation! Humans and aliens of all kinds, and— What? You mean you've never seen an alien?"

"No," says the beautiful dark-haired girl shyly. She who has faced rapes and pirates seems bedazzled by the other's account of civilized life.

"Oh, my goodness, Raven, we have to do something about this."

"Maybe there'll be an alien or two on FedBase," says Raven sleepily. He's preoccupied with a weird feeling of happiness. His girl, his girl he'd lost forever, is here. The fact that she's in two bodies seems only to make it richer, more complete . . . as though he had her very life.

He's playing with the idea of accompanying them on from FedBase; he can tell that the light Illyera has fired in the younger girl's eyes won't be quenched by a quick return to colony life. Why not go with them? His credit account would stand it handsomely, if he stays away from *rava*-down coats.

"Oh, Moom, and Swains," says Illyera loftily. "I mean *real* aliens."

"I'd love to," says Laine, wide-eyed. "You know so much. . . ."

"But we can't stay anywhere," Bobby puts in sharply. "You know we've got to get home to help with the harvest . . . if there's any left."

"That's right," says Laine. "Oh-h-h . . ."

"Don't worry about that," Raven tells them. "The Fed will send over a whole squad of help to put everything right, when people are attacked."

"They *will?*" Bobby is incredulous. "But we were told and told never to expect help."

"That's right, that's the normal rule of colonies. You have to make it on your own. The Fed'll evacuate you if you're dying, that's all. *But* when some disaster strikes that they're commissioned to guard you against, like raiders or alien attack, it's their duty to put you back on your feet. See? You're free to go sight-seeing. Plenty of volunteers from FedBase for bringing in a harvest."

"Will you go, Raven?" inquires Illyera, smiling that incredible, loving, teasing smile.

Raven snorts. He has been keeping one ear tuned to the muttering from the big far compartment. *Blackbird*'s open work tunnel is hitched to the stern exit of the old colony boat. Raven's wondering if he shouldn't go back and shut off the tunnel, in case Roy gets wanderlust. But no, Roy's too fat for that work lock.

"That's great!" Bobby has cheered up notably. He yawns. "D'you know, I'm falling asleep. Maybe I could go back and crawl in one of those chests for a nap? That's where—where *they* slept."

"Good. I'll escort you." Raven has no more formal doubts of the innocence of the two captives, but he has to move or fall asleep himself.

Back in the dim aft chamber they find Jangoman lounging in his bonds, on a sleep-chest by the single porthole. He has his face turned to the port, ignoring the fat Rama who is sitting beside him on the chest, hands clasped in prayer position, apparently talking to the pirate's back.

Bobby picks out a sleep-chest near the aft lock where *Blackbird*'s moored. "This is the one I used." He props the lid open and gets in. Raven checks that the prop is solid—that the lid seals airtight.

"I'll wake you at switch-over. Rest well."

"For the first time in a long while, Myr Raven," the young man replies somberly. "I'll never thank you right."

"So all's well that ends well," says Raven jovially. He wants to check on something he's seen.

But before he can get back forward, Roy calls to him.

"Myr Raven? I wonder if you could loosen one of this poor man's bonds? You can see he's in distress."

"This poor man," says Raven levelly, "has tortured, raped, and killed people."

"But look. You wouldn't treat an animal so," Roy points out.

Jangoman makes no move to show his trouble but continues to stare out at the starfield. But Raven can see, behind his back, that he has unduly tightened the wire around one arm. The hand is blue and swollen.

"All right. Call him an animal. . . . Bend over, if you want that fixed."

Jangoman makes no reply, but only lets his eyelids droop, as if to shut out an annoying sound.

"Please, Myr Jangoman," the fat priest begs. "You could lose that arm."

At this, the pirate gives a disdainful laugh. And as though a spell has been broken, he bends forward so Raven can cut the wires, saying in his high, nasal, oddly refined voice, "The flesh is weak."

"You realize that, my brother?" Roy asks eagerly. "Then you are on the first step on the Path."

"Path"? Ah, Raven has him now. This is a man of the Path, a Human-alien cult from the South. But Pathmen are supposed to take a poverty vow; the only other Pathman Raven has seen was in very plain gray, while that embroidered robe of Roy's is no poverty item. Things must have prospered with the Path.

"Flesh is dirt," says the pirate scornfully under Raven's ministrations. "Out there"—he jerks his chin at the starfields—"that's real. That's where I belong. Alone." His voice is strained, but not druggy.

"For a loner," says Raven, finishing the wire, "you've surrounded yourself with quite a pack of people. Whom, incidentally, you've led to their deaths."

"People are cattle," returns the pirate distantly. He turns his face back to the starfields and says over his shoulder, "When they . . . finish with me . . . do you suppose they could shoot the leavings back out there?"

"They may grant you a last request, though I don't see why."

The fat Rama is shaking his head mournfully, but he persists. "Beauty is out here . . . that's true. But don't you see, by denying your Humanity, you deny the very senses that appreciate the stars?"

Raven leaves them.

On his way back to the girls, he stops at the spot where the chamber narrows to the nose-section and flashes his torch around the top and sides of the hull. His other hand comes up with an iron prybar with which he prods and taps, giving grunts of confirmation.

"What's the matter?" Illyera calls languorously.

"Laine, did you know that this ship is a glued-together job?" Raven is fiddling with a worn plastic hanging beside the narrow waist. "Somebody welded an old freight booster onto the tail of a supply tug. This is the old air seal they used while they finished the job."

"I didn't know," Laine says. "I was too young when we came to Cambria, and I wasn't born when they first used it."

"Well, it is. That explains the position of the drive, and some other things. . . . Done a long while ago. It's leaking. I'd hate to be in here if we had a high-gee turn."

"J-Jangoman used to pull that old curtain across when he wanted to be alone—or—" the girl says, and shudders visibly. The gods knew what had happened to her behind this curtain, Raven thinks savagely.

Illyera hugs her gently. "Forget it, darling. Forget it all. It never happened. . . . I'll see that you forget it all—"

The girl gazes at her hopefully, the beginning of a smile on her face. It's a beautiful smile. But she doesn't have Illyera's magic, this nice colony girl who happens to be outrageously beautiful. There's no irony, no mischief in her. Her black curls are swaying toward Illyera's shoulder; she must be exhausted.

"Baby," says Illyera fondly. "I'll tell you something you won't believe. When I was your age and looked just like you, Raven and I were in love."

Laine's dark eyes open—a puzzled look crosses her face. But it is too much for the tired girl to take in. She smiles vaguely, and the dark curls nestle into Illyera's neck.

As Laine visibly drifts off to sleep, Illyera, stroking the black hair with loving fingers, beckons across it to Raven. He leans toward her.

"I remember—I remember *our* roses," Illyera whispers. The gilt-blond head shakes in wonder and reproach. "My dear, my dear . . . what a little oaf I was. . . ."

"Never," says Raven, choked up. Frantically he searches for distraction, and finds it.

"Speaking of high-gee turns, we seem to be heading pretty close to that little system ahead." He turns to the scope and sees a pair of small stars that seem to have planets. In that direction *Mira* had disappeared.

"Yes," Illyera says. "That must be where the alarms woke us, coming out. I guess he's sticking exactly to the trail back. He's had enough shortcuts!" She laughs that lovely low laugh.

The trail she's referring to is in the guidance computer. The tail of every ship, by regulation, carries a time-lapse camera that takes backviews of the starfields all along the route. To retrace your path, you simply take the record out and insert it in the guidance computer. It was *New Hope*'s trace record of her path from the "great junk-pile" that Raven had pocketed. Thinking of it now, he pats his pocket. That will be his next destination— But no, it won't. Not if he goes with Illyera. Well, junk can wait. He'll have to surrender it at FedBase, he guesses; but not without a copy. Oh, what could be in that accretion! He sighs, thinking of antique ships. . . .

Any problem with the close pass to that system ahead won't be coming up for some while. Time for a nap. But as he debates just stretching out on the chest, not bothering to get in the couch, it comes to him that he'd better check the fuel. It's holding out better than he expected, and it would be awkward to run out and have to switch drives while they're in the system's gravity field.

He gets up into the pilot's couch, starts checking *New Hope*'s readouts more carefully—and finds, beyond the main tank readout, the old indicators for the supply tug's own old tanks. Aha! So there is independent tankage, which is feeding into *New Hope*. He cuts the connection and realigns the supply for direct use. They are still accelerating; when *New Hope*'s supplies run out, the drive will now shift automatically to draw from the tug. In fact, the tug could fly on her own, if she were free. Even the oxy and water supplies are stored up here. . . .

Raven has leaned back and is contemplating the reconstruction possibilities of *New Hope,* conscious that he is dozing off. With half an ear he listens to the sweet voice of Illyera singing a lullaby. Again, the strange feeling of a happiness he can't recall steals over him. Dimly, he's aware that the fat Pathman has come up forward, apparently for more water. The gurgling, splashing sound strikes him as pleasant, too. . . .

And then, oh, gods—he's brutally awakened by the nastiest shock of his life.

A slithering something touches his forehead and, avoiding his drowsy hand, slips behind his neck—and tightens! Someone scuttles behind him, cloth slips from his grasp—girls scream—and he comes fully awake to find himself half-choking in what can only be a slave collar.

His hand, gingerly exploring, feels fine links—he has been caught by a new type of slave collar made of links! Easy to conceal in a seam or a Sticktite.

And now, too late, he recalls the thing he had forgotten—a careful search of Jangoman's torn suit.

As this flashes through his mind, his body has been reacting automatically to catch the culprit—he is lunging, arms out, as the fat man ducks back through the connecting waist and scuttles, half-floating, away down the hall. Raven makes to follow—but the thing on his neck contracts so savagely across his throat that he can only stop.

Ringing through the ship comes Jangoman's jeering laughter. The pirate, his arms free, stops working on the wires of his leg bonds to bray in triumph.

"Turn about, eh? Take it easy, new boy."

He brandishes something that could be a small transmitter and guffaws again as he bends to work on his leg knots.

Raven is speechless, sick with helpless fury. Fragments of questions tumble through his head. Has the fat priest simply betrayed them? Betrayed them for money—ransoms for the girls? Or been somehow convinced by Jangoman? Above all, what can he *do?* How to get out of this? And the girls—

As he backs away from the nose-cone opening he's conscious of a sudden slight loosening at his neck. Yes! He's now nearer that transmitter he stuck on *New Hope*'s outer hull so long ago—and it's still working. As long as it continues to send, Jangoman can't actually kill him. But it must run down soon. What can he *do?*

As if reading his mind, Jangoman calls again. "Something to keep you busy, new boy. Call that yacht and tell them I have their women. Tell 'em to turn back and meet me. And if they call the Feds, I'll take it out on you and the cunts."

A tweak at his collar tells him that the pirate is trying to show his power. Raven pretends to choke hard. When it's over, he goes docilely to the commo station.

"Oh, Raven, what's *happened?* What will we *do?*" Illyera asks. Laine, who has understood faster, is weeping.

"Wait. I don't know. I messed up. . . . *Mira Two? Mira Two? New Hope* calling *Mira.*" Just as bar Palladine's faint voice comes through, the proximity alarm jangles. Raven cuts it off and by reflex turns to the scope. Jangoman yells a query. His voice sounds closer, as if he'd hopped forward. Those knots of Raven's must be giving him trouble.

"A rock!" calls Raven. But it isn't a rock. It is, he slowly realizes, what could be their salvation: a huge dark gas planet, hanging out here beyond the twin suns. There's his gravity well, *if* he can think and move fast enough, and *if* great luck is with him. His one crazy chance. There'll be no other—and this one has a dozen ways to fail.

"I'm turning around it," he calls. Jangoman, thank the fates, seems to have no burning desire to take over driving the ship.

"Very well." The voice is near and piercing. To Raven's surprise, it's coming from the speakers. Jangoman must have found an old intercom. "And then you can send the women back here, Raven. One at a time. I think I'll try the new one first. I'm tired of wet-face. Tell Blondie I mix my tenderness with a certain amount of, ah, pain."

So strange is the tone of these repellant words that Raven wonders if the pirate also had a cache of drugs in that suit. He damns himself for a stupid, bloody clown; missing that suit.

But he has no time for self-reproach. Carefully, he aims *New Hope* straight at the gas giant and kicks in all drives.

"What are you doing, Raven?" comes Jangoman's voice.

"I told you. Running this big rock." Will Jangoman look out to check?

"Get on my message."

"Right." Raven almost chokes with relief. *"Mira Two?* Bad news." Curtly, Raven tells them that Jangoman has taken over the ship, that Roy is working with him, that he himself is a collar-prisoner, and that Jangoman claims to be holding the women for ransom. "And he threatens reprisals if you call FedBase. You will now turn back. Repeat: Turn back for rendezvous. Our coordinates will follow. Over.

"Shall I figure the coordinates, Jangoman, if you want to meet him?"

The field indicator is already showing the gas giant's gravity pull as a component of their acceleration. It will stay unnoticed in the ship since it's straight ahead. But it'll take time to get deep enough for Raven's wild purpose. And for that he wants the coordinates, too.

While he works the computer, he muffles the mike and beckons to Illyera, who has been watching him, wide-eyed with fear.

"Illyera darling—" he murmurs when the perfumed head comes close. "I'm going to make a fancy turn soon. I'm pretty sure I can shake that booster loose. I want you two to be ready to hold tight. And—suit up."

At that she turns to glance at her suit, and Raven sees his error. His fatal error. Here are her suit, and his—but Laine's is back in her sleep-chest. Two suits, three people. Oh, no.

Raven stares numbly at the suits. His head is throbbing with pain from the intermittent choking, he is tired to death, he can't believe this blow. And as he grunts like a man dealt a knock-out, he sees Laine has followed their gaze and guessed.

Two suits, three people.

The terrible logic assails him; involuntarily, he looks from one to the other—and sees that they sense that, too.

He is choosing between them.

He must.

For an instant that's the longest in Raven's life, he vacillates. It's only an eyeblink in the outer world, but a hundred things pass through his head. A young woman with her life before her, versus an old, old woman who has lived to the hilt—a naive, blank girl, versus his love, his love who remembers his roses, who is Illyera's real rich self—a colonist's healthy young grin, versus the magic smile that has haunted his dreams—a stranger, versus one so intimately his—and yet—and yet—

Meantime a thousand things seem to be happening at once. His fingers have come up by reflex with the coordinates of their position. Jangoman is yelling at him: Raven hears some rational part of him reply, "I'm going to turn back and put us in orbit around that rock, with your permission, so they can find us. Right?"

"Be careful, new boy."

He hears his own voice sending the coordinates to *Mira,* and their faint acknowledgment.

But his whole soul is dominated by the terror of the choice before him. The two women are staring at him. He hears Illyera whispering, "Take her, Raven. Take my girl. I've had—" and Laine cuts across her:

"No! I won't! Take her, she's my—" But he can't listen, can't "discuss" this. How can he bear to watch either of them die in a vacuum, as die one of them must when the nose-cone breaks away? Which one? *Which one?*

No! He can't.

His whole being refuses it. Neither must die.

Does that mean that he himself must? He will, if he gives up his suit. Is that the only way?

No, again. Impossibility.

There must be some other way. Only, what? And that planet is coming up fast. They're already deep in its gravity. He *must* move. . . . But what to do? A memory skitters across the chaos of his mind. Enough to gamble on?

Total frustration explodes in total action.

"Can either of you fly this thing? If not, you better learn fast. We're turning."

He leans forward and bashes the drive controls to send *New Hope* into a violent U-turn. Gravity reels. Amid screeching and groans of strained metal, Raven leaps from the pilot couch and lifts Laine bodily into it. "Take hold. Keep her pointed up. When you can get into orbit, start sending out that Mayday there. You'll be in a vacuum here in the nose-cone. Hold on till somebody comes. And"—he throws a suit at each woman—"suit up! Now!"

"No, Raven, no! Oh, no!" they cry, being buffeted by the force of the turn.

"Shut up and suit up. And you, Illyera, pull this curtain across after me, it'll slow things down." Crackings and squeals of the breaking weld are coming from the joint, air is already rushing to it as bolts tear loose. The gees of the turn slam him hard against the hull, but he rebounds into the already bending passageway, ramming a couple of fast pries at the tearing joint with his iron.

"Now close this up. I love you. *Move*—you godlost fools!"

On that, Raven starts the fastest, longest run of his life.

Back through the aft chamber toward *Blackbird* he goes. A fat figure is tottering at him, mouth open. He kicks it in the stomach as he goes by, half scrambling on the side of the hull, half momentarily helpless in glides. The booster shell is buckling around him, the outgoing air is fighting him, and the godlost collar is tightening, tightening as his distance from the hull transmitter grows.

Jangoman is ahead in the shadows; he has long ago released his transmitter. Puzzled that it fails to stop Raven, he wastes a precious moment fiddling with it before he leaps to intercept his captive, one leg still trailing wire. Too late—Raven springs hard, evades a hooking foot, and is past. But at that moment the collar grows tighter still, he can barely pull a thread of breath to continue his crazy flight. Already he can see *Blackbird*'s open tunnel port, just ahead.

The pirate behind him pauses, and Raven feels rather than hears a bullet whistle past. Just at his side a sleep-chest explodes. Oh, gods,

Bobby is in there. Death. But there's no time for dead men now—Raven's almost made it.

Too late! The collar constricts hard on his throat, nearly cutting his head off. Nightmare pain—with his last strength, all but dying, Raven twists inside the tunnel, yanks the work door shut, and makes himself dive into *Blackbird,* to live or die.

For a long, gasping moment he can hardly realize he's alive, the gamble won. The deathly collar has loosened, bathed in the frequency chord coming from under *Blackbird'*s couch, where a lifetime ago he had stowed the master transmitter. It's still sending.

For how long? Will it quit next moment or next hour? In the bucking turmoil and confusion of his ship, tied to the gyrating booster hull, Raven doesn't try to guess but only snatches up the transmitter and eases the relaxed collar-chain off himself.

Free! But the broken booster is dragging him down to death, the searing gases of the planet so close below are strong in the air. Raven struggles up into the pilot's couch, casting one quick glance upward as he grabs the controls. Over the curve of the planet he sees a spark—that could be the thrust-fires of the separated nose-cone, disappearing around the planet's limb. If all went well—if they got suited up in time—if the fuel held—they should be green. Has he actually saved them both, done the impossible?

Meanwhile his hands have automatically cut in the torque and re-troboosters that will literally unscrew *Blackbird'*s nose from what was *New Hope'*s stern, gripping hand- and leg-holds as he's flung about. Now everything depends on whether that frail work port holds shut; there's no time to go forward and dog the regular lock.

It holds. Suddenly a fat shadow that is the booster, gape-mouthed, is falling away from his ports. Jangoman and that fat betraying weasel, Roy, are dying or dead in there—a kinder death than they'd offered their victims. And poor Bobby's bullet-shredded corpse with them. Well, the lad went to sleep happy, and just never woke. No way Raven could have saved them all.

On that thought, he gets the crazy spin slowed and is able to stand *Blackbird* up on her own high-gee drive and start her climbing out of the giant planet's grip. . . . Now, for the first time in days, Raven has nothing to do but relax and wait.

Held-back panic grabs him by the spine, buckles his knees, sets his elbows shaking and jerking, kinks his gut in nauseated knots. A dozen feelings he'd had no time for jolt him now, sending sweat sluicing down his belly, make him shiver so violently his teeth rattle. His blood curdles with repressed fear at the same time as it bubbles with triumph. Visions stream and mingle in his head—Bobby's burst sleep-chest mixes with Illyera's silvery hair, Roy's broidered robe drapes over his gross belly above Laine's young legs, bar Palladine's hawk eyes half hide the instruments on his panel—he can feel the iron prybar in his hand, weakening the ship's joint, while the same hand feels Illyera's tender body through her suit; the acridity of sleep-gas mingles with remembered roses, his own voice echoes in his ears—too much, too much! Stop it!

As his little ship mounts higher he forces himself to a shuddery stillness, takes a long deep draught of air, and then another; works to relax his legs, which are still pounding *New Hope*'s hull in a race for life. A strange feeling emanating from somewhere inside is helping him quell the turmoil of reaction. His fingers, shakily tuning his caller for what he hopes to hear, grow steadier and calm. What is this? He doesn't know but only works over the bands until, suddenly, the call he wants is there —the echo of an unmistakable Mayday squeal.

Somewhere on the other side of the great planet, the women are blasting their SOS into space. They're all right.

He can't believe it, but the evidence's there. After his one awful stupidity, he's managed to work his craziest chance and save them. His love lives. All he has to do now is track down their Mayday and reach them.

There's a little green key on his panel that will set the job automatically, in case Raven needs to be free for emergency tasks along the route. Another neat gimmick he's not yet used.

But as his fingers seek the green key, Raven suddenly identifies the new strange lightness that has grown in him and helped him cancel the residues of terrors and heart-piercing pain.

It is—freedom.

This is what freedom felt like. Every contour of his old couch speaks of it to him now. How easy, how uncomplicated, how stressless on the heart! Nothing to concern him but that great Golconda of a junk-pile, waiting only he knows where!

The moment he presses that little green key, all this will be gone. In its place, of course, will be the ecstasies of Human love—the blissful puzzle of choice—the thrills and revels of Human life in the luxury of Fed Central—the forgotten dreams all come true. And nothing is irrevocable, freedom can be recaptured. But . . . but . . . he has it *now*. Until he presses that key.

He finds his hand has been fingering the pocket in which he'd stowed *New Hope*'s trail guide to the great junk-pile and angrily makes himself stop. Yet a thought occurs to him. That trail guide is no use without the latest link, the trail from where he is now back to where the three ships met and *New Hope*'s solo trail begins. And while they'd been coming here, *Blackbird* was being towed, her tail-holo disregarded because he'd been driving *New Hope,* now broken up. It would make no sense regretting a Golconda he couldn't get to anyway; why not check this out before he scrambles his head with any more idle thought? It's overtime to suit up and close the work tunnel properly, anyway.

As he clambers swiftly into his spare suit, two other thoughts occur to him. First, in all likelihood the women believe he's dead. They couldn't possibly have seen *Blackbird* come free from the falling booster. They may not even believe it had been possible—in fact, it barely was.

So they're probably mourning him right now, up there in that half a nose-cone, uncomfortably waiting for the Patrol or bar Palladine to reach them. The thought gives Raven a violent urge to drop all this and rush to them, to end the misery that was needlessly tormenting his love; but it fades.

The work lock secure, he goes aft to crawl down the access shaft to where the trail assembly sits. It's on the way that he has the second thought—not a thought, really, but just a flash of profound realization; how very hard it is to find a ship silent in space, especially if the ship's pilot doesn't care to be found. Not a new reflection, of course, but one that comes with peculiar urgency now. Hmm.

As he approaches the tail camera he hears a click— So the time-lapse record *has* been functioning all through the tow! And the cassette has not run out! Which means that the missing piece is in his grasp—he could start from here, right now, and follow the guidance back to where he met *Mira* and *New Hope*—and then follow *New Hope*'s record all the way to that monstrous what-is-it Laine and Bobby described!

Just as he reaches to open the cassette holder, the camera gives a chime and sets up the buzz that means the record has run out.

Whew! If he'd been a few minutes later in looking back here, all he'd have found would be a used-up record that had ended gods knew when and where, of no use at all to him.

With slightly shaky fingers, he extracts the old cassette and drops in a new. . . . Have the gods of chance been speaking to him?

But as he returns to the pilot area, bearing his two priceless trail tracks, he seems to hear—what is it? laughter? Sweet laughter in the stars. Are his ghost-girls laughing at him? Are they so sure of his heart? Or are they merely laughing to be on their way, to the glitter of FedBase and the glamour of Fed Central? Raven stares out into the starfield, seeing smoky eyes that change to far suns . . . and back to eyes again.

Freedom and love, love and freedom, wrestle in his brain. And he must soon get some sleep or risk falling asleep on a course to nowhere. Random thoughts veer about in his mind as he clears the panel.

How long would two beautiful women wait for a man they'd all but seen die? And that terrible eternity when he thought he would have to choose which one would have the suit. . . . What would he really have done, whom chosen? But wait—that wasn't entirely a dead question. By what right does he assume that he, Raven, now "has" both his loves, or both versions of his loves? With one a Galactically famous beauty, and the other her inheritrix? Isn't it more likely that those halcyon moments when he sat with them on the observer's seat, were *it?* Were the culmination and fulfillment of Raven's lost love, the love that Rehab had stolen to save his silly young life? And in fact, the mists of Rehab are stealing back, are perhaps some fraction of the overpowering need to sleep. The trouble is, there are *too many* of her.

Far away, yet so near, the echo of a Mayday trills, like the voices of long-ago Lorelei calling. Ghost-girls, their slender fingers tenderly reaching for the bonds of Raven's heart. . . . Positively, he must act now.

One hand lingers by the small green lever, the other holds the trail cassette ready to drop into the guidance comp. Ghost-eyes glow in the starfield, a star sweetly, richly hums an old, old tune. Raven's heart gives a lurch in his chest, like a newborn animal struggling to rise, in the closing mists of oncoming sleep.

He decides.

Long years later, a contented, still-young salvage officer taps out a little jingle on *Blackbird*'s keyboard:

> The night has a thousand eyes,
> So fine to see;
> What use is the heart's sunrise,
> If you are not free?*

---

\* With apologies to Francis William Bourdillon.

# The Library Desk _____

"**W**ell, well, well!" says Moa Blue as the young Comeno couple approach. "And how did you like our second tale? Different, wasn't it?"

"Oh, my yes. Why, Humans have so many various facets, just like us. There was even some humor!"

"Yes, Humans are known for that. If a situation permits a laugh, they'll have it. And *now*"—he drags up a heavy sheaf—"the treat! I only hope it *is* new to you. Were you aware that the Human-Ziello First Contact was written up as a living tale? And you Comenor are in it—not as copiously as I could wish, but there, and at a tragic moment of your history, too. Some of your very words!"

"Oh, my—how wonderful. But why didn't we find it? I'm sure we looked," the boy says.

"It turns me blue to say so," Moa replied, "but I found this whole text filed under 'History of Exploration.' You'll see why. But there were no fact/fiction refs leading in. Somebody has *got* to give those files a good shake-out."

"Oh, how kind of you to do all that looking," the little Comeno girl says admiringly. Moa notices that her gaze keeps straying to one of her upper hands, which she has pushed forward. He looks at it and sees why—a handsome Comeno mateship coronet is set on her wrist. The boy has one, too, Moa sees now, though he's holding it less conspicuously.

"Well, my goodness, I see congratulations are in order!" And Human history is temporarily forgotten as they go through the pleasant ceremonial phrases. Moa is genuinely pleased—in addition to his weakness for romance in general, he has developed a strong liking for this young couple who study so harmoniously together.

"I wish you could meet our third," the girl says shyly. "He's my godfather. You'd like him, he's a real scholar. In Xeno-arts. Myr-and-Ser Carricklee."

"Why, of course, I know him by reputation," says Moa, thinking to himself that his instincts were right; these young ones come of very good family.

"It's a pity you aren't Comeno," the girl says mischievously, "or we'd have asked you! Because you're partly responsible."

At that, Moa really does turn blue, his racial equivalent of a violent blush. Not only is he in neuter mode, but the Comenor, for all their gentle decorum at most times, are renowned for letting go with great fervor at their rare biological rituals.

"Oh, ah, why, thank you," he stutters.

"I was just teasing."

"But you, or rather the last tale you gave us, *are* partly to blame." The boy smiles, his snowy muzzle looking very handsome and hearty. "I—I found some echo of my feelings in the Human Raven's love for his Illyera, and it woke me up to the awful possibility that I might lose her when we graduate." His upper arms clasp those of his bride-to-be.

The girl laughs musically. "So I must be very careful never to have myself cloned, or he'll run off and leave the two of us!"

"Never say that," the boy says sternly, and hugs her again. Then he turns to the new sheaf. "So we're really in this? Funny—I can't recall what our first Human Contact was."

"I do," says the girl soberly. "It was with Black World Humans." She shudders.

"But how loathsome!"

"Yes," says Moa. "It just shows you what the wrongly socialized Human is capable of. I've always considered them extraordinarily malleable and pliant. And as you'll see, many Humans are profoundly conscious of this and the dangers it creates. The story is set so soon after the Human Last War. . . . And it's in the same Rift area as the others, but earlier; it's the oldest of the three.

"But you can have confidence in it—most of it was taken straight from messages and newscasts and other records of the events, and the final Human-Ziello section was most carefully reconstructed from depth-interviews with the survivors. *And* there's three or four sections set entirely among the Ziellor on Zieltan, with whom you're so familiar. The writers had extensive help from a Ziello participant on these—in fact, she was the young female referred to in the text. They will give you a test for estimating the true-to-lifeness of the Human parts.''

"Of course! How great.''

"She had quite a sense of humor, too; it comes straight across the ages.''

"They all do,'' said the boy, carefully wrapping the bulky sheaf of the third tale in their waterproof carry-all. "All the feelings, I mean. People were certainly—people, weren't they? I must say it was a great idea, writing up slices of history like this. I'll never look at a star-map again without thinking of the real, quirky, emotion-beset people who filled it all in, star by star.''

"Was it a Human idea?'' the girl asks.

"That's the supposition. They've certainly done a vast deal more of it than any other race. But you could probably find other antecedents, if you looked hard enough. As with almost everything.''

"Well, we certainly feel we've had a whole education since the day we first came in to bother you. We pictured like a paragraph or two, some colorful incident. Not like meeting whole, rounded-out people of those far-off days. I'll remember them long after the dates and places and who-had-FTL notes have disappeared! And''—she takes his scaly hand shyly—"we'll remember you. Won't we?''

"We certainly will.'' The boy smiles. "You've brought this great impersonal library alive for us, as well as Human history.''

Moa snuffles ferociously, trying to control both his sinuses and his heart. He loves his job, and at moments like this he loves the whole university, and Deneb, too. With relief he sees the Moom astrophysics student stalking in upon them; in a moment he would surely have heard his own scales rattle with unseemly emotion.

"Well, now, wait till you read this last before too many thanks are in order,'' he tells them, showing the glittering array of teeth that had carried his remote ancestors to dominance on his home planet of Hard Eggs. "And meanwhile, my dears, accept my very warmest wishes for your happiness. I come from a long-lived race, you know—maybe I'll have the joy of guiding one of your progeny to some reading of his own.''

"Oh, how wonderful!'' the girl exclaims. "Oh, I do hope so! And now good-bye, good-bye, dear Myr Blue, until our next return!''

# Third Tale
# Collision

The space-worn message pipe, looking like a tiny spaceship, noses its way up the incoming chute. Finally its sensor cap touches the communications antenna that has called it across the light-years to Human FedBase 900.

When it makes contact a beep sounds, far down below in the Communications office, where the extensive facilities of the Base are housed inside a great crystalline asteroid. Nine hundred is an old frontier base, and accordingly is fitted out with every convenience and luxury that can keep life functioning happily in the immense isolation of space.

At the beep, Pauna, the Commo officer, sighs resignedly. It's been a busy day. She waits for the Commo aide in the surface bubble above to detach the sensor cap and send the incomer down the chute to her.

While she waits she finishes sorting the routine P.M. intake: five for Navigation and Charts; two nonurgent for Medical; two for Terraforming; three long ones for Colony Services; and a personal commendation to Maintenance from a touring commander. Plus a late info-special to Exec, from FedBase 300, way out on the far northeast end of the Rift.

She glances over it. Some suspected Black Worlds activity there. The Black Worlds are a largely Human group of planets who refused to come in the Federation after the Last War. They give refuge to a lot of bad actors, and their cultures are pretty unsavory. They're outside Fed boundary, and no regular space routes run there, but they manage a small traffic in gemstones from their native mines. This message is of no concern to 900, but Exec will post it as a news item.

When the new message pipe thumps down, Pauna's eyes are drawn to its heavy space patina and the freckling of dents and scratches. This thing has been a long time en route. Is it from deep in the Rift? Or has it only spent time bumping its blind way around some enormous planet?

No telling. In Commo you get used to receiving strange things—even junk pipes built by kids back in Central to surprise a Far Base and bearing weird notes: "The storm is coming!" or, "Hass and Dahlia send love."

But this is no prank. It's an old, old realie, maybe from some mission that set out before her tour of duty. She pulls out its cassette—it's stuck in crooked, probably in haste—and threads it on her voder to sample for distribution and urgency.

A man's voice announces, "Message one, *R-R-One* to Base, at Beacon Alpha, Navigator Torrane recording." Which means nothing to Pauna.

He goes on to give the Standard date—why, that's over twenty years ago!—and rattles off their space coordinates. Pauna doesn't need her ephemeris to know that those specs are deep in the Rift. Whoever can this be from? It isn't a Charts mission, the pipe didn't carry Charts' bright black-and-yellow belly stripe. Maybe a lost ship?

"We have just established Beacon Alpha," Torrane goes on. "It's in orbit around the tenth planet of a big blue sun, mass approximately four point five Sol, luminosity two fifty. We are about to make a thirteen-degree course change to the Galactic northeast because our computer shows a concentration of electromagnetic transmissions in that direction. It should be a center of activity for whatever life-form systems lie across the Rift."

Across the Rift!

Aha, now Pauna gets it—*R-R-One* stands for Rift-Runner, the first cross-Rift exploration! It had started out while she was a child. And this must go straight to Exec, right now. She'll take it up herself; that way she just might get to hear some of it.

Even in her excitement, Pauna's lips quirk at the folly of Human hurry at the end of the pipe's slow years of travel. But the pipes are the only means of commo from the Rift—the changing density-gradients out there garble any EM transmission to unintelligibility after a very short distance.

She calls a messenger to deliver the routines—not without a little twinge of regret; like any good Commo officer, she has a keen ear for gossip, and she enjoys her daily after-work round—and gives a quick briefing to her night relief, who has just arrived. Then she's hastening up the spiral exercise-ramp she uses as a shortcut to the main view corridor, where Exec's office is.

When she gets to the big main view-port she stops for an instant to look out. Oh, how beautiful! Over the bleak surface of the asteroid the starfield is splendid, dramatically cut by the long black river of the Rift. It's almost all above the horizon and parallel to it, about twenty degrees wide and half the sky long. A very few bright stars stand out in it against the faint haze of starlight from the far side.

The Rift is not a rent or tear, of course, but only a relatively starless region, of the same nature as the starless regions between the Galactic arms. Many such abrupt local density fall-offs can be seen with scopes, but this rift is special because it serves as the northern border of the slowly expanding sphere of Federation space. The Rift has made Fed space quite lopsided to the north, so that 900, which isn't really very far from Central, is also a genuine frontier.

Several explorations have ventured far enough into the Rift to know that the normal starfields of the arm begin again on the far side. And their sensors have picked up definitely artificial transmissions. But all the near stars have proved planetless; it became clear that a complete crossing would have to be made to find sentient life. A generation ago the time was judged ripe, and *Rift-Runner One* set out.

It's nothing unusual as missions go—two women and three men, all multiply skilled, and including a keen Sensitive. And a redundancy of supplies and First Contact gear. The ship is a regular recon model, retrofitted with extra fuel tanks and super-long-range sensors, plus broad-spectrum radiation detectors. They also carry a few beacons to position at course changes, so that others can follow them. The ship is of course taking the regulation time-lapse aft-pointed holography, which can serve as computer guidance on their own trip home.

The only really unusual feature of the cross-Rift trip is the very long times spent in cold-sleep. But even that is not a record; longer sleeps have been done, some inadvertently, and no ill effects observed. There is only the incongruous youthfulness of the sleepers on emergency, because you don't age—or do anything else—in cold-sleep.

And now comes their first message. Pauna's pace quickens as she catches sight of the Exec's deputy at their office door. Like many dedicated specialists, Pauna is quite unaware of the expressions her face is radiating, or that she's leaving behind her a trail of smiles and curious looks. Fred, the deputy, catches sight of her face and sighs in his turn.

He, too, has had a long day, escorting a pod of Sfermini all over the great Base.

He holds the door open for Pauna.

"Oh, Fred, thank you. Is Exec in?"

"And waiting for you. I caught the message as you came."

"Oh?" Flustered, she puzzles over this, gives it up. "Fred, the first signal from the cross-Rift mission just came in! I knew you'd want it now."

"Cross-Rift. . . . Oh! Yes indeedy."

They go in, to be greeted by the Exec, a solidly built gray-haired woman with sharp eyes and a fine smile.

"You have an info-alert about Black Worlders from FedBase Three hundred coming up by messenger, but I thought you'd want this before closing time."

Fred has opened their voder and is holding out his hand for the cassette.

"May I thread it, please?" Pauna asks. "It wasn't put in straight. It's not hurt as far as I can tell, but they're delicate."

"By all means."

Exec's sharp eyes have picked up Pauna's radiant excitement, and she takes pity on the girl. "Would you like to stay and hear it?"

"Oh, yes!" The blinding smile makes Exec ashamed of herself for teasing. Funny, she thinks, how much more appealing curiosity is in the young and pretty than in the old and worn.

The recorded voice of Navigator Torrane is starting. As he proceeds through the part she has heard, the deputy starts to frown. After Torrane gives the blue sun's specs there's a pause.

"Sounds nervous," Fred observes.

Exec nods.

Pauna reproaches herself sharply. She'd missed that. Now she hears it, too, the breathing, the tone. And Torrane had started improperly, with an abbreviation—and the jammed-in cassette. Curse her over-excitedness. But—is there trouble? Has anything gone wrong? Oh, please, no!

Torrane gives the course change and then goes on. "By the way, there seems to be a lot more transmission activity than we expected. There may be something pretty big over there."

Exec's eyebrows go up, then meet in a frown. She's listening intently, but her gaze seems to be fixed on some vistas beyond the voder.

"I wonder how much briefing those kids got," she says quietly to Fred as Torrane pauses. He looks at her thoughtfully and nods.

But the next words drive all this from Pauna's mind. Torrane takes another audible breath, then blurts out, "Something weird is happening to us, I think—but I don't know how to say it!"

At that same moment—insofar as simultaneity can be affirmed over such vast distances—far away on the other side of the Rift, which is here called the River Darkness, another but non-Human message is being heard. This message, too, has come automatically to its destination, the planet Zieltan, headquarters of the Harmony. But it has not come so long a way or over so much time. It identifies its origin as a group of colonies at the far northeast end of the River Darkness. These colonies are not of the dominant Ziello race, but of another, the Comenor, who are also in the Harmony.

It is being listened to by an assembly of the Advisers of Zieltan, who are clustered around a great table in the brilliant afternoon sunlight, their large single eyes intent upon the strange-looking mechanism, which shows the scars of its perilous journey.

"Help!" cries the recorded Comeno voice. "Help in the name of the Oversoul!"

It is the ultimate appeal; the Advisers raise their distinguished heads, tensely attending to the alien accents.

"Help us or we die—and others, many others, after us. We have been attacked by an unknown alien race, who descend upon our colonies and capture, murder, and enslave us by torturing our children. Every world they touch on is captured or extinguished. It has taken us years and lives to contrive to send this message. When you receive it we may be gone, too. The attackers are infiltrating around the east end of the River, from the south. They are repugnant in aspect, and call themselves the Zhumans or Zhumanor.

"In the name of the Harmony, send help to wipe out these monsters, even if we die with them. Death is better than life under their rule. They will not stop with us."

As the message runs out, the Chief Adviser comes painfully to his aged feet.

"We must convene a full Council at once, and our young Administrator must attend." He brushes the gray exudate of grief from his eye. "This is terrible. Terrible. . . . Never did I think I would say such a thing, but I thank the Oversoul that we did not destroy all the dread weapons of the Last War."

Around the table, indrawn breaths of realization as the full import of his words strikes home.

Back in the Executive office at Human FedBase 900, the three Humans look with sudden sharpness at the cassette from which Torrane had just uttered his strange words.

"Weird," he repeats. "I've got to tell you. Maybe if I just say it like it happened . . . The others are all back in cold-sleep now, there's no hurry. But I wish I knew who's listening to this. If the Exec is still Myr Rabeson, I know how he feels about Sensitives and hallucinations. Believe me, I'd give anything not to send this. But I have to."

Exec smiles very faintly. Her name is Myr Jonne.

Torrane takes another loud breath.

"Well, I was awakened according to plan when the computer decided we should change course, and I proceeded to put out a beacon and take scope holos. But first I checked everything, according to regs. All instruments were green, go. But when I checked the crew, well, that's when the first strange thing happened, when I looked at Kathy, uh, Lieutenant Ekaterina Ku. Her vital signs were fine.

"But I, well, it was like somebody was thinking for me, I said to myself, like whispering, 'Her spots are too pale.'

"*Spots.* I was looking at her through the front vision plate, and of course she doesn't have spots any more than I have. She has a lot of freckles, sure. But I was looking for big blotches like dark brownish, about three–four centimeters' diameter. Especially she should have one on the bridge of her nose. Then I thought, I'm crazy, I'm still asleep— what gives me the idea Kathy should have spots? And yet it meant something, too.

"So I went on checking out the others—and they all looked a little queer to me. Their colors were wrong—mostly too pale. And when I saw Captain Asch's neck it looked completely wrong to me. Please, I'm not crazy. Or if I am, it's not only me, you'll see in a minim. Anyway, when I saw his neck— Oh, I can't say it."

Comes the sound of Torrane swallowing.

"Funny, water tastes bad. . . . Damn. I have to. All right—*I thought he should have like extra little arms.* Little arms where his neck joins his shoulders, on the collarbone. And he was too short there.

"Wait, please—I can tell what you must be thinking. Only please wait.

"Well, I choked those thoughts down—there were others, about Dinger and Shara, see. Different things wrong. About faces and eyes, yes, eyes most. But all of them were green on their vital signs. I was

pretty scared about myself, I wondered should I wake Captain Asch
and tell him I was unfit for duty.

"Because thinking these things wasn't all. I was clumsy. I mean, out
of cold-sleep you expect a little slow reflex, but this was—is—different.
I keep reaching for things with hands that aren't there, and finding I'm
too short or small to fit where I expect—and the worst is, this is hard to
say . . . I keep trying to brace myself . . . like with a tail. A tail, I
mean, like an animal. A picture came in my mind sort of, I saw it once,
an animal called a Roo, or a Kangroo, with a big thick tail like a third
leg. That's what I felt I should look like. *Be* like.

"Meanwhile I was doing my work in spite of the clumsiness. I put out
the beacon and examined the area the computer had headed us for, and
found a high-density region of GO suns. A lot of signal activity was
coming from there. Too garbled to get anything, of course, but I did
catch voice sounds not too different from Human.

"I was feeling a little more normal then, except sometimes when I
went to use the stylus I tried to pick it up with a hand that wasn't there.
I mean a little hand and arm like I'd imagined on Asch. And just when
I was coming to where I had to decide about myself, a shower of small
rocks hit us, plus one large one that holed the cargo bay. And the
alarms went off and everybody was waking up."

He pauses again; the listeners hear him gag. Realune, Exec's aide, has
come in quietly with a sheaf of papers; Exec nods for her to stay.

" 'Scuse me. Well, we did the routine and it was nothing, just a teeny
hole by the aft scope. I want to make a note here, somebody please
record. There ought to be reinforcement there. If a rock bounces off the
rear scope housing just right, it can hit a single weld. That's what
happened to us. But we had the sealant right there and made permanent
repairs in seven minim. And I reset course, because the jet of the leak
had moved us a hair off.

"But what I want to say, why it took us seven minim, was because
everybody else was clumsy, too. During sleep we all wear as much as we
can tolerate, in case we wake up in vac alarm, so there was only like
pulling up and closing in to do. But people had trouble. Captain Asch
and Shara were cursing their suits, and Dinger said, 'Some joker had
one too many bright ideas; where do I stow my tail?' But he like broke
off as he said it. And Kathy said, 'You, too?' while we were all rushing
and scrambling to check the leak. And I saw a couple people *hopping;* if
we hadn't been zero gee we'd have broken our necks. Kathy seemed to
be the worst off; I saw her standing with her hands at her sides, wiggling her shoulders, as if her helmet ought to be coming down by itself,

saying, 'Oh, oh, oh.' But what with the alarms and the leak and the confusion, I was about in panic myself. I figured I might be hearing and seeing things as well as feeling them.

"Then after we fixed the leak and everyone was checking their assigned areas as per regs, I got Asch aside and told him I'd been feeling and seeing funny things and maybe the cold-sleep was affecting my mind. He didn't say anything for the longest while, just kept looking at me like I was, well, slipping in and out of focus. Then he suddenly turned to the whole crew and asked, 'Have any of you noticed any unusual subjective phenomena?'

"There was kind of a gasp, like people had been holding their breaths, and Dinger said, 'Oh, man! Have I. Yes!' And then it came out all at once, they'd all been feeling just like I had, that they had missing hands, and a tail, and everybody looked and felt wrong. And Kathy said, 'I am the spotted one! I shall do the Ritual if we make it!' And she was crying and laughing together. I tell you, it's weird—like something had got at our minds. Shara even said, 'Shall we turn back? Abort?' "

Torrane is breathing hard with the effort of telling the strange tale. They hear him drink again.

"Even water tastes terrible," he complains. "Usually after cold-sleep you can't get enough. . . . Well.

"So then Asch, who hasn't been saying much, speaks up in his official voice, slowly. 'All right. So we're all experiencing the same type of illusory sensations, as if we had different bodies. I have heard of one another such phenomenon, though I can't at the moment recall any more than that, I do recall that it wore off after the region had been passed through. It may be that this is normal for this particular region of space as well. And although it slows us down a little, it doesn't prevent us carrying out our duties. That's the crucial point. And somebody's got to explore this area sooner or later. We're here. I propose going on. But I realize some of you may be more affected than I, so we can take a vote. Lieutenant Dingañar?'

"Well, Dinger voted yes, and so did the others, but when it came to me I told him I had reservations. 'I don't know exactly, but it's like there was some danger to Kathy—Lieutenant Ku.' I should say here, Kathy is our Sensitive. My specs show I'm part Sensitive, but it's not reliable.

"Captain Asch thought this over and then asked me if I felt strongly enough to force an abort. You know a vote like that has to be unanimous. That was the toughest decision I ever had to make. And Kathy kept saying, 'Oh, *no*, Torry, not for me,' and grinning so I lost my feeling of fear. So I just said, 'Abstain,' which wouldn't abort, and it was decided. They all got back in their chests.

"I didn't want to strain matters by asking Asch if I should send all this, but he knows I have to report the course change and leak. Maybe he guesses I'll put the rest in.

"I guess that's all. Except just now I took a look in Kathy's sleep-chest and for a minute I could have sworn she has this big spot, over her nose. And like this voice whispering in my ear, 'She's the one who'll have to do the pool ritual if we land green.' And I felt terribly afraid—and yet at the same time *happy,* like it was great for her. But it can't be. I wish, I wish we'd turned back. . . . Oh, lords, let me not be crazy . . . I don't *feel* crazy, but they say the worst ones never know it. But Asch did say . . ."

He chokes off, then comes back stolidly.

"I'll send this now, after I take a roll of holos of the whole starfield from Beacon Alpha for Charts. Another will follow when we're halfway to target. Lieutenant Torrane of *Rift-Runner One* signing off."

In the Executive office there is silence for a minim; then Exec clears her throat and turns to Pauna and Realune.

"You two can probably guess what I'm going to say. We simply have no evidence on which to judge the seriousness of Lieutenant Torrane's report. And it'll be years before we do. I want you to remain entirely silent on the so-called subjective phenomena he or they experienced—spots, tails, rituals, little arms, clumsiness, and all. During the years before *Rift-Runner's* return, a loose word could get magnified into the rumor that you grow tails if you go too far into the Rift. Maybe you do, but not at the distances we use. Pauna, I want you to prepare an extract for me to post, about the beacon and the blue sun and the leak, and so on, but use the voder up here in my antechamber and do not let that cassette out of your sight. Realune will help. Rea, I can count on you.

"Now run along and leave the worrying to those who will come after us. Chances are everything's green by now, and they'll come home with the story of the century to tell. Rea, I won't need you again today."

She smiles her great smile and the two junior officers depart.

Exec and her deputy sit in reflective silence for a few moments. Then she sighs and says broodingly, "An hour ago we were effectively alone in the Galaxy, Fred. Now . . . we're going to meet the neighbors, like it or not. I don't know . . . I'm wondering if Asch was wise to ball on in. If only we could message them."

"You're thinking of Torrane's remark about the volume of transmissions on the other side? Implying that there might be another organization there, not just single worlds?"

"Yes . . . that, and the, ah, subjective phenomena. Fred, I've met Torrane, once briefly, to be sure, but my impression was, a solid type. If they're all getting this business, the only explanation I can think of is that there's a race over there psychically powerful enough to throw some kind of mental beam or field. Of course I'll take this up with theorists more qualified than I, but I don't see how you can get away from the idea of some kind of *influence*. Frankly it has me a little spooked."

"It would be good to know what Asch was referring to," Fred says, "when he said he'd heard of one other such phenomenon. I'll inquire around."

"Ah, good thought. That might help us a lot." She smiles, then sobers.

Watching her face, Fred comments, "You're wondering . . . what would happen if they react with hostility? Or, if *they* came to *us?*"

She nods grimly. "Fred . . . I find myself wondering an appalling thought: How much of that war matériel we dumped out west is still viable? I can scarcely believe I'd ever ask that."

In a rare gesture of personal sympathy, the deputy pats one of her strong hands. He knew what that thought must cost someone who had lived through the last stages of the war.

"After all, we have time. You could initiate a confidential consideration of this at the Exec's Council, with Central participation."

She makes a wry face. "I feel like Torrane. How would they take my story of tails and little arms?"

"People like Exec Starheim and Exec Cabrisco have enough imagination to grasp the problem," he tells her reassuringly. "And I can put in an advance word through the deputies' grapevine." He smiles.

"Thanks, Fred." She brushes imaginary dust off her desk, straightens her shoulders. "You've just given a superb demonstration of the stabilizing powers of the professional deputy. . . . I've always thought I was very lucky in getting you."

"I, too, have enjoyed our years together," he replies gravely, and they prepare to leave.

Many light-years away, on far Zieltan, it is early morning. Kanaklee, chief of Message Section, is opening his office for the day. The night staff is gone; there will be a few quiet moments while other offices open, before they develop traffic. The incoming day crew is taking over.

Kanaklee lingers in the ground-floor rooms, savoring the clean bright day.

Outside the windows the covered way is filled with government people on their way to work. Most are Ziellor; there're a few aliens, probably workers at Archives/History, or one of their embassy chancelleries.

Suddenly Kanaklee sees his little friend Zillanoy, of the Alien Affairs Section. She's hopping along at a good clip, looking as usual pleasurably excited about something. Kanaklee taps on the vitrines.

To his surprise, she turns and hops straight for the doors, evidently intending to visit him. He pushes wide a flange of the big double doors.

"Oh, Kanak, *the* most exciting!" she bursts out.

"It's always the most exciting, little one. What is it this time?"

"Oh, I'm forgetting my manners. How are you? And how is Leiloy? And your parents?"

Leiloy is his bride and intended coparent. He assures Zillanoy that everyone is well. "But what is your news?"

"Well! You know those warships they sent out east to save those poor Comeno people? Of course you do."

"We had a message in last night," he tells her soberly, "saying they've found a devastated planet on the very borders of the Harmony, Zilla. This trouble is bigger than we thought."

She, too, sobers briefly. "That makes my plan even more promising, Kanak. You see, Navy has to send a supply fleet to service and fuel the fighters. And Headquarters has been allotted six places on the main ship. And I've applied for one of them! I'm sure I'll get it. Oh, Kanak, isn't that tremendous?"

He is taken aback. "Great suns, Zilla—whatever *for?*"

"To learn the Zhuman language! At least, learn as much as I can before we send them all to rejoin the Oversoul. Don't you think that's a noble idea? No one else will know it, I'll be our expert on that alien tongue and culture!"

"Sounds like a nasty thing to be an expert in. And besides, hopefully they'll soon be extinct. Our Navy won't care to keep those types separated from the Oversoul very long," he says wryly.

"But there must be more Zhumanor someplace. We'll meet them again, and then they'll need me. And I'm young enough to wait."

"And you'll be younger than ever to me, after this trip. How many years will you be asleep?"

"Only about seven, overall. I'll be able to pick up and go on easily."

"Well, if you really want this. But I still think it's mad."

"It's my chance to be something really *different,*" she says earnestly, her large eye almost luminous with the intensity of her enthusiasm. "To *be* somebody, to make a little name for myself! And don't think it won't be hard work. I have no illusions; I could fail. I'll be dealing with such horrible creatures, too—and Navy regulations . . ." She looks away, shaking her neatly chiseled head, with its retroussé snout. "And I'll miss you so, dear Kanak. No, to be honest, I guess I'll be mostly asleep —but I'll miss you terribly when I'm not! There'll be a million problems I'll wish for your advice on. You have such a wonderful feel for aliens— you should have taken the Aliens office, and been my chief. Probably you'd hate me if I worked for you, always going off on my own tangents! Now, mind you take care of yourself. Can I come 'round to say good-bye to Leiloy?"

"She'd be most hurt if you didn't, little one."

His workers have been filtering in; time to get at it. As he walks Zillanoy to the door, she says, "Oh! Why, if all goes well, your *baby* will be born and starting school when I get back. I'll really miss seeing all the early part."

"If all goes well," he agrees.

"It will! I just *know* it."

They tap tails in affectionate parting, and she blows him a kiss with one hand-arm as she hurries out.

His office is on the second floor up; he decides to hop it instead of taking the lift. Must keep fit. As he goes up the long risers, he can feel his pouch beginning to itch slightly. His midriff feels heavy, too—a reminder of the sex-animal now growing within him. It seems to be growing even faster than he expected. Does that mean it will be healthy and strong?

As he passes floor one he has a moment of quiet panic; the oncoming birth of the Murnoo looms up as a terribly painful and frightening ordeal, which he can't possibly avoid, delay, or hasten. The sex-animal is alive inside him, growing on its own terms without regard for his desires. But the panicky moment passes quickly as he hops on up. He's heard in health class that new fathers often have such moods.

Instead, he turns to wondering what it will look like. What color will it be? Spotted like himself, or white like its mother Leiloy, or golden brown like most? He hopes it will be white. White excites him and would make the final reproductive act go easily. But white is the rarest, too much to hope for. If it isn't, Leiloy's whiteness will do for two.

And then there's that mysterious final product, their future child. Supposing *it's* white, like Leiloy; what a darling picture they would make! If the sex-animal is white—but it would be called a nurser then—

the baby would have a better chance of being white, too. But any color will do, just so long as it isn't spotted, like himself.

And how mysterious it all is! So complicated yet so precise. If they ever get to the final stages, what a supreme thrill!

Coming up to his floor, he smiles, remembering the kid's manual of sex instructions his father had given him. He can see it as if it were yesterday: *What You Should Know About Reproduction.*

It told him that his race, the Ziello, was unique. "There are other races which need three partners in order to reproduce, but only in the Ziello the third partner is actually created by the original pair. This is true of all the animal life on the beautiful planet of Zieltan.

"The first step," it went on, "is when a male and a female have special body contact, in a way your parents will tell you about. They exchange genetic material, and an embryo begins to grow in the male's pouch. It is the embryo of a Murnoo, often called a 'sex-animal.' The Murnoo is a very important part of the Ziello race, but it isn't a Ziello. You may remember the Murnoo who nursed you when you were a baby. The Murnoo grows very fast, and as soon as it releases the teat in the male's pouch it is born—a tiny furry helpless creature who requires care at first, but grows very fast.

"In only about three years it is full grown, but it doesn't look much like its Ziello father and mother. It's much shorter, with a rounded face and ears, rudimentary upper arms, and a short tail. At this point it is ready for the original male and female to undertake another special body-contact with it and each other. They must be the original pair; if one or both of the partners is different, either nothing will happen or a monster will be born." (Here Kanaklee recalls the shudder of fascinated horror that touched him at those words.)

"During this second and final contact, more genetic material is exchanged, and the embryo of a Ziello baby begins to grow in the mother's pouch. It carries full sets of genes from its father and mother, and an incomplete but vital third set of genes originally from them but transmitted via the Murnoo.

"After about a month, the tiny Ziello infant releases the teat in its mother's pouch, and she transfers it to the pouch of the Murnoo, who is now called a nurser, because it has developed a special, much stronger milk. The baby Ziello grows to normal baby size in the Murnoo's pouch, and then begins to release the teat and crawl up into the Murnoo's arms.

"The Murnoo cradles it night and day most lovingly, and soon the infant stays permanently outside the pouch. The Murnoo cares for it intensively, sometimes even forgetting to eat and care for itself. Soon the baby is crawling, and the Murnoo teaches it to walk and do the other simple things that it knows. But the Murnoo is now rapidly aging and becoming feeble. At about the time the young Ziello is ready to start nursery school, the Murnoo retreats to a corner and soon dies quietly of old age. Lucky is the child whose nurser lives to help it through the first year of school.

"In the old, uncivilized days people used to treat the Murnoo callously, as if it were a robot or an animal. And when it aged they cruelly turned it out to die. But now we regard it as an honored member of our race, and educate it up to the level of its abilities, and return its care with love. Some Murnoos have proved surprisingly intelligent, although none are able to speak very well because of the different structure of their mouth and throat.

"When you meet other races, you will be impressed by our good fortune in having this strange little second life-form, who is incapable of life on its own—Murnoos cannot, of course, reproduce—and who lives only to love and care for us when we are very young."

Brooding on these matters, Kanaklee had automatically entered his office and stationed himself at his big desk. His aide follows him in and waits a moment for his absorbed chief to look up.

"Chief," he says. Kanaklee rouses and looks up, grinning guiltily. "Chief, we need your guidance. We've got to figure a way to handle this big increase in Navy traffic. Look"—he points to a pile on the rolling-stand—"they're starting already."

"I know," says Kanaklee, definitely guilty now. "We can't just go running everything over by courier as it comes in. My thought is, ah, that I should contact Captain Navraneen and arrange for them to station a body with us, to sort their traffic right at input. That way there'd be no risk of delaying anything urgent."

"Or getting blamed for it," says his aide with a knowing twinkle. "Great."

"I'll get right on it," Kanaklee tells him. The day is starting well.

Life at Human FedBase 900 continues well, too. The work of the various offices goes on as usual, long months of routine punctuated by times of high interest. Colony Services oversees the fitting-out and departure of three new Human colonies plus a colony of the space-faring Swain people, and optimistic first reports filter back. It is Federation policy to prevent overpopulation and the degradation of environments by draining off breeding-stock to new planets, so long as the supply holds out; the fringe areas of the Rift show a good number of promising star-systems.

The Terraforming office is called on to help transform four new worlds, and for a while traffic is heavy between 900 and the new sites. Charts and Navigation fills in a commendable count of blank spaces, in the process discovering a likely group of GO suns. Alien Liaison entertains a steady flow of visitors from within the Fed, and one race of water-dwellers from the west who are just making up their minds to join the Federation. Their accommodation in mobile tanks puts demands on Engineering.

Logistics and Supply services 900's fleet of reconnaissance and work ships; Maintenance keeps them flying and retrofits the older models with the latest modifications. The discovery of a very old space derelict, evidently belonging to an unknown, possibly extinct race, provides a point of excitement. The small Research office has been playing around with an idea to solve the perennial quest for a means of sending message pipes from the surface of a planet, so that missions won't be out of contact when not space-borne. Their idea suddenly starts to show promise, and the team sends a rep with their data to Fed Central, to see what those massive resources can do with it.

And all personnel cooperate in the reception of a brilliant new androgyne Gridworld star—it being Federation policy to give the Far Bases first crack at the newest and best in entertainment. His/her troupe puts on shows for several nights and leaves behind a few cases of heartburn in the staff.

And all through the years, studded in among these zestful activities, comes a trickle of dark spots—a slowly increasing number of reports from FedBase 300, far to the east, on the doings of Black Worlders, of the sightings or traces of an unknown fleet, and, twice, of colony planets suddenly gone dead on the bands and found to have been exploded, whether by natural catastrophe or unknown planet-breaker missiles. Exec Jonne develops a tiny vertical crease between her brows.

In due course a new communication arrives from *Rift-Runner One*— this time striped yellow and black, which signifies that it is of interest to Charts alone. They are, it seems, at a point about halfway between Beacon Alpha and their target and making a minor course adjustment toward the center of EM traffic ahead. Their target is now tentatively identified as a world whose transmissions start with the computer-analyzed syllables "Zeel-tan." No other message or anything bearing on the crew's hallucinations at Beacon Alpha is included, save for Captain Asch's scrawled note: "Personnel green—S.Q.A.," meaning *status quo ante.* But which "ante," that of their departure or of Beacon Alpha? No one can tell.

Exec Jonne continues also to worry over the implications of *Rift-Runner One*'s first message, which seemed to imply some mental influence from an unknown source. Her deputy is as good as his word; he prepares the ground for her among the other Base Executive offices, so that when she comes to broach the problem to her fellow Execs she gets a serious reception. With the inevitable exception of a couple of the ultra hard-nosed, they all agree that the phenomenon demands close attention, and that if such a capability were to be found in the possession of a hostile race, it would pose a very great threat to the Federation. Central invites all concerned to submit suggestions for devising research on ways of meeting such a mental threat.

The whole problem is given credence by a colorful fact unearthed by 900's deputy. He had also promised to look into Captain Asch's remark about having heard of some sort of similar thing, and he sends out a barrage of inquiries through the Spacers' and pilots' network. The answer comes back: the Red Eft Effect.

It seems that a mission exploring far to the south had once crossed a small region of starlessness, an area of low density like a fragment of the Rift. In it they encountered hallucinations; the crew felt that they were, or should be, *lizardlike* in form, and bright shiny red in color, like giant versions of the bright little animal known on earth as red efts, or young newts.

The effect wore off as they came back into normal starfields, but it was a manifestation of something real; another crew who crossed the space on a different course met it also. When it was encountered a third time, a careful charting was made. But nothing was found in the area, beyond two white dwarf stars, the remains of former suns that had gone nova.

"Do you suppose that a race once lived on planets that were destroyed?" Exec Jonne asks. "And they had the power to form or throw such a field—maybe reflecting their own forms? And the field, or what's left of it, remains, in that undisturbed starless region?"

"Sounds plausible," one of her colleagues replies. "I think we might query Central about sending a couple of strong Sensitives down there. Extraordinary, to think we might be receiving impressions of a bygone race. . . ."

And so it is left.

But Exec Jonne has nightmares. She is no Sensitive, only very prescient, and she's never free from a lurking, shapeless dread. Her nightmares are of planets, green and pleasant, toward which fly dark alien ships with missiles that can tear worlds apart or scorch to ashes every living thing. And other ships attacking these, on and on, until every hand is against every other hand—or fin or flipper or wing or claw. . . . And the innocent faces, Human and alien, of those about to die in a conflagration they had no part in starting, which will have no end until all life is gone. Burnt, disintegrated, poisoned, crushed in an abyss of broken planets, exploding suns, torn to bloody shards and flamed to flecks in lava; gone, dead, extinguished, inanimate, and silent for all time. . . .

Mostly she associates these dreams with the troubling, enigmatic reports of destruction far to the east. But some of them, she knows, too, center on the tiny spark of Human life driving, all unaware of evil, toward this planet that may be named Zeel-tan.

During these same years, a young-looking Zillanoy returns to Zieltan from her trip east with the fleet, where she had gone to learn the language of the invading Zhumanor. She arrives at her office in the evening hours and as soon as she can goes calling on her old friend Kanaklee.

"Zilla! I thought you might be on that warship that landed today. Ah, it's good to see you back!"

"Oh, Kanak, how are you? How's Leiloy? I have so many—" And there follows the mutual outburst of greetings, inquiries, fragments of news, so-much-to-tell-that-we-can't-get-it-all-out that besets the meetings of star-traveling friends all over the Galaxy. Kanaklee's child, Zillanoy's work, events of the day—all tumble out in a frustrated rush, until Kanaklee finally gets out a straight question: "Zilla, did you really succeed in learning enough of the Zhumanor language to justify the years?"

Zillanoy calms down. "Oh, absolutely, yes. But it was hard, very hard. How much dialogue can you record from a being isolated in a bare metal hexagon? That's how the Navy keeps its prisoners. There's nothing to point to and name, unless you bring it. And the fleet's very strict—they wanted to search me every time I went to the cells. These were the slavers they picked up alive, see. Horrible types. But luckily some of them knew quite a few words of Ziellan, from their Comeno captives.

"And then the prisoners nearly all died from lack of—you won't believe this—*water!* It seems they need it in huge quantities. If I hadn't been there, they never would have found out. As it was, they lost several, including one of my best subjects, before they recognized it. And when they saw how much was needed—*every day*—the ship's lab just gave up and said they couldn't make that much. So they told me to select one and they'd send the rest to join the Oversoul.

"But I persuaded them to first let them all mix together, for two days, to talk where I could record it. And in the end Captain Krimheen let me keep two, and I got a he and a she, I think, with enough water. After that I could use the language-teaching kit and things went really well. I have translations of all that group chatter, for instance. But so much of it was slang and swearing, I couldn't have done a thing without an informant.

"When they got a new lot in from a ship we captured, I was actually able to converse a little. Our kit is very good, Kanak. It's the first time it's ever had such a test—a totally unknown, unrelated language! I have some improvements I'm going to suggest."

"I see you haven't lost a *stip* of your enthusiasm, little one. And now I must think about closing this office for the day, and arranging when you will come to us for a meal."

"Oh, I'd love it!" Zilla is hopping down the stairs, her large eye momentarily thoughtful. "Kanak, they were so *loathsome,* those Zhumanor. I couldn't wait for some of them to be sent to the Oversoul. *Killed.* If you'd seen what they did to those poor Comeno people, and their little colonies. Maximum dishonor isn't bad enough for them. . . . The Oversoul teaches us not to be revengeful, but I kept wondering if this means creatures like that. Whewf! Well, anyway, you'll be glad to hear that my work turned out actually useful to the Navy. Captain Krimheen's people were able to question them and find out where their bases were. And we did discover one fact that's going to fascinate Life Sciences: They claim that they and all their related life-forms actually derive from salt water; they're full of it themselves, almost like bags. Yet they're strictly land-life. Isn't that weird? And they truly are from across the River, across the River Darkness."

"Astonishing."

"And, Kanak"—she ducks her head under an upper hand, like a kid —"I got a letter of commend. Beautiful. Isn't that something?"

"Why, good for you, my dear little friend." Kanaklee gives her a playful tail-flip as they reach the doors. "Well! Would you look at that? It's raining!"

"Yes, it looked strange when I started out. I brought my gear."

"Curse it, I wanted to go to my station by way of the Shrine."

"What, haven't they roofed the Fortunate Way *yet?*"

"No. Look, I really must. Is your gear strong enough, or shall I leave you here on the covered way?"

"It's fine. I'll go by the Shrine with you and go to my station from there."

"Splendid."

They buckle on their tail-sheaths and boots and close up their hooded cloaks.

When they come out to the covered way it is, of course, crowded, so they hop straight to the nearest stairs to take the open way shortcut above. It is known as the Fortunate because it passes the Shrine, which is a convenient place of worship for the large Zieltan denomination to which both Kanaklee and Zilla adhere, in a tolerant way.

The Harmony contains many religions, and after the bloody horror of the Last War, great care is taken never to emphasize one above another, and to give major reverence to the ecumenical concept finally agreed on, the Oversoul which unites all.

Kanaklee's mind is never far from one subject. "Our baby is white," he confides to Zilla as they hop warily along in the drizzle.

"Oh, how beautiful! Watch out, Kanak, the flooring is damp there. . . . What color is the nurser?"

"Well, as a sex-animal it turned out a strange cream shade, quite lovely, with red ears and paws. Red like you. A real genetic oddity. We quite gave up hope of a white baby, but afterward"—here Kanaklee blushes perceptibly around his muzzle—"afterward it paled quite a lot. And the baby was white from the start. We couldn't believe our eyes."

"How wonderful." She hops a puddle. "I remember you were so gloomy, insisting it was going to be spotted like you. I never quite understood, because we're told the Oversoul has a special fondness for those who are spotted. And I think Leiloy might have preferred it."

"Ah, my spots. Actually those spots are why I never got to be a Spacer."

"*What?* You never told me that."

"Oh, I will, if you're interested. But in a drier place."

His mind skips back to the childhood day when he had announced that he wanted to train for space. His parents had firmly discouraged him.

"Just think," said his mother, Kanakloy, after whom he was named. "Supposing there was a new, far mission. You'd be sure to get on it. And supposing it was a great success, such as to deserve a Ritual. And you the most spotted member of the crew! You'd jump at the chance."

"And supposing the ship turned into a giant *Magglegg* fruit!" young

Kanak had retorted frivolously. "So what, if I were to return to the Oversoul in such a highly honorable way? You'd still have my sister—"

"Ah, yes," cut in his father. "But it so happens that we are very fond of this little expression of the Oversoul in his present dry form. Son, I share your mother's feelings. Study languages and codes, you know you like them, too, and let space missions go. They're just a routine like any other, these days."

So Kanaklee had obeyed, and seldom regretted it. In the present calm state of the Harmony, space wasn't very exciting, as his father had said. And here as Message chief he was daily dealing with more of space and aliens than he could hope to know as a Spacer.

They are nearing the Shrine.

"Oh, look! How beautiful—and how it's grown while I was away!" Zillanoy exclaims.

The great raised offerings-floor is truly gorgeous, almost mature. Many people stop here, and there seems to be a high level of artistry.

They go in out of the rain to the preparatory steps and remove their tail-sheaths to inspect their own colors. At the tip of Kanaklee's tail is a pleasing soft green powdering of feces. Now, where should this go? He feels it important that this should be a fortunate placement and studies the huge offerings-design carefully.

On the sunrise side, someone—more likely a group—has been working up a structure of dark red lines. And there are other symmetrical arrangements. He will not disturb them. Finally he spots a sketchy patch to the right between a heap of bright blue crystals and an orange line. There.

He turns and levers the open tip of his big tail delicately over the design to the unfinished spot. Careful, now. Delicately he squeezes, blows gently, and sees a small cloud of green-gray excrement extruding right into the site he's selected. There—lovely. Now to get his long tail back without dripping green crystals on the near part of the design or fanning too much air. Luckily the moisture in the air has partially cemented all the offerings, making the great rug quite stable; he gets his tail safely away and pauses to observe the effect. Excellent!

Meanwhile Zillanoy has been adding yellow powder to a large golden triangle that's been started at the rear. Yellow is quite rare; perhaps it comes from the shipboard food she's been eating.

Before going out, they pause a moment to appreciate the unity-in-diversity represented here, the harmony of life-essences offered to the Oversoul. Some people become overabsorbed in the artistry of the Ritual, Kanaklee thinks. Devout souls who live for weeks on exotic diets that produce rare colors, crystalline feces of violet, vermillion, even white. But that's perhaps a little untrue to the spirit; after all, the idea is to work with what you honestly are. He's quite satisfied with his softly glowing area of gray green that enhances the neighboring blue and orange. Honesty, modesty, and harmony.

As they prepare to leave, a nurser bustles up with a girl-child in tow.

" 'Scuse, 'scuse," it says importantly, and reaches in its vest to extract a neck-chain bearing a plaque. Kanaklee takes it and reads:

> "This child and nurser belong to Amblevoy III and Plazeen of the office of Base Maintenance. Their Names are Fitzloy and Chanlo. If they are in trouble, please call TH-O-86 or EM-&-117. Your help is deeply appreciated.
> In Harmony, Amblevoy III"

Chanlo, the nurse-animal, waits impatiently for Kanaklee to inscribe the numbers on his noter. As he replaces the nurser's neck-chain, it points outside and says worriedly, "Lain! Lain! T'ouble!" and exhibits a child's torn rain-cloak.

The little girl appears about three years old; she watches Zilla and Kanaklee with a large, excited eye, her small tail thumping. When Kanaklee turns to the Shrine's caller, the child holds up the tail to show Zillanoy. There is a quite large raw spot, through which bright green baby feces are crystallizing. Apparently the parents had underestimated the likelihood of this rare rain and allowed the child's rain-gear to go unchecked.

Zilla shows the corrosion to Kanaklee, who is rolling Amblevoy III's code on the caller. When he gets through to her she thanks him profusely.

"I'll be right up to get them, Kenta Kanaklee. No need for you to wait, the nurser is very responsible, although it doesn't talk too well. Just tell it to wait there—better yet, let me talk to it and you run right along. And thank you so much again—"

But the caller is too high for Chanlo; they must stay to help. Kanaklee holds the speaker down to where the animal can grasp it in its feathery, Ziello-like paw. It's already growing dark with age.

"Kenta Amblov? Lain! Lain-clo' ha' hole," it says urgently. Amusing to see it imitate people's mannerisms.

They wait while Amblevoy directs it, in order to hang the speaker back up.

"Than' you. I use this!" it says proudly to Kanaklee. "Bu' he'e too high."

"Yes, that's fine." They pat the nurser on its soft shoulder and wave good-bye to little Fitzloy, before taking themselves out in the rain. It's coming down harder now, they can barely see the separate drops. Under the edges of the rain-cloud a sunset is casting gold-and-blue shadows over the web of walkways between the tall Administration buildings. Beautiful . . . Beautiful Zieltan, the Garden of the Oversoul. . . .

Zillanoy must leave him now, to go to her home transit station. Affectionate farewells; and Kanaklee hops on alone, watching the lights come on in the buildings alongside. Just beside him is the Alien Affairs Section, where Zilla works. As he passes it the lights come up in the huge three-di display of the Harmony, colored to show the star-systems of all the allied races, of which the green of Ziello are far the most numerous. The stars are connected by the thin golden lines of regular transport routes. It really is impressive, a great hive-shaped brilliance sitting atop a long blackness to the south that represents the River Darkness.

Kanaklee pauses for a moment to look and notices that someone has already wired in some little red flashers among the Comenor's colonies at the far east end. These must stand for the Zhuman incursions. To his imagination they look ominous, expanding.

Beyond them, around the end of the River, begins the unknown. The Zhumanor must come from there. Zilla has just told him that the fleet is seeking authority to proceed into that area in search of Zhuman bases. Well, it's no use stamping out the sparks and leaving the source to spread. But Kanaklee flinches mentally; horrible that even the suggestion of war should be raised again. He is just old enough to remember some of the ceremonies of the Great Peace, when the warships were flown away to lie dead forever on a far-away, airless rock. Dreadful that they should fly again, now. But what choice is there? These appalling Zhuman invaders, stealthily killing colony after colony in their ruthless pursuit of riches—they *have* to be stopped.

But what lies beyond them? Are they perhaps the leading edge of some savage alien empire, which might have the power to retaliate?

Shaking his head to clear it of dark thoughts, Kanaklee moves on toward his station, His dear little Zillanoy seems really to have done well, getting a Navy commendation. That must be from this Captain Krimheen, who seems to be second in command of the whole fleet, as well as captain of the great warship that sits out there on the field. He has returned to get reinforcements, and to argue in person before the Council for permission to extend operations into the unknown. The good captain had apparently taken quite an interest in little Zilla and her language work.

As he hops into the shelter of the transit station, the monorail car for his home area is just approaching. Good. And good for little Zilla. This dreadful war in the east has at least brought some good to his friend. He had been wrong about her plan; it now looks as if she's chosen her field of special knowledge very well.

Back behind him, beyond the Shrine, the night lights of his own offices are on. The duty clerk is just filing a routine message on his desk for the morning shift. It's from a southern Ziello world in the River's fringes, which has just spotted a small unidentified ship that refuses or is unable to acknowledge signals. And it's apparently coming from the River Darkness.

Meanwhile the calendars at Human FedBase 900 have clicked onward, bringing their quota of stimulating events. But all are overshadowed now by increasingly ominous reports of trouble in the far east sector. Three hundred's scoutships sensors persistently report the presence of elusive somethings out beyond clear range: entities fast-moving, purposive, emphatically not the natural movements of stray rocks or other phenomena of nature. Three more colonies go silent, and their worlds are found destroyed. EM traffic is picked up at extreme distance. It looks more and more as though the operations of some life-form inimical to the Federation are coming closer and more close.

As the bad news reaches Central, responses are evoked. Nine hundred hears that an expedition is sent out to recover and refit the Class Y warships, long lying abandoned on a dead planet to the south. FedBase 300 turns four of its reconnaissance ships into crudely armed scouts, and six new ones are under construction at Central.

These doings almost eclipse what would have been the exciting rumors of a new breakthrough of some kind at Central Research. Those who attend to them consider grimly that the advances may come in time to help in a new Last War—provided the unknown enemy hasn't got them, too.

At FedBase 900, the old deputy retires. His replacement is a young man who is the clone of a man who had been deputy at 900 three generations back. The cloning of particularly successful deputies is quite customary, since their success depends primarily on temperamental qualities, and the job is so important to a Base's equilibrium. His nickname is also Fred, that being the informal way of addressing all deputies—short for Federation Regulatory Executive Deputy.

Exec Jonne is still too young to think of retiring, despite her nightmares. Thus she is still on duty when the third message pipe from *Rift-Runner One* falls into the incoming chute.

Down below, Pauna is now chief Signals officer. With a thud of her still excitable heart she opens the battered pipe and threads the message on her voder.

Again she hears the voice of Navigator Torrane, sounding surprisingly young—he has been in cold-sleep these many years: *"Rift-Runner One* to FedBase Nine hundred, message three. We are in the northern fringes of the Rift, approaching the planet tentatively identified as Zeeltan. Their EM traffic is very heavy—"

This must go at once to Exec. A call brings a quick appointment, and Pauna is trotting up the exercise ramp; her aide handles routine traffic now. She's considering the quality of Torrane's voice: more composed, but strained, she decides.

The decades-old scene reassembles itself in Exec's office. This time Realune, now gray-haired, is invited in from the start. Exec turns to her new deputy:

"Fred, you'll recall the briefing about *Rift-Runner One* when you first came aboard. Their first message, from their Beacon Alpha, showed them very disturbed by feelings, or hallucinations, that their body shapes were wrong, or should or would change. Specifically, they were too small and short, they were missing an upper pair of smaller arms and hands, and a tail heavy enough to brace them or be used in a hopping gait. Torrane did all the talking; he claimed that the others had similar disturbances, but we have no way of knowing for sure if this is so or whether Torrane alone was hallucinating. However, we have uncovered a similar phenomenon, with a different body pattern, down south and also in a starless region.

*"Rift-Runner*'s second message was purely technical, except for Captain Asch's *'Status quo ante.'* Here is message three. Pauna says they've reached the starfields on the far north side of the Rift and are approaching their computer-chosen target, a center of EM transmission activity. Green? Very well, here we go."

Torrane's voice comes on, very calm and formal. "We can now confirm that the fourth planet of this white-star system is a hub of signal activity, both transmitting and receiving. The syllables 'Zeel-tan' are clearly audible at the start of transmissions. There is also quite a volume of traffic between it and its two large moons, suggesting that some industry has been moved off-planet, as Human worlds have done.

"This is a high-density volume of space. We have counted at least fifteen systems originating traffic with Zeel-tan. Some ship-to-ship traffic is also probable, but we're outside the range of reliable detection."

"So formal?" whispers Pauna. "I guess he's making up for last time."

"The poor lad," says Exec. "He may believe we think he's crazy."

"—one highly significant phenomenon," Torrane is saying. "At regular daily intervals—planetary rotation is close to twenty-three hours Standard—all traffic falls off abruptly, and Zeel-tan originates a single powerful transmission. This is immediately picked up and rebroadcast outward to systems beyond; we've counted at least five such relays. We guess that this is a daily government news broadcast, suggesting that this is one big unified system extending beyond our sensor range.

"The really significant thing here is the speed of pick-up and retransmission. Until we can get more instruments on it, we are tentatively suggesting that they have some faster-than-light means of commo."

"Whew!" The deputy whistles. Exec just looks more intent and grave.

"I am now closing down while we near the planet. Our plan is to approach within orbital range, broadcasting standard First Contact signals. If there is no hostile response, we will spiral in and land wherever seems suitable. Navigator Torrane signing—"

There is another voice in the background, and then Torrane says, "Oh. Yes, well, I wish I didn't have to say this. The former hallucinations, or, uh, whatever, are still with us. It's almost as though we have imaginary outer bodies. But we're getting better at ignoring these symptoms. As Captain Asch says, they don't really interfere with carrying out our duties. Kathy—Lieutenant Ekaterina Ku—says that she thinks hers are getting weaker, or easier to live with, as we get into populated space." His voice has relaxed now. "We have a strong feeling that the people out here, the people on Zeel-tan, must look like we feel—for whatever that's worth.

"I will now lay this aside while we go closer. The maneuvers will put us near the end of our allotment of outbound fuel, but this is certainly the best target we can reach. If for any reason we have to use more, we can always get back to Beacon Alpha and wait there to be rescued. . . . Navigator Torrane out."

Clicks and more clicks from the voder. Suddenly another, deeper voice speaks.

"This is Captain Asch, commanding. It occurs to me that while we go in, you might welcome confirmation of the subjective phenomena

Navigator Torrane has reported. His description of imaginary outer bodies is very apt. In my case, the hallucinatory impression that I have a, er, a muscular, ah, *tail* strong enough to brace me or even propel me is intense enough to make me stumble occasionally, even in our minimal gee. My normal Human body seems to feel as if I were in some ways crippled or missing parts. And I wish to record here a general commendation for the crew, and Lieutenant Torrane in particular, who met these symptoms alone, for constancy and perseverance to duty in the face of a seriously disorienting and stressful challenge. Asch out."

A female voice replaces him.

"Lieutenant Sharana here, linguist and logistics. Everything Torry says is true. Everybody looks weird to me, arms missing, wrong faces, too many eyes, no tails—it's weird. And if I try to pick one more thing up with my imaginary hands, I'll—well, no I won't. It's just as bad for everyone. Shara out. Oh, our Asch-o has been tremendous."

Another woman takes over.

"Lieutenant Ku, copilot and Sensitive. Yes, it's all so. I may have felt it more strongly than others, I've been almost paralyzed for a while. Everything is so *wrong*. But now I'm feeling more like it's normal, only I'm so clumsy. And I hear voices, every so often I can understand what they say. Like about the Oversoul." Her tone has an odd tinge of involuntary reverence or awe. "Some of the others tell me they hear things, too, in a kind of whisper or mumble, like they *should* be able to understand. It's my strong belief that the nature of the life-forms here is transmitting itself to us. . . . Kathy Ku out."

The last member is Lieutenant Dingañar, engineer and paramed.

"Yeah, it's all true. I'm afraid I'll fall all over myself when we get in real gee. I figure this type body normally hops. Or has a tripedal gait, using the tail. Maybe the arms that correspond to our regular ones are occasionally used for support, too. And somebody should mention that it's hard to drink enough water. It feels dangerous, like it'd be corrosive. Whoever this is must sure be a dry type. . . . That's all, except I really hope this wears off soon. And Cap'n and the others have been great. Dinger out."

The voder clicks off.

Exec nods, satisfied, and puffs a breath up through her fluffy gray mop of hair.

"That confirms Torrane," the deputy agrees.

"Yes. . . . Frankly, though, I think I'd rather have had one mad navigator than what this implies. *And* with FTL transmission."

The voder comes back on; Torrane.

"Seventy-five Standard hours later. Approach completed. Deceleration and spiral to landing orbit. No reaction of any sort observed from the planet. We have had what appeared to be hailing signals as we came through the outer systems a day or so back. We are starting standard First Contact hailing broadcast, with extra time on most used planetary frequencies. Computer analysis of all transmissions in the area so far appears to indicate that there are no video signals. Maybe they don't have this technology. But FTL transmission appears more and more likely.

"Ah. Answering hail, we're pretty sure. It starts with a pretty good imitation of 'Rift-Runner One.' But beyond that we can't get a thing. . . . They seem to be trying different languages now. Still nothing remotely familiar. But the voice sounds themselves sound a lot like Human . . . and there's this feeling we *should* understand it.

"We see two spaceports. The largest is near or in the largest city; we'll land there. There are no bodies of water on the whole planet, only a dust of some kind of ice at one pole. The place looks dry. If we didn't see and hear them, I'd say it looks an unlikely place for life.

"The scope just found what looks like a warship sitting on that port. Missile racks tentatively confirmed. Plus some small type of ship that could be armed scouts. . . . There are several other large ships on that port, and a lot of activity everywhere. Oh, hey—there's one of those probable newscast things starting right now!"

He pauses.

"What it comes to, I guess, is that we're approaching a large civilization, maybe very large, certainly well linked up together, and armed; possibly at war somewhere. Possibly with FTL transmission, maybe FTL transport, and with the approach mined with some peculiar confusing mental effect. Whew. . . . Funny, I feel as if I shouldn't joke. I get a feeling of, well, reverence. Maybe that's my unreliable Sensitivity —no, Kathy is signaling she gets it, too."

He pauses, then says with a peculiar slow accent, "The Garden . . . the Garden of the . . . Oversoul . . . Ah—"

"Out," snaps Captain Asch's voice.

"Yes . . . sir," says Torrane. "We'll dispatch . . . this now."

The voder controls click.

"I believe that's all," says Pauna. "I'll run it all to be sure, but that was the cassette control snapping off. The other item that was in the pipe are some starfield holos; I'll run them over to Charts."

There's a silence.

"Big and armed and technologically advanced," says Exec heavily.

"And we're entirely unable to communicate with them. It's vital that this contact come off peacefully, that we don't provoke hostilities or leave a hostile impression. And we've got five untrained, uninstructed star-hoppers crashing in. Oh, gods—how short-sighted whoever laid on this mission was!

"If we could only communicate—no, *have communicated,* this is all long in the past. Whatever was going to happen has happened. . . . Do we start setting up defenses? What in the hells is happening *right now?"*

Pauna and Realune stare at Exec, curious and a little frightened. It's the first time either has known her to lose her cool. A sense of the reality of danger, of genuine gravity, begins to percolate through to them.

Meanwhile the deputy is saying something to her in a low voice. Visibly, effortfully, she regains her calm and glances at the others, smiling again.

"All right, girls. I'm an old worrier. Remember I'm paid to worry. You're not. All we have to do is to wait, constructively.

"Pauna, can you make a copy of this, leaving out all the body-hallucinations stuff? I'd like to have it posted in the main lounge before dinner tonight. And Realune, we'll get back on that communication to the Ammourabi, green? I'll be with you in a minim, as soon as I ask Fred something."

Renewed smiles all around.

As the two women leave, they hear her say, "Fred, will you encode the gist of this for rush transmission to Central and to the other section Execs? And never forgetting the deputies' grapevine."

"ZIELTAN TO ALL-HARMONY, TWENTY ULANTAN, YOUR REPORTER IS FAVONEEN. FROM THE GARDEN OF THE OVERSOUL, A FORTUNATE MORNING TO YOU! IT IS NOW JUST OH-SEVEN HUNDRED HOURS ON A BEAUTIFUL CLEAR DAY.

"OUR FIRST ITEM IS A FOLLOW-UP ON YESTERDAY'S FLASH. CAPTAIN KRIMHEEN OF THE EASTERN FLEET HAS LANDED AND IS DEEP IN CONFERENCE WITH THE COUNCIL, DISCUSSING THE LATEST DEVELOPMENTS IN THE EAST COMENO REGION, WHERE THE ATROCITIES COMMITTED BY THE ZHUMAN RAIDERS ARE APPARENTLY MUCH MORE WIDESPREAD THAN WE THOUGHT. HE FLEW HIS WARSHIP, THE *GUARDIAN,* TO ZIELTAN IN RECORD TIME, BRINGING WITH HIM PICTURES AND DETAILS OF THE ZHUMANOR AND THE BRUTAL METHODS THEY USED TO SUBDUE THE COMENO COLONY WORLDS. THE PIC-

TURES WILL BE TRANSMITTED VIA OUR LATEST DIGITAL TECHNOL-
OGY AT THE END OF THIS BROADCAST FOR REPRINT IN YOUR LOCAL
PRESS, AND NO ONE WHO SEES THE DEVASTATION AND THE PITIABLE
PLIGHT OF THE COMENO CAPTIVES CAN FAIL TO BE MOVED. ONE OF
THEIR MAIN METHODS WAS TO TAKE HOSTAGE THE COMENOR CHIL-
DREN AND BY SYSTEMATICALLY ABUSING THEM THEY FORCED THE
COMENOR TO ABANDON THEIR VITAL AGRICULTURE AND DIG GEM-
STONES FOR THE RAIDERS. ANOTHER CRUEL TECHNIQUE WAS TO PUT
TIGHT COLLARS ON THE CAPTIVES, WHICH COULD BE CONTRACTED
BY RADIO SIGNAL, THUS CHOKING THE UNFORTUNATE CAPTIVE TO
DEATH IF HE DID NOT WORK HARD ENOUGH. BY THESE MEANS THEY
FORCED THE PRISONERS BEYOND THEIR STRENGTH, LITERALLY
WORKING THEM TO DEATH. AND THE NEGLECT OF THEIR CROPS
MEANT THAT THEY WOULD STARVE. BUT THE BESTIAL ZHUMANOR
TOOK NO CHANCES: WHEN THE GEMSTONE LODES WERE EXHAUSTED
THEY SLAUGHTERED ALL SURVIVORS AND DESTROYED ALL TRANS-
MITTING EQUIPMENT, WHICH IS WHY THESE OUTRAGES HAVE GONE
ON SO LONG UNKNOWN TO THE REST OF THE HARMONY.

"HOWEVER, OUR FLEET'S LAST OPERATION AGAINST A CAPTIVE
COLONY HAS MET WITH SUCCESS. OVER A DOZEN RAIDERS WERE
CAUGHT WITHOUT THEIR SHIP—THEY ARE, IT SEEMS, SHORT OF SHIPS
—AND THEIR PRISONERS RESCUED ALIVE. ALSO, TWO GROUPS OF FU-
GITIVE COMENOR WERE FOUND AND RESCUED IN CRITICAL CONDI-
TION. THEIR NEED IS GREAT. FOR ANY WHO CARE TO CONTRIBUTE TO
THE RELIEF OF THESE SUFFERING PEOPLE, COMENOR-RELIEF BOXES
ARE BEING SET UP IN EVERY ALIEN AFFAIRS OFFICE. THE ZIELLO
GOVERNMENT WILL OF COURSE DO ALL IT CAN, TOO. BUT THE RELIEF
AND REBUILDING OF THE COMENO COLONIES WILL STRAIN OUR RE-
SOURCES.

"AMONG THE RESULTS OBTAINED FROM THE ZHUMANOR PRISON-
ERS IS THE PINPOINTING OF MORE ZHUMAN BASES. A BIG CONCEN-
TRATION OF ZHUMANOR APPARENTLY LIES TO THE EAST AND SOUTH
OF THE RIVER DARKNESS, IN UNKNOWN SPACE. CAPTAIN KRIMHEEN
IS RIGHT NOW WORKING FOR PERMISSION TO FOLLOW UP THESE
LEADS, IN ORDER TO WIPE OUT THE NESTS FROM WHICH THESE MON-
STERS COME. THIS NEWSCAST IS OF COURSE PROHIBITED FROM TAK-
ING SIDES IN AN UNDECIDED ISSUE, BUT SURELY I AS AN INDIVIDUAL
WILL BE FORGIVEN FOR EXPRESSING THE PURELY PERSONAL HOPE
THAT HIS BRAVE EFFORT SUCCEEDS. THE OVERSOUL COMMANDS US
NOT TO SEEK REVENGE, BUT I FEEL IT DOES NOT FORBID US FROM
CLEARING OUR HOMES OF DESTRUCTIVE ANIMALS, AND THAT IS HOW

I VIEW THESE ZHUMANOR. AND I SPEAK FOR ALL ZIELTAN IN SEND-
ING OUR UTMOST SYMPATHY TO OUR COMENO MEMBERS OF THE
HARMONY.

"OH—I HAVE HERE AN INTERESTING SIDELIGHT ON EVENTS IN
HIGH ADMINISTRATIVE CIRCLES. IT SEEMS OUR YOUNG ADMINISTRA-
TOR IS SO MOVED BY THESE HAPPENINGS THAT HE HAS ASKED TO GO
TO THE FLEET AND TAKE PART HIMSELF! OUR SYMPATHY TO THIS
BRAVE YOUNG MAN, WHOSE FUTURE POSITION CONFINES HIM TO PUR-
SUITS WHICH DO NOT ENDANGER HIM.

"FLASH! OUR SPACEPORT HAS JUST TOLD US THAT AN UNIDENTI-
FIED NON-ZIELLO SHIP OF LIGHT RECONNAISSANCE TYPE IS ORBITING
IN TO ZIELTAN FOR LANDING. THEY APPARENTLY CANNOT RESPOND
TO OUR HAIL, OR RATHER, THEY ARE RESPONDING IN A LANGUAGE
UNKNOWN HERE. IF ANY OF OUR ALLIES IS MISSING SUCH A SHIP,
POSSIBLY A PRIVATE VESSEL WHICH HAS LOST ITS WAY, KINDLY GO
TO THE NEAREST CALLER AND ROLL THE ADMIN INTERPLANETARY
NUMBER GO-1-1119 TO REPORT IT. THAT'S GO-1-1119.

"AND NOW WE BRING YOU A ROUND-UP OF THE SCORES IN THE
CURRENT ALL-HARMONY TAIL-BALL GAMES PLAYED LAST NIGHT
ON ELEZEER, MANHO, AND PERRUTAN. . . ."

Only five days after the arrival of *Rift-Runner*'s third message at
FedBase 900, message number four drops down the chute to Pauna. A
few minim later she is in Exec's office, with the group assembled to
listen.

"*Rift-Runner One* to FedBase Nine hundred," comes Torrane's voice.
"We're starting this as we come in for landing on Zeel-tan, although it
can't be sent till we're back in space again.

"We've just done, ah, what might be regarded as, ah, a strange thing.
Telling it sounds weirder than doing it. Anyway, on the way in, Kathy
—Lieutenant Ku—got very disturbed. She kept looking at us as if she
wanted to say something, and then going off into kind of a trance like,
you know, the way Sensitives do. Finally Captain Asch asked her what
was wrong.

" 'You are!' she sort of burst out. 'I mean, we are! All wrong. Look,
I'd never forgive myself if I don't warn you. After all, this is my job,
isn't it? That's why I'm along, to pick up stuff? Well, what I've picked
up is that if we land looking like we do, we'll be in terrible danger.
Maybe killed. There's a feeling of hate for us—for our forms—that's so
thick I can't see why no one else gets it. From all over! Don't you pick
up anything, Torry?' she asks me.

"Well, to tell the truth, I *had* been picking up something just like this, only I know I'm unreliable. So I told her. She sighs, like greatly relieved. 'Yes. Captain Asch, I'm formally requesting that we disguise our appearance. . . . And I know just how to do it, too.' She points to our bundle of tents, you know, those long thin pointy duffels.

" 'We take our ground-suits, and those tent brace-cases and sew them on, and maybe tie one brace around our waists to go inside with padding, they're flexible. And put some wads of stuff inside the chests, like arms folded up inside, and do something about our eyes. Makeup. Oh, we won't look exactly like Ziello—now where did I get that? Oh, from Zeel-tan—but we'll look, you know, Zeel*loid,* like the races around old Terra look Humanoid. See?'

" 'Huh?' says Dinger. Captain Asch just watches her. 'Tie 'em on—where? What for?' Dinger asks, and Shara joins in.

" 'To look like *tails,* of course. Like we feel.'

"Well, we went 'round and 'round it, but in the end Captain agreed that was what she'd been picked for and we should go along. My confirmation seemed to carry weight, too, I guess—frankly the idea seemed great, to me. I hated the thought of facing whoever was down there just as I was. And we've been spending days ever since we waked up maneuvering and dodging those tails that don't exist, and trying to remember we don't have spare arms.

"So we spent the time coming in doing just like she said, and it works pretty well. They really do look like real tails, of course, not prehensile or strong, but sticking out flexible, like alive. Shara got laughing and we all broke up. But really, they feel natural. And Kathy painted a few spots on her face, right where I thought they should be.

"Now I'm going to put this aside until we're down, and then keep a log to send you when we're up again. Lords, I wish somebody would come up with that atmosphere-to-space pipe they're always predicting. There's nothing new to report from out here, except that warship on the port is confirmed. The scope picks up the armor and missile racks. The smaller racks are empty, but they're carrying eight big ones, like planet-busters. Oh, and for the time we've been observing, the weather has been completely stable. Dry and clear, no rain at all. Torrane out."

The voder clicks.

Pauna looks at Exec with a half grin at the idea of those tails but sobers when she sees the older woman's face. Exec is imperceptibly nodding her head, as if to say yes, quite somberly.

"A chance they'll never connect that ship with us, if anything goes wrong," the deputy says, low-voiced. Exec nods definitively.

Torrane's voice comes back.

"Well, here we are on Zeel-tan. Down at eight twenty-four fifteen, eleven hundred hours Terratime, that's early morning here.

"We got a good look at the ships here as we came in. Their drive is definitely different from ours, and their fuel tanks are huge. Possibly indicating less fuel efficiency. We identify a probable tractor-beam head on that warship, too.

"We're getting a pretty cool reception, no interest at all. These people must be used to receiving unidentified alien ships. The air samples proved out green, but very dry, so we cracked the port and rolled the gangway half out. We're all wearing our modified work suits. Dinger finished up those tails really nice.

"Shara and I prepared a selection of First Contact materials as per regs, three sets of basic picture-talkies and three advanced. It looks like we can't hope for any verbal commo whatever. The picture-talkies should help, they're the new models with a small hand-held video cassette that shows a moving picture on the plate to illustrate each spoken word when you press the button. If you learn one, you have a basic pidgin-Galactic, no pronouns or prepositions or tenses or any trimming at all. The thing is, you have to learn it yourself to use it, we've all been doing that.

"Then Shara and I pulled a sequence of fish-eye shots of the starfields all the way from our side of the Rift to a scope close-up of Zeel-tan. Captain Asch said that in view of the apparent size and unknown nature of this system, we should omit the holos showing exactly where Base Nine hundred is. So we start with a general one that's clearly in the fringes of the Rift seen from our side."

Here Exec sighs relievedly.

"So far all we've seen is a port crew, who pointed to where we should park, and took off before we opened up. They put us on a spot covered with, like big lichens, probably not much used. And their body shapes, as far as we could see, are just like what we expected—taller and bigger than us, extra pair of upper arms, one big single eye, and a long heavy pointed tail they brace on. Their skins are covered with very short fur, like that cloth, velvet. Mostly brownish gold. We took all the holos we could.

"Aha— Here comes a port official, or somebody in what looks like a staff car. Much rounder shape than ours, more headroom. And insignia on the side like a big jointed wreath. The driver is alone. He's getting out now. Captain Asch will greet him from the top of the gangway, with us behind him as a back-up."

The voder clicks off—on.

"Well, that was something! We let the gangway down and turned out as planned, and this official hops right up to the captain, giving us a kind of perfunctory once-over, as if he'd seen everything and we were just one more. Captain Asch salutes, and gives a real short speech in Galactic, the official clearly not understanding a word. When Asch finishes he says something incomprehensible that sounds like 'Same to you.'

"Then he just hops straight at Asch as if he expected Asch to step back and let him by and into the ship, through us. Asch didn't want this booger loose in there, so he says low, 'Close up,' and just stands there with us jammed up behind him. The alien grunts, and fishes in his suit and flashes some kind of badge, as if that gives him the right to enter. But Asch just stands there with us behind him, and Dinger pulls the inner port closed.

"So the alien says something like Asch was being ornery about some standard regulation, with lots of irritated-sounding grunts. But Asch pulls out a big fancy gold Federation pilots' ID and flashes that, saying, 'No way, Myr Three-legs.'

"And just when things are getting a little sticky, another vehicle arrives. This one has the same wreath; it's bigger, with a driver. There gets out two aliens in long blue robes, and a third in what looks like a uniform, bright orange.

"The port official starts bitching to them, but Asch cuts through with his short official speech, of which they plainly get nothing. Then he signals Shara and me to go forward to them and present a set of our materials, which we do. I try to show them how the holos are in series, ending with Zeel-tan. But when Shara shows them the movie-talkie they're fascinated—I guess they really don't have video—but they just press buttons at random, apparently making no effort to learn. Asch finally gestures to them to take the set away with them.

"Then the officer and the two robed types—maybe priests?—start arguing over who should have the things, and in the end Asch takes the chance of giving them another whole set, leaving us one more. He figures they will probably go up through different offices or chains of command.

"It looks like we're going to have trouble getting to meet any of the big honchos of this world.

"But Shara got a lot of good out of her interview. The planet is definitely 'Zieltan,' with a little 'i' sound in it, and they are the 'Ziello,' I mean the 'Ziellor,' 'r' or 'or' is their plural. And she's got 'yes' and 'no' and a probable 'this,' and indications that they raise the tone up for a question just like we do; I guess that's one reason their speech sounds so familiar. She's putting in a little cassette with her findings, just in case this is all you get back from us and somebody has to meet them again."

Realune gives a little gasp at that. Exec pats her hand and says quietly, "They did get off safely, Rea, we have the pipe." Then she quickly turns back to the voder, because Torrane is saying:

"—strange thing happened. When Shara told them we were Humans, one of the robed ones kind of burst out, 'Yoo-manz—Zhumanor? Zhumanor—' and some stuff I can't say right. They have trouble with 'h,' Shara says. And they all make the negative sound, as if denying that we could be Humans, see. And the officer gets quite worked up when Shara insists, so she goes back to the pictures. And then the really weird thing happens.

"Kathy has been inconspicuously photographing everything of interest. All of a sudden she pushes the camera into my hands and runs after the aliens as they start getting back in their car.

" 'The Ritual!' she cries. 'Remember the Ritual!' And she pulls the top of her suit open, and we see she's drawn big spots all over chest and shoulders, too. She looks up and calls out something in a strange voice —alien words, like. I feel I half-understand. Like she's calling to the sky over their heads.

"The robed aliens turn back to her, seeming to understand. One of them replies something, bowing his head. And the officer says their 'yes.' Then they get in and drive straight off.

"The port official has kind of faded into the background while we talked with the others. Now he says something to Kathy, pointing to the sun and moving his hand like he means afternoon. Then he gets in his car and leaves, too.

"By this time Kathy is kneeling on the hot ground with her face to her hands. We think she's crying, but when Captain Asch goes out and helps her up, we see she's smiling, like trembling, as if she's crying for joy. Her face has a weird exalted look.

" 'What was that about, Kathy?' I ask when she comes in the ship. And yet I feel like I almost know.

" 'The Thanksgiving,' she says. 'We reached here.'

" 'That's right,' Dinger says. Then he like shakes himself and blinks.

" 'There are strange influences here,' Shara says, putting her little cassette on the voder. 'I want to practice these alien sounds. I'm sure we got a "Who are you?" ' Shara's good.

"Then Asch indicates he has something to say. I'll put it on the recorder."

The captain's voice comes on, deeper and grave.

"This seems to be a world where things that are nonrational in our terms go on. I'm not certain that we, including myself, are entirely ourselves here. Now, there's some explanation for all this. We just don't know it yet. We just have to keep remembering who we are, and that we're contacting something totally new in Human experience. *And* that nothing suspends the laws of nature. Then we simply go on and play it as it comes.

"However, I feel it best that we remain prepared to take off unexpectedly. A lot depends on whether they locate somebody here who can communicate with us. At the moment it looks unlikely. If they don't, I think we should take off tomorrow noon. Federation can send a second, better-equipped expedition now we know what's here.

"Meanwhile we should collect as many observations of this place as we can. It might even be worth making an expedition to the port office to collect more speech samples for Shara's base, so the experts back home will have something to work with."

The voder clicks, and then Torrane's voice comes back.

"Later. Well, that settled us all down. And nothing happens for a while. Dinger and I made a trip outside to collect specimens of the lichen and any insect life he could catch. We're all feeling the effects of the total dryness everywhere. Even the ground acts funny; if you spit on bare earth, it boils.

"Dinger's preliminary analysis of the plant life shows it just the reverse of Terroid: it gives off $CO_2$, carbon dioxide. Maybe that accounts for the high percentage of $CO_2$ in this atmosphere. Dinger says you can smell it if you put your nose down at plant level. I'll bet Life Sciences will love the biochemistry here.

"We watched some ships take off or land and picked up their transmissions, and we were thinking of going over to the port office, when a heavy vehicle drives up beside our ramp. It's loaded with construction equipment. The boss shouts something to Captain Asch, and then his crew gets out and starts building something just beyond our gangway. Since it isn't touching the ship or in our way, the captain doesn't interfere. It turns out to be an obviously temporary low scaffolding, not menacing as far as we can see. On the scaffold they set up a big basin, like a child's wading-pool. Then they lift out of the truck several carboys of clear liquid, like you'd store chemicals in, and start filling up the basin. That's what they're doing now. To judge from their cautious behavior, the stuff must be corrosive.

"Captain and Shara are going down to check on it. . . . Crew are waving them to keep back. Shara has a piece of sample cloth, and she manages to dunk one end in the liquid. They're bringing it back to the ship."

"If it wasn't for the way these people are acting," comes Captain Asch's voice, "I'd say it was water or some mild basic solution. Dinger's doing a quick electrophoresis."

"Look, Captain," says Torrane, "here comes another delegation. Why don't I just record live?"

"Green. Dinger, you finish that. The rest of you come out with me."

"Five aliens are getting out. Looks like the same two in robes—no, these look bigger and older. Three more types holding gadgets of some sort—could be musical instruments? Everybody's out now.

"The aliens are lined up by the scaffolding. You'll hear—"

A definitely alien voice speaks, or intones, from farther away.

Then—*Moo-oo Hoo-La-La—LAA-AA-Hoo*—a blast of what must be music comes from the voder. Over it Torrane is shouting:

"Two of them are singing to musical accompaniment—Oh, by the gods—" And there is a rising babble of Human voices while the music wails on.

"I feel funny— Oh, no—"

"The music! Stop the godlost music!"

"My Ritual! It's my Ritual, can't you *see?* Let me by!"

"Kathy! Kathy, stop! Oh—"

"Kathy, you can't go down there stark naked—"

"Lieutenant Ku!" roars Asch's voice. "Halt!"

"Stop her!"

A confusion of voices and sounds, moving farther away amid the braying music. "Kathy, Kathy—"

"It's just water," Dinger's voice shouts. "Plain water!"

Clamor of voices, slap and slosh of splashing, the hoots of music, and through it a high female voice yelling, "Help! Help! Hold me down, I can't—" More splashes. "Get her out! Get her out!" shouts Asch. "Here, I—" The music gets louder.

Far away, in Exec's office at FedBase 900, the hearers look at the voder, look at each other, while the minims tick away filled with incomprehensible uproar.

Then come heavy footsteps on the ramp. The music quits.

"Get her to the med station," says Asch's voice.

"She hasn't been breathing for—for—"

As the footsteps pass, someone clicks off the recorder.

In a minim it clicks on again.

"It is now about three hours later," says Torrane shakenly. "Captain Asch will speak."

"Lieutenant Ekaterina Ku is dead," Asch says stiffly. "Dead by drowning. We were unable to revive her before irreversible brain damage had occurred. The cause of her death was partially self-induced. When she jumped into the water-pond, she first attempted to drown herself by holding herself facedown in the relatively shallow tank. When she failed in this she called to us to help her by holding her under water. Some of her words were, 'Help me, I must die so the Ritual will be right! It's my chance!' She seemed to feel some good end would be served by her death.

"We on the contrary attempted to pull her out, or at least hold her head out. But in the crowded quarters and the slippery tank, and the clumsiness of our actions—and not helped by Kathy's—by the lieutenant's"—his voice chokes—"long dark hair, we somehow pressed her upper body farther into the water, facedown. The influence of the alien music on our perceptions and actions was very great. I consider we were temporarily deranged by it.

"After too long a time we realized that her lungs were full of water—she must have deliberately inhaled while she was under—and she was no longer breathing. At that point the alien music stopped. We quickly got Ka—Lieutenant Ku into the ship's emergency apparatus. But as I said, it was too late.

"We have placed her body in the appropriate refrigeration compartment and held a brief service. In ending I should say that there is no question that Lieutenant Ku perished in the line of duty. Her dedication to our mission was complete, and as a high-order Sensitive she was subject to inimical influences peculiar to this area. The disaster that befell her should be taken as a warning in selecting personnel for future missions here. This is not to say that Sensitives should be avoided; on the contrary, her perceptions have, I feel, been invaluable. But great care must be exercised by the commanding officer in the event that self-destructive patterns become imprinted on the mind.

"It is clear in retrospect that something of this Ritual pattern was perceived or imprinted on Lieutenant Ku as far back as Beacon Alpha. And it was not confined to her. All of us in some degree *expected* and both welcomed and feared just some event. It appears to be the alien custom of ritual sacrifice in thanksgiving for a safe voyage. Lieutenant

Torrane was also heard to say, when the alien influence was strong, 'The spotted ones are preferred.' There was also the general idea, in all our minds, of joining with, or rejoining in death, some great supernal power—call it the Oversoul—under conditions of great honor. Thus the vital force of these aliens is such that their psychic patterns are to some degree imprinted upon all our minds.

"Except under extraordinary conditions, however, such as the playing of that music, I believe we are still capable of functioning Humanly and carrying out our mission. I propose to depart tomorrow, which should give them time to come up with a Galactic translator, if one exists here. I may say that none of us have any premonitions of further alien happenings ahead.

"In closing, I blame myself very severely for not having faced and taken seriously the earlier presentiments about this Ritual by Lieutenant Ku and others. My negligence in this matter must be considered an indirect cause of her death. . . . Asch out."

Exec's eyes are grave.

"To lose a crew member like that, the first day," says her deputy.

"He shouldn't blame himself," Realune protests. "Who could guess she intended to try to die in a kid's wading-pool?"

"That's what captains are for," says Exec shortly, and they turn back to the voder, where Torrane's voice has come on.

"—wants me to tell you. We couldn't help noticing even in the—the confusion, and our sort of paralyzed minds—that the aliens were also very excited. Both the big shots and the construction crew crowded in close, like they couldn't believe their eyes, pointing at our wet legs and arms and all, and confirming we were actually in the tank. They themselves jumped back to avoid every splash, and took extreme care not to step on any damp, boiling places. Water is evidently dangerous to these people. We think they expected Kathy to die just by going in it. And we think they were confused and thought that the Human shape of Lieutenant Ku's, uh, nude body was damage caused by the water. We still had our work suits on, see, with the tails, and, like extra arms folded in.

"I don't think we'll try any more contact today, unless somebody comes to us. We're taking in the gangway, and making use of the one-gee-minus here to grab a little real sleep. None of us rest too good in zero-grav. This is all for this cassette, I'll start a new one. Torrane out."

Pauna gets up. "I have the second cassette here." She opens the voder.

"I don't know," says Exec thoughtfully. "Asch appears perfectly functional, and yet . . . I feel he's somehow not a hundred percent himself. Don't ask me why. Unless possibly I'd have been happier to see him lift off right then and forget about waiting for a nonexistent translator. . . . But yet they've come all that way, it would seem a shame to leave without learning more about this great new alien complex. If only its size and extent."

Fred nods understandingly. "This does confirm all that was implied by the third message prelanding. That warship is operational. If it'd been converted to civilian use, it wouldn't go about with planet-breakers racked up. Hence they *are* fighting, or preparing to fight, somewhere. Perhaps they are still having religious wars, as we did.

"On the other hand, we have those reports of vanished planets from down Sector Three hundred way, and here's a live alien ship with probable world-blasters at about the same time. And only the gods know what's been happening down there since we heard. . . . Our hope is that they have enough on their plates not to desire more hostilities. Or even to welcome a possible ally. It would be good if our people are able to depart as they came, apparently unnoticed."

"Umm," says Exec. "Fred, what do you make of the first group's reaction to the crews' claim that they were Human? Does somebody there know what Humans look like? Is it even common knowledge, say, that we don't have tails?"

"We're ready to go, ma'am," says Pauna. "The second half."

And the voder starts to spin.

On far Zieltan, it is evening of the day Kathy Ku died. Zillanoy of Alien Languages is recording a courier letter to her friend Kanaklee, chief of Messages, who is home with an inflamed eye.

"Oh, Kanak, my dear, I shall simply explode if I can't vent this! Maybe it'll amuse you on your bed of pain. I know you can't read so I'm doing this. Give my love to Leiloy and the little one and prepare to listen to an outrage.

"It's about what's happening with that alien ship that just landed, what Admin has done—or rather, not done! Honestly, it's so shameful it makes me stamp, but I'll try to be coherent. And we do have quite a puzzle on our hands, you'll be interested.

"You know your office sent me a transcript of that hailing broadcast they put out on their way in—thanks, dear Kanak, without you this place would go straight to max entropy! Well, I could actually get some of it, although the accent is strange as can be.

"I recognized several instances of the word *yooman,* which could be a form of 'Zhuman.' And they referred to a *federation,* which I picked up as something those eastern Zhumanor were afraid of. A bad thing. And *we come in peece* may mean that they're just a piece or part of a group of ships out there. Definitely, it's similar to the Zhuman tongue, or, as I'm beginning to think, of a larger language the Zhumanor and others use. Anyway, I sent a flash up to Admin saying that I recognized a Zhuman affinity, and to send every bit of recorded speech to me, top priority. Our good boss Kenta Graveen authorizing. And, since the Zhumanor are such bad actors, to watch themselves—of course I said it in officialese.

"Well, I guess that flash is still moldering in some upper official's in-pot— Really, that whole top echelon below the Council is purely useless and hopeless and ought to be fired. They just slow everything to a standstill— 'Scuse, where was I? Oh, yes.

"So the port heard nothing, and they just went ahead with a Class D reception—the aliens refused arms inspection, by the way—until the aliens demanded a Ritual. They've clearly come a long way. They claim to be from across the River Darkness, I don't believe that, of course. They haven't got the fuel tanks for it. But I'm jumping ahead.

"Anyway, at the Ritual—with only *three* musicians, and a pool so small it looked like a child's sandbox. Which it probably was, Reception is conserving funds for the big All-Harmony Conference next Dusedan —at their Ritual, *all* the aliens *got into the water* with the Ritual person. Just hopped in and splashed! Imagine!

"That's tolerance to water, see—a Zhuman trait. The Zhumanor claim they and all life on their worlds originated in water— Did you know that? Weird. So, when I heard this, I thought, Zhuman for sure. And what goes on? Here we are hunting them all around the east of the River, and a shipload of them lands right on our door-pads!

"But I got Kenta Graveen to get me some pictures—the driver had been taking pictures to sell to the news services—and these aliens aren't Zhumanor at all. They look like little cartoons of us, kind of limp and sickly.

"But I'm forgetting the main thing, Kanak. The aliens presented Reception with two sets of the most marvelous artifacts! In each set was a packet of wide-angle holographs of the whole skyfield at intervals on their trip. I've seen one group over at Charts, that's where they finally ended. The Charts person told me the early ones seem to show the sky from the far side of the River, but of course that's a hoax or an extrapolation. But the things are of superb quality. Charts says they're priceless. I don't know where the second set is, or rather, I can guess. I only hope they're both the same.

"But it's the second artifacts that are the marvel and the crying shame. Each one is a little folding cassette, with a speaker at one end and a shiny plate at the other. And when you press a button, the speaker says a word, several times and—listen!—the plate lights up and shows a *moving* picture! Showing what the word means, see? Some are holographs, some are diagrams, or drawings. About a hundred and fifty different ones, at a wild guess. Absolutely exquisite, way beyond the state of any art here. And what it is, it's both a teacher *and* a message, I'm positive.

"Now here's the crying part. Reception sent these things up to the Council, probably by slow freight. And when they finally got them, the stupid Councillors spent the time playing with them! Just *playing* with them. As if they were personal gifts! Punching buttons in any order, to see the pretty pictures, not learning anything and *not getting their message!* Oh, Kanak—how do you bear it? The little Administrator was with them, but you can forgive him, he's a real boy. But the others are grown-ups—supposed to be our wisest people!

"So here sits the alien ship, and there lies their messages, being played with by a covey of ancient dolts and a little boy! Honestly.

"Well, the gods know how long this would have gone on, but my good chief Graveen got wind of them, and he just kept boring in till he got through the dust layer—that's what I call the upper echelon—and a couple of the Councillors *finally* had the bright idea that maybe some expert ought to get a look at these things. So they sent a packet of holos down to Charts. And one cassette went to Research, who tried to take it apart and promptly broke it. And Graveen brought the second cassette to me, and I'm about to start a night's work on it. Kanak, I think this thing has over a hundred words and pictures in it! Oh, I hope the two were identical—but we'll never know now, will we?

"What's clear at once is that these things were never prepared en route. That means they have a home office where such things are made, for use in contacting strangers. Which in turn implies a lot of things. Oh, Kanak, I have a hunch, as though things I can't see clearly are connecting up. Like the Zhumanor in the east and these people coming here—and I think the Navy should be in on it.

"I'm going to pluck up my nerve and get in touch with Captain Krimheen, he's the big commander who brought our ship here, and he's a live light. I should say there was some junior fleet officer went out to look them over for weapons, but he didn't see anything. But what occurs to me is, if this is the state of their technology, would we recognize their weapons if we saw them? But it's funny, what I'm concerned with isn't weapons on that little ship. It's what's behind it all. To use a military term I learned, I think the problem here isn't tactical. It's *strategic.* Meaning bigger and deeper and maybe indirect.

"So there's my bedtime story for you, Kanak dear. Can you see why I got mad? And who'd have thought, when we said good-bye for me to go study an obscure, possibly extinct language out east, that a week after I got home the language would be right here on our main landing-field!

"Rest well, get better quick, and love again to Leiloy and little Kanlie. Fondly, your friend Zilla."

In Exec's office at Human FedBase 900, the second part of that long-ago message begins to unreel on the voder. It's Torrane.

"We were pretty depressed about Kathy. Shara and I collected her things and stowed them away. And we rolled in the gangway, and took off our wet work suits and hung them in the cabin to dry. The moisture in the air really felt good. And nothing else happened from outside, so we had chow and turned in early, taking one last look around the spaceport from the lock.

"I guess I didn't tell you it's all surrounded with a covered roadway, with roofed alleys out to the different hardstands. These people must be really leery of rain. So far we haven't seen any change in the weather at all, just high cirrus. And there's a lot of dust in the air that makes the sunsets something to see. We watched the lights come on. The port office down at the end looks busy; the military vessel only has standby lights.

"In the morning we start preparing for lift-off, securing the cabin, and taking the back-starfield holo strip out of the aft camera and threading it in the computer so we can go on automatic guidance in a hurry if need be. More of Kathy's little stuff turns up. We still can't believe she's gone, stiff and cold back there. . . . 'Scuse.

"Anyway, no outside action at all, until a little before noon, when a big staff car drives up. It has the thing we think is a government symbol on the doors, and also two little orange flags on the front, and the driver is sitting outside. Maybe big shots.

"Out gets a big male in orange uniform. He's got up fancier than the other uniformed type, with a line of what could be medals. Then comes a smaller male in a plain uniform, with shoulder loops; he acts like an aide. And then a still smaller, red-colored alien dressed in some kind of silky outfit that suggests it's a female. It turns out that's right.

"She hops out and makes a beeline for the ship, and slaps the side with her tail. Pow!—we just have the lock cracked, see. And she calls out, 'Herroo! Herroo, Herro? You come out? I come in!'

"By the gods, they've got a Galactic speaker here at last! We whip open the port and let down the gangway. She bounces straight up to meet Asch, holding out one of her top hands with a glove on it.

" 'Me Zillanoy,' she announces, pointing to herself. 'Zilla. Fee-male.'

" 'Hello, Zilla,' we all say, and she gives a chortle, like it's all great, and shakes all 'round, getting names. While this goes on I'm busy setting up another recorder. I figure there's going to be an extended talk in pidgin-Galactic and I'll put that on a separate record so you can have the whole thing verbatim. I'll just give the gist of it here.

"She introduces the big alien as Something Krim-heen, probably like a title, 'Captain,' because she says, 'Big chief fight-ship.' Captain Asch offers to shake hands, but she slaps at him with her gloved hand. 'No, no! *Kifa!* Bad *kifa.*'

"At this Shara points to the water flask in our mess rack and asks, *'Kifa?'*

" 'Yess,' says the alien, 'Wa-ta. Wa-ta bad *na* Ziello.' I get it; it's the moisture in our skins they fear.

" 'There's something strange about her accent,' Shara says. 'And she knows the word *chief.* That isn't in our Basic.'

"By this time we're all in the ship, except for the aide, whom Captain Krimheen sends back to the car. We settle around the mess table as well as we can, with their size, and all those tails. And I lay out a ready-ref spread of the talking-pictures kit, and a big holo showing the whole Rift and both sides. All this seems to delight Zilla; she goes off in peals of laughter that sounds a lot like ours, although at first we thought she was choking. She seems like a nice girl. 'Go-od! Class-ee!' she says at the spread.

"Captain Asch starts off by introducing us formally as Humans from the Federation, coming in peace on an exploration mission. 'We come look what here,' he says, pointing to his eyes and all around. 'Zeel-tan big!'

"But Zilla is staring at him with that big single eye, all giggles gone. So is Krimheen.

" 'Yoomanss? Zhumanor? No!' she explodes. And gives us a blast I'll try to reproduce. 'You no Zhumanor! I know Zhumanss! Zhumanor kill people, come Comeno planetss, do bad things. Catch people, make dig di-monss, zara-navths, kill Comenor. Ziello ship come, catch two—three Zhumanor, no ship. Ziellor kill Zhumanor, look more. Look much Zhumanor, kill all! Look ship, Zhumanor fly, Ziellor catch. Look

Zhumanor base, blow up— *Pzeh!* Zhumanor want shipss, want di-monss. Kill all Zhumanor! Yess!'

"Well, this about knocks us flat.

" 'That's a Black Worlds accent,' Shara exclaims.

"And that's the key. After a lot of go-round, you'll get it on the other cassette, we figure it out. Black Worlds Humans have been getting into them out east, capturing and killing an allied race called the Comenor. The Ziello have gone to their rescue, chasing and killing the Black Worlders. That's where Zilla learned her scraps of Galactic; she's sort of an official translator.

"Anyway, all Zeel-tan hates what they call the Zhumanor. At one point Zilla gets up and scoots out to the car—those hoppers can really travel when they're in a hurry—and comes back with a folded, printed-looking kind of kidskin stuff—a daily paper. Two big photos front and center: one shows a clearly Human Black Worlds type with pointy hair, crouching and pointing a stunner at the camera. The photographer must have been right with the troops. The other is a pathetic huddle of corpses, or creatures nearly dead. They look partly like little Ziellos and partly like big rabbits.

" 'Comenor!' says Zilla. 'Zhu-man! Pfeh!'

"Well, with those photos in everybody's hands, it's obvious that if we'd landed in our natural forms, we'd probably have been lynched on sight. That must have been what Kathy and I picked up. Kathy saved our lives all right. . . . But now what do we do?

"All this time, big Captain Krimheen never really softens up. He's giving everything the hard look-over, and while Zilla's talking, he gets up and studies our controls, and all the instrument banks. Captain Asch quietly keeps an eye on him.

"It's also apparent that the two females can communicate much better than the rest of us, natural since Shara's a linguist and I think Zilla is, too, and she'd talked with Galactic speakers before. (We give her the advanced movie-talkie cassette, too.) So Captain Asch lets Shara do the explaining, how we are *good* Humans from the *good* Federation, we don't kill or enslave people and we don't want diamonds or zaranaveths. And the Humans she's seen aren't from the Federation but from the Black Worlds outside, and we hate them, too.

"That gets a response. Zilla says thoughtfully, 'I lis-ten, black pla-netss. Yess.'

"But that sets her off on a new tack. 'I think Zhumanor do bad things you,' she exclaims. 'I think you Yoomanor want come *na Allowateera!*

Much people come *na Allowateera*—good, good! Why you talk fekey, talk you Zhumanor?'

"It takes all Shara's skill to unscramble this. It seems Zilla now has the idea that we come from a race that's been persecuted by the Black Worlders, and are seeking refuge in their alliance, or union, or whatever the *Allowateera* means. But the best Shara can do is to keep the question open whether our 'Yooman' is really the same as 'Zhumanor,' which is how they pronounce Black Worlders.

"Captain Asch is using a stylus on the big holo to show where the Federation is, and draw in our cross-Rift trip. But Krimheen takes the stylus and pinpoints some systems out east.

" 'Zhumanor here,' he says. Then, watching Asch through his narrowed eye, he drags the stylus along from the east through the southern fringes of the Rift, to Zeel-tan. 'You come *na* this, here, I think,' he says dryly.

" 'No! No!' we all say.

"But he just gets up and goes out and down the ramp. We see him conferring with his aide, who picks up what could be a caller in the car, in the flash I get of it.

" 'I don't like this,' mutters Asch. Neither do I.

"But when he comes back he seems quite affable, and makes a little speech. It's an invitation to us to come into the city with him to meet some people we gather are government high officials. Zilla is enthusiastic. 'You look Zieltan, is good! You look *Allowateera* big shits!' she says in her hair-raising mix of Galactic and Black World lingo. 'Good you come look!'

"Well, it's pretty tempting after the endless time cooped up here. Captain Asch agrees to go, with Shara and me, leaving Dinger to guard the ship.

"We all troop out to the car with him, and Krimheen directs me to sit out in front with the driver. He's being real cordial; he personally opens and closes the door for me.

"This disconcerts me so that it's a minim before I realize he's slammed the thing on the tip of my fake tail, which should be, I guess, excruciating. As quick as I can, I make to flinch and holler. But I was slow, slow. Does this big devil suspect it's a fake? He gives no sign. But looking back, I seem to recall his nudging or bumping myself and Dinger quite a bit. I'd put it down to the cramped quarters. . . . Oh, no—this is bad! How do I get word to Asch, closed in the back with him and the aide and the girls?

"And the car has started. In no time we're in the middle of the port.

It's clouded up. Zilla is happily explaining something to Shara, when suddenly Captain Asch's caller blats. I hear Dinger's voice.

" 'Mayday! Mayday! They're draining the fuel from our tank!'

"At that very instant, the driver beside me screams. Really *screams*. I see a couple of drops of rain have hit the windscreen. He slams to a stop and starts to pull up curtains.

" 'Everybody out! Run for it!' shouts Asch.

"We tumble out and start pounding as fast as we can. But it would have been pathetic—those hoppers can fly. I didn't dare look back, but I hear what sounds like a stun-bolt go by my ear. And some orange figures—troops—in the walkway to my right, start out into the field to cut us off.

"But—talk about crazy luck—the whole field lights up with a thunderclap and a blast of rain hits us. We race on. But I see the soldiers skid to a halt and hightail it back to shelter, where they start yanking out some rain-gear. No sounds of pursuit behind us.

"As we near the ship we see three or four more soldiers by the tubes, struggling into stuff. The gangway is half up. One of the soldiers tries a shot at us, but he's half into his gear and I guess the rain is burning him. I can hear one actually crying out with pain. But one big fellow is about dressed. He blocks the way.

"For a convinced pacifist, our Captain Asch has a mean body-hook. He decks the big hopper, and Dinger drops the gangway right on top of him. We scoot up it and Asch throws himself into the pilot couch. Dinger has everything set. In two minim we're digging air, clawing our way up off Zeel-tan—I hope for keeps.

"I waste a second hoping Zilla didn't get burned too badly. By the time I can see down, the port's almost gone. So is the rain, and the thunderhead is thinning out below. They seem to have these little thermal storms that come from nowhere and disperse at once.

"Dinger tells us that as soon as we were on our way, this squad of soldiers appeared and surrounded the ship. They located the outer fuel cap, opened it up, and stuck a hose down it so they could siphon without Dinger being able to use the choke-off. Dinger goes out to try to stop them, but the leader pulls a weapon and points it at his head, waving him to get back in.

"So he does—and grabs the waste-water hose and extends it to the port, below their line of sight. And he drenches them good, and hoses down the tank input area with suds. That way he saves most of the fuel —they were out to drain us dry, making the ship a neat jail for us. And of course that blessed shower came just in the nick.

"On the way up, their hose blew off, and we're using the emergency choke until somebody can go EVA and replace the cap. We've lost a lot, though. We'll have to do some figuring.

"We'll send this as soon as we have a fuel estimate. And— Oh, oh, Dinger says the scope is showing some activity below, around that warship. Are they preparing to take off after us? This is going to take some close instrument work, we can't hang around to watch. *Rift-Runner* temporarily out."

Vast distances away and forward in time, the voder in Base 900 clicks. Off— On.

"It is now forty-five minim later. Take-off of a massive vessel confirmed. It looks as if we have that warship on our tail, with a thirty-nine-minim lead.

"And we have a fuel check. We do not, repeat not, have enough left to get back to Base. But we can make Beacon Alpha. . . . In a way it doesn't matter, because Captain Asch is not about to lead that battleship armed with planet-breakers into the Federation, if they follow us all that way. Of course, they may overhaul us earlier and grab us with that tractor-beam, which I guess is what Krimheen intends to do. If that happens, we'll try to get off a message before we're hauled in. We'll set all kinds of alarms, and keep a pipe ready for update, but this may be the last you hear from *Rift-Runner One.*

"The best outcome, we figure, is that we reach Beacon Alpha ahead of him and then play an evade-and-wait game there, hoping you can send some kind of relief. Ah, the captain has a word."

"Asch here," says the deeper voice. "I am sorry to have to record that this peaceful exploration mission ends with us running for our lives from unprovoked hostilities. I wish to point out that something has been seriously amiss in Sector Three hundred, who are supposed to keep a watch on the Black Worlds beyond. Their reports, when I left, stated that no off-planet activity was observed, and the population was supposed to be diminishing. But as near as I can judge, these Black Worlds raids on the race called Comenos were already starting. There is also the possibility that they were emigrating out to attractive worlds in that area, hence the, quotes, diminishing population. Those Black Worlds activities are poisoning the minds of people against Humans all along the south edge of the Rift, and maybe beyond. Distasteful as the thought is, I strongly suggest that the Black Worlders be reduced or eliminated—and steps taken to separate them from the Federation and Federation Humans, in alien minds.

"Now, when and if you come to our relief at Beacon Alpha, do not underestimate the probable Ziello strength there. Depending on the time elapsed, they may have called in reinforcements. Above all, I do not wish that more Human lives be endangered by our mission.

"Our plight may well be judged my fault for having insisted that we were Human, in the face of the Ziellos' apparent feelings, and our Sensitive's earlier warning that Humanity was 'hateful.'

"We will have forwarded all the useful information we have been able to obtain on this mission, especially if we succeed in doing as I intend, which is to include estimates of fuel use, speed, and other flight characteristics and Ziello capabilities, in the event of our being overtaken and captured. No useful aim would be served by endangering people to rescue our persons, beyond the humanitarian one. And in considering this, I insist that you give weight to our desire to have no more Human deaths on our consciences.

"I will now turn this back to Lieutenants Sharana, Dingañar, and Torrane for their provisional and preferably private farewells. . . . As to my own mate, now in cold-sleep, I believe she has recorded her wishes in the event of my nonreturn.

"Lutho Asch, commanding, out."

In FedBase 900, Pauna has caught Exec's glance; she jumps up and switches off as the voder clicks.

"We can defer the rest until after receipt of any message reporting their capture," says Exec quietly. "Or until so much time has elapsed that we must believe they are lost."

All four Humans sit for a time in silence. Exec's chin is on her fist, her expression grim. Just as Fred is about to dismiss Pauna and Realune, she speaks.

"Well . . . the worst outcome. I've already said all I feel. Fred, we'll have to get at some careful planning tonight.

"Meanwhile, Pauna, I want you to run a careful check back to the times of sending and arrival of messages one, two, and three, to get an estimate of the time it will take *Rift-Runner* to get to Beacon Alpha. And Charts has their starfield holos for the whole trip; please drop by and warn them I'm going to be needing their best estimates of the same thing, plus—important—the distance from here to the beacon. Thus we'll have two independent estimates. The one thing I don't want is to have those people dodging a battleship or worse around Alpha for years, waiting for us to get to them.

"And Realune, ask Charts to make a set of close-ups of the Alpha region, so our rescue mission can locate them promptly if they're not transmitting."

"Will that be all, Myr Exec?"

"Right. Thank you."

As they leave they hear her say, "Fred, even if we start yesterday, we're going to be late. Maybe too late. . . . I wonder—we've been hearing these rumors out of Central. If by any chance they have something that works . . . we need it. I'm going to start hammering on some doors, life-or-death priority."

On far Zieltan, while that message is being recorded above them, Alien Languages Officer Zillanoy is calling up her friend Kanaklee, at his office.

"Oh, Kanak— Something so exciting! I'm going into space on a real mission! I wish I could say a proper good-bye, but Captain Krimheen says I must get myself aboard in thirty *stor* or be left behind. Of course they wouldn't leave me, because I'm the only Zhuman speaker they have, but I just will not hold them up.

"You see, nobody knows the speed of the aliens' ship. Of course our big warship will catch it easily, but he wants to make it a short chase so he can get back east.

"Oh, I wish I could tell you all the excitement, with them running away and taking off in the midst of that rainstorm! I got two big water-burns, but they're nothing. Only I have to save the details till I get back. To tell you the truth, though, I was delighted they got away. Captain Krimheen is so grim and suspicious. Real war must make everybody like that. He didn't tell me he planned to trap them by taking out their fuel.

"What I called about, aside from good-bye, my dear: It occurs to me that we should take a Ritual person with us in case we have to offer Thanksgiving. Or we might have a Ritual when we return, if we have many adventures. Which I have a hunch we will. The aliens might fight, or who knows what. Just between us, I think it'll be a longer chase than Captain Krimheen does. And I believe they've come a longer way than he thinks. They're surprising!

"So I thought of your old nurser, Tomlo. It must be getting pretty old and feeble now that Kanlie's so far in school. And I think it's educated enough to appreciate a beautiful return to the Oversoul with honor, don't you? What do you think? . . .

"Oh, I'm so glad, I thought you'd agree. Then if it's all right, I'll just pick it up at your home on my way to the port, and I can say good-bye to Leiloy, too.

"I'm so fond of Tomlo, you know I'll take good care of it to the end. And I do think it likes me, don't you, Kanak? . . .

"Great! Now I must hop and fly. Imagine, we never thought when I went east to study that awful Zhuman language, it'd get me taking off on a *combat* mission, chasing aliens! Good-bye, dear Kanaklee, good-bye. Could you tell Leiloy I'll be by as soon as I pack a couple of tail-bows? Oh, right—and prepare to have your ears talked off when I get back! Love and good-bye, good-bye!"

The years pass. . . .
In the dark of space, in the depths of the empty Rift, a beacon's soundless voice wails.

Drawn by that voice, the silvery fish that is a Human spaceship approaches. It begins to decelerate. The beacon—Beacon Alpha—is circling a big ice-planet, which in turn is in far slow orbit around a great blue sun.

But the little ship is not alone. Behind it, almost out of sensor range, there follows a much bigger ship. A warship of the Ziello from Zieltan, nosing implacably down the trail.

In the small ship, four Human bodies tumble out of sleep-chests. Their first thought is fear; have they been wakened by an alarm? Is the warship closing in? But the alarms are still. Only the amplified wail of Beacon Alpha sounds in the bridge.

Lieutenant Dingañar flings himself at the scope, rubbing the last mists of cold-sleep from his eyes. He scans around quickly, glances up at mass-proximity indicators, swivels the space-radar, goes back to the scope.

"We've lost her!" he shouts. "Those indications at Beacon Beta were true, she can't match our running speed. Oh, joy, oh, boy."

"That is a big help," says Captain Asch soberly, to the general jubilation. When they had last clocked the warship, before fatigue had forced them to rest, the computer had given them a good probability of outrunning their pursuer. It was only a probability then. Now it's certain.

But it's not salvation. Only a help, as Asch has said, in the game of outwaiting the warship at Beacon Alpha. There is no hope of losing her, of holing up and hiding; they are leaving an ion trail in virtually virgin space. However they double and hide, sooner or later the enemy will be coming down on them.

"What now?" Dinger asks.

"Now I take us off course and tuck us back of that planet to wait," says Asch. "And then we play kittimousle with that thing. Around the beacon, around the planet, around the star . . . until help comes. Only we can't; we haven't the fuel. So my plan is to evade her for a while until we get good estimates of her turning radius, acceleration, and other flight characteristics. Then, if they seem to be serious about catching us . . . then I intend to try to parley."

"They know we don't have much fuel," Dinger comments. "Maybe they don't, either. But unless they're real short, why should they bother to parley?"

"We have to figure they have a resupply coming," says Asch. "If I were that captain, Captain Krimheen, I guess, messaging for reinforcements and supply would be the first thing I'd do once I saw I was heading into the Rift. Especially if I had FTL commo. Whatever we do, we should do it before any reinforcements show up."

"So?"

"We have one threat," Asch says slowly. "I think we'll find we have enough extra speed and mobility to ram them. Suicide-style. We could probably remove them as a threat to the Federation. Of course there'd be enough scraps left so that their reinforcements could guess what happened. But their command would be gone. And we'd tell Base our intentions. But do we mean it? That's what I need your vote on: Do we in fact ram, before letting ourselves be taken? Think over the implications; would that bring us closer to war?"

A silence, as each considered years in an alien prison on a waterless planet, interrogations, the possibilities of the Base's rescue mission, their personal lives and hopes.

"I say ram," Dinger says at length.

"Ram," says Shara. "Pfoo!"

"There's this, too," says Torrane. "His reinforcements, if and when they get here, might not be able to figure what happened. They might conclude we had some superweapon, and get a healthy scare. I vote ram, while we still have enough fuel to afford a miss or two."

"So let it be recorded," Asch says somberly. "Lieutenant Torrane, will you cut a message to Nine hundred outlining our plan? We'll send it as soon as we can add a few specs on the capabilities of that ship. Lieutenant Sharana, I'll need a lot of help on composing a parley message in pidgin. General idea is peace, not war; inviting them to Base—preferably minus their planet-breakers—and a later exchange of trade goods. We have our video technology, they have FTL transmission, for starters. Do you think you can get all that?"

"Assuming that little Zilla-something is aboard, and she's looked at the advanced language-pack. I better make a simple one in case she's not." Shara's moving up to the copilot's couch. "Oh, whew, by the gods!—do you feel it? We've lost those extra imaginary bodies and tails and all!"

"Hey, yes!"

"Great!"

"Oh, it's wonderful not to feel so *clumsy!*" Shara cuts a cartwheel through the rotating compartment that holds their sleep-chests; its spin provides a minimal gee to keep them healthy during the long sleeps.

"I don't know," says Dinger the joker. "I may miss that tail. It was interesting."

"We've apparently run out of the Ziello influence," Asch observes. "But why? It set in at the beacon here. No, wait—we're on the Base side of the planet's orbit now. Could we have cut it that fine by chance, to locate the beacon right on the border of the, ah, influence?"

"Stranger things have happened," Dinger remarks.

"I have a theory," says Shara, irrepressibly cheerful. "Maybe we Humans put out a field, too! Why not? And if we're right where they overlap, mightn't that give a really sharp border? And maybe it kind of fluctuates back and forth a little."

Captain Asch is rummaging through the software. "There's an E and E program here. Evasion and escape. We'll have to run it by hand until we know that ship's maneuverability and what constraints to put in. Unless they've loaded on some smaller stuff, we don't have to worry about being shot at; those planet-buster missiles are too big and slow to hit a small mobile target. I'm assuming they aim to pick us up with that tractor beam. Range and strength, unknown; we better estimate one fifty percent of ours, just to be safe. . . . It'll be a while before we get much sleep, at least all at the same time."

"They may knock out the beacon. Run over it," reflects Dinger, still at the scope. "But we could put out another. . . . If they get to breaking up planets to keep us from using them as temporary hidey-holes, the debris will serve just as well, for a while. . . . Oh, by the gods, it's a crime the way things have turned out. There're some great planets here for meeting and trade, just at the halfway point, too. . . ."

"That's the way things have turned out," Asch says grimly.

"Reverting to my theory," says Shara, "I still don't see why Humans couldn't be putting out a field of influence, too."

"Our alien visitors would have reported it," says Torrane from where he's readying the message pipe.

"Maybe not," Shara persists. "Because maybe these things work only in real empty space. And nobody comes to us through the Rift. Didn't you say your red-lizard thing was in an empty place like a piece of Rift, Captain?"

"Possibly so, I can't be certain. It's a nice theory, Shara, but . . ."

"But don't measure your velocity until you're sure your engines start, as Mama used to say, huh? Sure. . . . But I'd like to think Humans have everything anybody else has. Hey—maybe every race throws a field, some stronger, some weaker—but they're only noticeable if they're near a real low-density region! . . . If it turns out the Ziello in that ship are feeling like imaginary Humans—remember you heard it here first. And *I* better get to work. Our grim pursuer should be showing up pretty soon."

"When it does," Asch says to Dinger, "take a reading so we'll know where any reinforcements will be likely to appear."

"Message recorded through status so far," says Torrane. "Including the intent to ram, if the attempt at parley fails. . . . Does anybody have any objections to naming that big blue sun 'Ekaterina'?"

General approval. But at the memory of the girl now lying frozen and lifeless in their cargo, the temporary euphoria vanishes. What's ahead looms bleak—a life-and-death contest of maneuver with a largely unknown enemy, which may indeed have to end with self-inflicted death. And their home-haven, to which they dare not point the enemy, so relatively near. And all so needless, so nearly inexplicable—having for enemies the alien peoples who should have been met with friendship; the terrible prospect of interstellar war overshadows all—a crime, as Dinger had said. A crime of which they're entirely innocent, the pawns of evil fortune. . . . The words of the little interpreter: "Kill all Humans!" echo in their heads.

"Got her!" says Dinger, pointing to his instruments. "There she comes. . . . If her sensors are as good as ours, she ought to start decelerating pretty soon. . . . I'm getting a trace of excess I.R.—could be caused by personnel in the cargo-bay."

"Marines in cold-sleep, at a guess," says Asch.

"The seeing's very good—I could be getting those missile racks in a minim or two."

By this time the great warship is a naked-eye object, a bright splinter barreling along on their former course past the beacon.

"I intend to wait until they've picked us up and are headed right at us," says Asch. "Then I'll bust out about at one seventy-five degrees to them, put the planet between us, and make a U-turn around the next planet in and wait for him again. Give Torry the missile data as soon as you pick it up, and we'll send the pipe after we're in motion, on his off side. Green?"

"Green."

They wait. The warship is decelerating now, its retros bursting on the night like great blossoms. Dinger picks up the smaller missile racks. They're empty; the warship is still armed only with the eight probable planet-breakers.

"Little uneven on the navigation there," says Asch critically.

Their enemy is making a wide turn, evidently questing for their spoor. As they watch, it straightens out on a course from which they must be plainly visible. Then there's another flare, and as it clears they see it heading straight at them. But it isn't a clean aim; the alien pilot makes two—no, three course corrections. Asch is frowning.

As the enemy warship grows in the view-port, he says, "Get ready for a quickie." Closer and bigger yet it comes, until Shara can't help glancing nervously at Asch, poised like a hawk over the controls. Bigger, closer—and suddenly the giant fist of acceleration is punching them down, as Asch cuts everything into a dash past the bigger ship and back along its course.

"He should swing around on that planet," Asch says, and straining to look back, they can see the enemy warship doing just that. All can see, too, that there's a raggedness in his maneuver.

"I'm not going to park by any more planets. Makes it too easy for him to turn," Asch says, frowning at himself. They accelerate out of there as the other ship comes out of its turn, following them.

"Message pipe released," Torry says. "I think I sent it off while we were out of his field."

They run straight for a time, with the big ship falling ever-farther behind. "Curse the fuel," Asch mutters. "This could be fun. . . . I'm going to get on his tail to talk. How're you coming with my speech, Shara?"

The beacon's wail is growing faint. Dinger turns it up.

"Don't want to lose track of that," Asch says. He starts a swing to the northeast, watching his pursuer. At the instant the warship's jets flare to turn with him, Asch rams on his opposing thrusters, knocking them around a hundred and eighty degrees, accelerating.

"Now show us what you've got," he tells the enemy under his breath.

The big ship torches by, still turning the wrong way. Asch fires another turn that sends stuff winging and banging all over the cabin. A correction—and they end up following the warship's tail. "That was easier than it should have been," Asch comments, frowning harder.

"For what it's worth, I . . ." Torrane speaks up, hesitates.

"Yes, what? You picking up something?"

"I don't know. Just trouble, faint. Faint . . . Oh, devils, probably I'm crazy."

"No. They're not reacting right."

Shara hands her noter-recorder to him. "Here's a draft of what you could say. All words are in the basic movie-talkie pack."

"Umm . . . good. Gods, it's like baby-talk, isn't it?"

"Pidgin is almost a language. I've tried to exploit their distinction between 'Zhuman' and 'Yooman,' see. It's to our advantage. And I thought you should repeat the whole thing so they get a second crack at it. You won't want to read it twice, just record it—flip that switch when you start to speak—and replay."

"Green. I don't see anything here to change. All right, go." He thumbs the caller open. "*Rift-Runner*—Federation ship *Rift-Runner* here. Federation Yoomanor calling Ziello fight-ship. Federation Yoomanor calling you. Come in, Ziello ship. You hear? Captain Krimheen, you hear?"

No reply from the receiver except a shuffling, jangling sound. Then there is what might be a faint grunt. "At least they have their pick-up open," Torrane says.

"Captain Krimheen?" Asch repeats. Then he quickly puts his hand over the caller and says to the others, "Listen, you guys . . . I'd be obliged if you sort of don't listen to this. I feel a perfect fool!"

"Right." All turn ostentatiously to other tasks, and Asch starts his speech. Despite their best efforts, his authoritative tones cut through.

"We want talk. We want talk you, we no want fight. Why you fight? Why you make war with Federation? Federation no want war, want peace. Federation no do bad things. We from Federation, no same Black Worlds Zhumanor. Black Worlds Zhumanor do bad things. Catch people, kill people. Make people dig dimons, zaranavths. We no want dimons. We want peace with Ziello. We fight with Black Worlds Zhumanor . . ." And on and on, to an invitation to an exchange of visits— "You come Federation, say hello. Federation come Zieltan, say hello." And a final vista of trade and a warning of the horrors of war.

In spite of Asch's professed scorn, he really puts his heart into the peroration. "You catch us, kill us; Federation come catch you, kill you. You come Federation, blow up Base, kill all people—Federation come Zieltan, blow up Zieltan, kill all. You come Federation, blow up many bases—Federation come you, blow up more Ziello planets, kill more— Ziello big, Federation big! All peoples kill all peoples! War, war, war, long war. Bad, bad war no finish. Why we start war? We want talk, we want make peace."

Even as he speaks, faint sounds are coming from the receiver. Without pausing, Asch gestures Torrane to come closer, put his ear to it.

"Now talk come two time," Asch signs off, and puts the recorder to the caller. "Whew! What're you getting, Torry?"

In reply Torrane turns the volume up. Nothing—and then a childish voice says, "He'p!"

Asch picks up the caller. "What? Say more!"

"He'p," cries the little voice. "Come he'p? Big peopre sick. Big peopre ve'y ve'y sick. . . . Go O'ersou' now. . . . He'p, come."

There is a sound like things falling. No more voice.

The Humans stare at each other. "What do we make of *that?*"

"Some kind of trick?" Shara wonders.

"If it's a trap, it's a good one." Asch turns to the caller. "Who are you? Identify, identify yourself. Are you calling *Rift-Runner?*"

But the little voice, childish but no Human child, only says again weakly, "He'p . . . Come he'p."

"You want us to come to your ship?"

No answer but vague scratching.

Asch draws a breath, turns to face the others. "I'm inclined to think something *is* wrong. But I could be fooled. I can't risk all your lives."

"I vote we go help them," Shara says.

"Yeah," says Dinger. "Better'n ramming, anyway."

"Oh, the hells." Torrane makes the motion of slapping a flipped coin, peeking under his hand. "Yes."

"Well . . . green, then," says Asch. "Provided we carry weapons."

"Weapons—" Dinger paws into the stowage. "Where'd I put those stunners? Ah!"

"And one more thing," says Asch in his captain's tone. "We have to realize these Ziello have only met Black World Humans. They know how Black Worlders operate. Maybe they've learned from them, maybe they have some cute tricks of their own. If this is a trap, we're doing for free exactly what they looked to do with that tractor beam—walking right in. Now, what if they decide to get our further cooperation the easy way, by taking a hostage or two?"

Grunts, as they think this over.

"I don't know about you, but I do *not* guarantee my continued resistance if they start mutilating one of you. Blinding, say. . . ."

"For once I'm ahead of you, Captain," says Shara. "I thought I was a likely hostage. So I remembered our emergency stuff." She pats her jaw. "It's going to make eating a little tricky, though."

"You've already got that trick tooth in place?" Asch is surprised. "Well, good for you. May you never have to think about using it. All right—Torry, Dinger, that goes for us, too. You do have your drop-deads with you?"

"Yeah."

"We put 'em in place now. Shara, take the controls a minim—and keep your ears open for any whisper from that ship. Let's hope she doesn't move."

They get up and make for their duffel compartments.

When they return they are waggling their jaws experimentally around the little weapon of self-deliverance. "I feel like a hologrid star," Dinger complains. "But I guess it's the practical thing."

"It is," Asch assures him. "And the gods are with us; that ship hasn't accelerated. I guess they want us." He starts the maneuver that will bring *Rift-Runner* alongside.

"Their caller is still open," Shara reports, "but I haven't heard a thing except a set of uneven footsteps, fading away. . . . Oh, wait— Somebody groaned, very faint."

"Artistic," Asch comments dryly. "Look at the size of that port. I just hope our flanges cover it."

The warship is gently rolling, or wallowing, on her course. It takes all Asch's skill to match with her and grapple their smaller port flange into a tight dock.

Just as they do so, there comes a clashing rattle through the linked hulls. Shara, suiting up by the view-port, sees one of the warship's big missiles detach itself in a burst of silent fire. They all watch as it goes hurtling off on its course to nowhere.

"Looks like somebody sick and crazy," comments Asch. "Not to mention hostile. . . . All right. Let's open up and try to go on in. Take your safeties off when we get their port open."

But getting the big ship's port open proves not so easy. The emergency handle that should permit ingress won't engage.

"Open your port! Open up!" Asch calls.

"Shall we go EVA and look in a viewer?" Shara asks.

But clickings are coming from the other side. The childish voice cries "I t'y! I t'y open."

And finally the port gives. They open it quietly and slip into a big, empty, silent lock. As they cross the threshold of the joined ships, they hit the jolt of almost full gravity.

"Artificial gee," Dinger whispers. "The lucky so-and-sos."

The inner port is ajar; oxygen-rich air is drifting out. Asch pushes it open, stunner ready. He looks right, looks left—and then stands staring at the sight before him. The others crowd in behind.

The big bridge is almost empty. To their right and forward is the pilot's well, with two Ziello figures slumped, half-off the couches. To their left is the front of a lighted herbarium—not a hydroponics set-up, among these water-shy people—which somehow looks wrong. Directly in front of them, on the floor, is a small creamy-furred alien which seems to be feebly trying to crawl toward the herbarium. It is visibly gasping for breath. Huge sleep-chests, with occupancy lights on, stand against the far side of the hull.

"Hello!" says Asch. "We come help. What, ah, what bad thing here?"

But the figure on the deck makes no response, only gasps harder.

Dinger and Shara go to it. It's an attractive little creature, rather like the antique toy called a teddy bear; but its pink mouth is open, its face screwed up as though strangling. To their questions it says nothing but only continues to try to crawl toward the shelves of plants.

"Let us help you," Shara says. They each put a gloved arm under the alien's upper arms—it is shaped like a big Ziello, though only about half its height—and start to carry it toward the bank of plant trays. As they lift its head it makes a sound of protest, so they let it drag and merely pull it toward the trays.

Once there, the creature suddenly writhes from their hands and rises up, thrusting its snout and head in among the lichenlike, reddish plants and breathing deeply.

"Something's wrong with their set-up—look, the stuff is almost all dead!" Dinger waves a hand over the stand of plants, and they suddenly crumble to powder in the wake of his moving arm. "They're just dust, standing there!"

"The trouble must be lack of whatever these put out. Look, they've rigged an emergency collector." Asch points to a long air-scoop along the front of the bank, which feeds into a funnel-shaped duct. "That runs over to the pilot couches."

"What those things put out is CO two," says Dinger. "Carbon dioxide. At least the ones I examined did. That makes sense, see, that fan is driving the stuff toward this front edge. It's heavier than air, so it would flow down into this collector. They must *need* CO two in their air-mix. Something happened to their set-up and they're dying without it."

"What has carbon dioxide in it?" asks Shara practically. "I know— our breaths!" Her faceplate is open. She stoops to the gasping little alien and gently exhales across its muzzle. The creature suddenly inhales greedily and lifts its face to almost touch her nose.

Captain Asch and Torrane have been investigating the big aliens in the pilot well.

"It's Zilla and Krimheen," Torrane tells them. "They're semiconscious. Wearing nose-masks connected to that collector. Krimheen has a death-grip on some kind of gun."

"I don't think those masks are doing them much good by now," Dinger observes. "There's only a few plants left alive in here. It's $CO_2$ they're short of. I'll try disconnecting those hoses and you each breathe into one. Our exhaled breath has about four percent $CO_2$; that must be pretty close to their atmosphere. If it'd been over five, we'd have felt it."

"Our analysis showed three point six," Asch confirms him.

Dinger has unscrewed Zilla's hose from the central pipe. "Here, Torry."

Torrane takes the hose and blows into it. As his breath reaches Zilla, she gives a convulsive gasp, and another. In a minim her eyes open, focus wonderingly on them. Her mouth is free to talk.

"Zhumanor!" she exclaims feebly. "No do bad thing!"

"We Yoomans, no Zhumanor," Asch tells her. "We no do bad things."

Dinger has the big alien captain's hose free. He hands it to Asch. "Rank hath its privilege," he quotes wryly. Asch takes it, and presently Krimheen stirs and wakes.

His first move is to jerk loose the hose and point the weapon at Asch. "I catch you!"

"Oh, mother," says Dinger disgustedly. As Krimheen chokes, strangles, and slumps back into unconsciousness, Asch disengages the gun and lays it atop the control board. Dinger gives the big alien measured breaths.

"You'll have to take him over, Captain," he tells Asch. "I've got to go get a bunch of supplies—fire extinguishers, one of the $CO_2$ canisters for our hydroponics, plus anything I can think of."

"I've thought of . . . something. But someone . . . will have to go EVA," says Torrane between breaths. "That dry ice . . . around our vent. If . . . it's in the shade."

Dinger runs to the alien's big view-port. "By the gods, it is. It'll keep till I get the easy stuff rigged. Torry, you're a genius. I should have thought of that!"

"Only at . . . times," says Torrane. "The prospect of giving mouth-to-mouth . . . resuscitation for a couple of years . . . stimulated me."

There follows an awkward, hectic time of trying to arrange the aliens in some reasonable manner so that a conference can be had. It becomes soon apparent that Torrane's vision of prolonged mouth-to-mouth revival is only for emergencies; the aliens' noses are becoming painfully burned by the moisture in the Humans' breaths. Zilla shows them this; Captain Krimheen remains scornfully stoic and silent, watching their every move. After Zilla has replenished her $CO_2$ levels, she finds that she can be without it for brief periods and volunteers to go to their medical supplies for some salve, "good thing nose."

But when she rises to hurry across the deck, her usual fluid hopping gait has changed to a shuffling run. Moreover, her upper arms hang limp, and her tail flails about loosely.

"Why me same you?" she demands. "Same Zhumanor? No arms! See —you same!" She points to Captain Krimheen, and they realize he has kept his normally active upper arms folded close to his body. Yes, he had held the weapon in one of his larger, rough-work lower hands, too, and his tail hangs limp.

"They're getting Human hallucinations!" Shara exclaims. "Remember?"

"It certainly looks like it," Asch admits.

As Zilla roots her pot of salve out of a drawer in the aft wall, they try to explain to her their own reverse problem in this part of space. "We think we same you, on Zieltan." Krimheen, silent, is following intently. "We make tails same, we think." Something of the idea apparently gets across, but they have no common word for "feeling."

When Zilla, starting to gasp, stumbles back with her salve, her illusion is so strong that the image of a red-skinned girl running across the deck flickers in Torrane's head. She snatches up their interconnecting hose and fairly sucks at his breath. Breath of my breath, he thinks, and for an instant feels an intense protectiveness. The little being is far from home, at the mercy of aliens for her very life. He beams at her; maybe this gets across a little, too. The idea of war between them looms behind Krimheen. An obscenity.

Krimheen haughtily accepts the burn salve from Zilla, but when it comes to the idea that they should get their heads down lower, where $CO_2$ is accumulating, he is adamant. Zilla, however, is acquiescent and stretches out comfortably, hand-moving her tail, on a carpeted area of the well. "It's a natural heavy gas-sink," Dinger says. "Thank the lords they weren't up high, or they'd be dead."

He is arranging fire-extinguisher foam in the gas-collector funnel. "There's a slow fan in that duct," he tells them. "It goes in by gravity, and then the fan pushes it to them. Nice. Try them on it now. Screw your ends into that central pipe. If it seems like they have enough, Shara, you can bring your patient over and hook it in, too. I saw an extra nose-piece down there."

They do this, and the arrangement seems to work well, provided some Human stands by to refill the $CO_2$ input.

When Shara carries the strange little alien over, its big eye is oozing a bluish powder. "Pain from its muzzle, I think," Shara says. "Its name is Tomlo."

Zilla swabs salve on its mouth burns from Shara's breath. "Is Murnoo," she tells them. "Murnoo for Ziello, eh, children. Is Ziello but no same. Good Murnoo," she assures it. "Die soon."

"I ca', I ta'k he'p," the thing says feebly but proudly.

"It saved your lives," Shara says indignantly. "I mean, it help you no die."

"Yes, good Tomlo. Is old, die soon."

The mystery remains.

As to what happened to the air-plant, this also is obscure. Zilla seems to be trying to say that the plants unexpectedly formed flowers and seed, and died at the end of that cycle, an apparently rare event. "Probably they expected to be in cold-sleep, or back at Zieltan," Torrane says. "I think she's saying that it'll regrow; there do seem to be seedlings coming. . . . This crisis may come to an end if the whole bank regenerates."

"And that reminds me!" Dinger slaps his head. "Brain, wake up!" He hastens out the big port and back into *Rift-Runner* while Torrane and Shara are getting Tomlo into a nose-piece and showing it how to draw from the central duct.

Dinger returns with a big plastic wad, which proves to contain the plants he dug up at the spaceport.

"Good for air? I put in there?" he asks the alien captain. Krimheen unbends enough to give the Ziello affirmative chin-jerk. Zilla is ecstatic. "Oh, good! Oh, good! Come more quick now!" She shuffle-hops over to help him bury the roots of the first one, then buries her nose in it. "Zieltan," she says lovingly. "Beau-ti-ful Zieltan," before she gasps and has to return to the well.

"You talk Galactic more good," Torrane tells her.

"We learn, we work, learn," she replies. "Before sleep."

"All right," says Asch, who has been quietly and thoroughly examining the bridge and its workings. "Now is time we talk. I want talk. You listen, ah, you want hear me?" His question to Krimheen hangs in the air, finally getting a reluctant assent-nod from the alien. "Good."

But he notices that Krimheen has been glancing at the row of sleep-chests, in which presumably are the rest of the crew. Zilla has intimated that they went in when the plants first started to go bad. Two on the right end are dark; it is the lighted one next to these that Krimheen seems concerned with. Asch walks over and points to it. "Trouble?" he asks.

Krimheen gives a curt "no" chin-point. But Zilla says, "Malloreen sick." She puts her hand on her long chest and makes a fast, flapping movement, at the same time pantomiming a person gasping for air. "No go box quick e-nough."

Krimheen grunts disgustedly at these admissions to the enemy.

Asch considers. A struggle with asphyxiation can mean trouble for a wonky heart—assuming these aliens have pumps for whatever flows in their veins, as most of them do.

But . . . "Do we have enough CO two for one more Ziello?" he asks Dinger. "Can you estimate time?"

Dinger looks sharply at the slowly sinking foam level in the collector and calculates their reserves.

"I'd say . . . with four, two days. Forty-eight hours. But then something *has* to happen. Like, they all get in the chests."

Asch walks back and approaches Krimheen, holding up a sheet of plastic to protect the alien from the water vapor of his breath.

"Captain Krimheen. We want help. No do bad thing. If sick people" —he repeats Zilla's flapping-heart gesture—"sick people go in sleep-box, is no good. Bad. You know I say true?" Krimheen watches him grimly. "We have good air for four Ziello for two days, if this people come out. Four Ziellor, two days. Now: You think you number-two ship"—he points back at their course—"you fuel ship come in two days? Have more good air for you?"

If Krimheen is surprised that they have guessed that he has reinforcements coming, he shows no sign but only remains staring hard at Asch with his great single eye above the nose-piece.

"All right." Asch sighs. "Try another way. Now you know how much air you have. . . . You want we open box, help Malloreen?"

"Captain," says Dinger as the alien stirs, frowns, "I think he's too uncomfortable, tied down to that nose-tube. Suppose I get them some dry ice in a bag, so they can move around?"

"Good thought."

"I'll go with you," says Shara. "We're almost suited up." They had kept on the clumsy suits as the easiest way of avoiding moisture-burning the aliens.

They go out through the big port so they can use *Rift-Runner*'s EVA exit. While they're gone, Torrane tries to tell Zilla what they're up to and teaches her the name "see-oh-two" by a series of gestures that has her giggling. He's pleased to see she hasn't lost the chortling laugh he remembers from Zieltan; finds himself thinking of her as a girl rather than an alien. Her work suit is an attractive silky stuff, nicer than theirs.

Dinger and Shara return with four deep insulated tumblers and a bundle of dry-ice chips in a quilted bag.

"We've got to move our ship in a couple of hours, or that vent will be in sunlight," Dinger warns.

Shara tries to explain that the stuff will turn to gas without making a liquid, but the concept of subliming is beyond their language capability. The aliens seem unfamiliar with frozen $CO_2$. "Well, they're not chemists or engineers," Torrane says. "How many of us have seen frozen oxygen?"

They hand each alien a tumbler containing chips of dry ice, pantomime that they are to sniff it as needed. "Cold! Very cold! No touch!"

But Zilla has already probed the mysterious stuff; a squeal, and she puts her finger in her mouth. Shara hugs her and goes for the salve. The finger is startlingly Human.

"I do bad thing," Zilla says. "Same children." From Krimheen comes a faint snort. He now removes his nose-piece, picks up the tumbler cautiously, and shuffle-walks with as much dignity as he can over to the sleep-chest holding the supposedly sick Malloreen.

As Dinger had guessed, the regained freedom to move has loosened his reserve. "Yes," he says slowly. "O-pen." And stands back, waiting for the Humans to obey.

Asch steps back with him, thinking that his guess of Ziellan reinforcements is now a certainty. Within two days—possibly much sooner —they will be outnumbered, maybe outrun, and under fire. Not good.

Zilla shows Torrane and Dinger how the big sleep-chest works and punches it onto waking-opening cycle. Apparently it doesn't decant its occupant, as the Human ones do; when the cycle is over, the heavy outer lid lifts, revealing a light inner cover. Presumably it has injected or otherwise administered a hibernation-stasis breaker to Malloreen. But the inner cover heaves, falls back; Malloreen is too weak to throw it open. Dinger grabs it and flings it wide, revealing a reddish-colored Ziello twisting and starting to choke, Dinger whips a tumbler of dry ice under the alien's nose and holds his head, while Zilla bends over him, speaking reassurances. As the $CO_2$ gets to him, Malloreen relaxes and lies back. They can see that he looks unhealthy; his brown velvet fur is staring and lusterless, his big eye is hollow and half-closed.

Dinger has produced a stethoscope. He applies it first to Zilla's clothed chest to hear a normal Ziellan heart, and then brings it down to Malloreen's.

"Oo-oof. Bad. If he were a Human, I'd say a goner without help. Heart's ragged and fluttery; instead of a steady thrum I'm getting clusters, and some kind of crazy PTL beats." He addresses Zilla and Krimheen. "You have good thing for heart?"

"N-no. . . ." Krimheen chin-points negatively.

"Who is people for sick, here?"

Zilla points in the sleep-chest. "Malloreen."

"It would be. Cap'n, I think Malloreen's their medico. . . . If he were a Human, I'd try digitalis. There's no chance that drug is native to Zieltan, it's originally from a Terran plant. But maybe anything's better than watching him pass out." He bends to the med-kit, extracts a vial.

"Captain Krimheen, here is Human thing, good for heart. But I think no good for Ziello. No is bad thing, see—" He cracks half a tab and swallows it. "You have no thing for Ziello. He very bad, no live. You want I try this?"

Krimheen approaches the chest, looks down. Dinger hands him the stethoscope, with which he seems familiar, and motions to him to listen through it. His face changes to what even the Humans can read as a bleak expression.

"Shall I try this?" Dinger asks.

Krimheen's eyelid droops. Slowly he nods his chin: affirmative. Then he stoops over and says something in Ziellan to Malloreen, brief and grave.

"Oh, gods," whispers Shara. "I think he's saying good-bye."

"I don't want him to die in there," says Asch. "Shara, fix up that place in the well where Zilla was; that'll give him the best air."

Dinger has managed to get a tab of digitalis into the alien's mouth, with Zilla persuading him to swallow. He gives one puzzled, despairing look about but is too weak to care why aliens he thinks of as evil Zhumanor are ministering to him. His eye closes, nor does it open while they lift him gently out of the chest and carry him over to the well. He is half suited-up; they pull the stiff fabric off to ease him and put a thin pillow under his head, in the deeper part of the well. He is slight, slender, perhaps quite young. Dinger pulls one of the nose-pieces over and ties it on him, and Zilla tries to tell him to breathe through it about every ten breaths. But it's doubtful he understands.

All they can do for him now is wait. And every minim brings that Ziellan ship, or ships, closer. Captain Asch must parley with Krimheen now.

Krimheen has returned to his pilot's chair, turned so he can keep an eye on Malloreen. Asch seats himself on the well's step.

"Captain Krimheen. Number one, we no catch you. We come help you, no more. And we want talk. No fight. When you no sick, we go to our ship"—he points, gestures—"and we go. We give you all our CO two. We go. You go, where you want. You hear?" he asks, trying to convey cordiality.

But as he speaks, he realizes he cannot mean this. To turn Krimheen loose in his present frame of mind would be to risk the terrible danger that he might follow someone or something to FedBase—blow it up on sight—and go on a glory-trip through the Federation, blowing up colonies until his missiles ran out. Or, if he returned to Zieltan, he might well return with a hostile force. . . . No; Asch must somehow soften him up, keep him in contact.

"We want you come Federation, look Federation, say hello. Federation no do bad things you. No catch you. Federation want peace. No fighting, no war—" And here Asch delivers a shortened version of his speech that was never heard.

Krimheen listens impassively. He seems abstracted, as though half his mind is on something else. On Malloreen, Asch hopes.

Shara has jumped up meanwhile and gone over to their ship. She returns with an armful of holographs. "Maybe he'd like to see Base," she whispers to Asch. "And I brought a starfield of the Rift."

This gives Asch an idea. He stands the big holo up before Krimheen and comes beside him, taking care with his breath. "Captain, see. Here we are. Here is Zieltan, and the—give me the word, Shar—the Allowateera." He draws a big vague circle on the northern side of the Rift. "And here"—he makes a similar circle on the south—"is Federation. My Base here, more Bases here, here, here." His finger runs along the fringes, eastward. "And *here*"—he points to the far southeast—"*here* are the Black Worlds Zhumanor. Black Worlds no in Federation. Is bad people. Federation fight Black Worlds. And here"—he points to the Ziello side of them—"I think here is your fleet. Your ships fighting Zhumanor. Yes?" Krimheen only blinks once. "Anyway, I think so. Now look. Is good way for you to go home—" Oops, he has overrun the captain's Galactic word-power. But Zilla has come beside them and translates.

"You come to Nine hundred with me, say hello. Then you go east on Federation side, say hello at Bases here, here, here, get fuel, air, whatever you need, and come to your ships here. More good than go back long way—" He traces the route back to Zieltan and through Ziellan space around to far southeast. "See is more long? Go back by Federation more quick. More good. Yes?"

Krimheen seems to come out of his trance. "Is good plan," he says carefully. But Asch detects some overtone, as though the alien were deciding a purely hypothetical question. Uneasily, Asch sits back.

"Show him the Base holos, Shara. I'm gibbered dry."

With help from Zilla, Shara starts handing him the colorful holographs. "This topside landing . . . this number-one port . . . this meeting-hall, er, place . . . this big chief in office, name Exec. . . . This Captain Asch's mate—mate, Zilla? Yes. She in cold-sleep now. . . . Place for eating . . . Place for people who come see, say hello. You like stay in this place?"

Zilla is exclaiming excitedly at the exotic scenes. But Krimheen glances at the guest rooms critically and points to a fountain. "This . . . wa-teh?"

"Oh, yes, I forgot—you no want, we stop it quick."

The show winds to an end. Asch gets up to confront Krimheen.

"Well, what you think, Captain Krimheen? You want come to FedBase with me, go back to your ships by Federation?"

To his surprise, Krimheen again inclines his head yes, saying judiciously, "Good plan." But again, it is as if in abstract approval. Well, Asch has done all he can on the big issues. Base diplomatics will have to take it from here. Now for their practical problem—fuel.

Krimheen's resupply of fuel will obviously arrive first; theirs may not come for . . . years—don't think of it. So Asch will have to persuade Krimheen to let him hook on and, when he is refueled, tow *Rift-Runner* to FedBase. No problem with that in space, once acceleration has been achieved; and surely this huge craft can manage.

"Good. Now, how we get to Base?" he begins. "I no have fuel, you no have fuel. Federation come here, but your number-two ship come more quick."

Krimheen is listening with sudden intensity. Asch makes the motion of joining two ships together with his hands. "You want use that big port for you fuel ship, I think?" and he goes on to the complex question of where and how to hook up, in which Dinger joins them.

"We have to move our ship now," he says. "Bad for sun to come on ship. CO two go!"

With Zilla's and Shara's help, the concept is explained, and the question of where to dock their ship is put to the alien, who is keenly attentive. He takes up his dry-ice tumbler and goes to the port to examine their docking mechanism. Then he seems to consult some inner complexities and comes back to the well, where he points to the hull alongside and behind the pilot's chair.

"Is port, for, ah, for trouble. You come here."

"An emergency port. He thinks our lock will fit it. Good thing! And it's on the shady side. Let's move her right now, Captain."

"Green. Right, Dinger, I think you and I can do it. Captain Krimheen, my ship come here now?"

"Yes." With emphatic chin-nod.

And in a very few minim Torrane and Shara find themselves alone in the alien bridge, watching through the big view-port as *Rift-Runner*, looking very small, pulls away.

After a lonely time, there comes a grating jar at the warship's bow. They go behind the pilot's chair and remove some equipment and padding, revealing an emergency lock. From beyond it sound grindings and clankings.

"Open up!" comes Asch's muffled voice. They do, revealing a tunnel crawl-through onto which *Rift-Runner* is docked and locked.

Captain Asch crawls through to them, looking pleased. "All secure. I think that'll hold her on through a gravity vortex. This ship is old, but her fittings are well made. Captain Krimheen, your ship good ship!"

But Krimheen has turned away and is suddenly intent on his sensor bank. When he turns back, he is a changed being, all abstractedness gone. He picks up his caller and barks a phrase in Ziellan. There is an answering faint voice from the receiver.

"My fuel ship come," he announces. There is an odd gleam in his eye.

"Well, good!" says Shara. "Now we all go to FedBase. When we start?"

Captain Asch says nothing but watches Krimheen.

Krimheen gets ponderously to his feet.

"You plan good," he says heavily. "You plan . . . very . . . good—for *you*. You Zhumanor catch me, catch two ships. Very good for you. But I think, no!"

With a sudden uncoiling movement he has grabbed Shara around the neck and next instant is holding a small weapon to her head.

"You . . . now . . . go . . . in . . . sleep-boxes. Yes! You think you catch me. I catch you. You go to Zieltan!"

In the astounded silence, Zillanoy cries, "No! What for, this?" Then she switches to Ziellan and fires protests at Krimheen.

"Oh, by the All!" exclaims Dinger disgustedly.

A stunner has leapt into Captain Asch's fist. But Krimheen has Shara over his front, covering him. No attempt at a shootout will work, with that thing at Shara's head. Even if they could take over the warship from him, it's out of fuel. And his relief ship is near. They can't get away.

Sick at heart, blazingly angry with himself for having been fooled, Asch tries to think coolly. Their whole effort has failed—the big alien captain hasn't changed his mind-set. He still believes they may be some kind of Black Worlds operation. Even if he has some doubts, they only strengthen his intention to get the Humans back to Zieltan, where all can be straightened out—under Ziello control.

And that would mean years of imprisonment, of interrogation; chances are they'd never see home again. Neither he nor the others will endure that. Well, they have the means, the means of desperation, to avoid it. He tongues the lethal little fake tooth. Has it really come to this?

Once they consent to go in the sleep-chests, they're helpless. They'll wake up in Zieltan, under guard. And *Rift-Runner* has no fuel; there's no hope of escape in her. Which means, no hope.

And worse—when the Federation gets here and finds everyone gone, they'll assume he was destroyed or taken. Which is true—they *are* taken. The Fed will assume that the Ziellor are at war with them up here, in addition to the shootings out east. So the Fed will arm, and think about retaliation. . . . Has *Rift-Runner* started Galactic war? It looks like it.

What can he do? What can he do, but talk as long as he can?—to this obtusely suspicious military alien. Talk that's already failed once.

If it fails again, there's nothing to do but bite down on the deadly little thing in their jaws.

As these thoughts race through Asch's head, Krimheen is saying: "I want guns. Zillanoy!"

Zilla is staring at the scene, eye wide with astonishment and dismay. Now she starts to protest in Ziellan, but the big alien tightens his grip so that Shara involuntarily yelps, gasping for air against his powerful lower arm.

"No! No!" Zilla cries. Krimheen hisses something at her in Ziellan and tightens his grip still more. Reluctantly, Zilla goes to Asch, holding out her hand. He gives her the weapon.

"Two more," says Krimheen. Dingañar and Torrane surrender their stunners.

"Now! You go in sleep-boxes! Go, *na* I kill this one. Finish with Zhuman thing!"

"Don't . . . let him . . . blackmail you," Shara gasps. "I'll die . . . first."

"No talk!" snaps Krimheen. "Go!"

But Asch says gently, "No heroics yet, Lieutenant Sharana. Krimheen! I no go. You want kill me? What good this?"

"I won't go, either," says Dinger, and Torrane says, "No."

"Go!" Krimheen tightens his grip until Shara cries out again.

"Captain Krimheen," says Asch desperately, "you no know Yoomans. We want die, we die. If you do bad things, we die. You have four dead Yoomans, one small ship—Federation give you ship same that—what good? If you do bad thing Shara, she die. Why you do bad thing? We saved your cursed lives—we help you no die, we give you all our CO two. Why you make war?"

Krimheen only blinks a couple of times, as if a fly were bothering him. Zilla chatters at him. Incongruously, he has to take a sniff of breath from the Human tumbler he holds in his upper hand.

"So die," he says. But not, Asch thinks, with full conviction.

Just then Dinger gives an exclamation.

"Look at Malloreen, hey!" and runs to the well beside Krimheen and Shara.

All turn to see. Malloreen is moving, is propping himself up on an elbow. Dinger puts his stethoscope to the young alien's chest and whistles. "By the gods—his heart's compensated! It's almost steady."

He looks up at Krimheen and Shara. She has taken advantage of the distraction to get a hand behind Krimheen's arm and is trying to look down at Malloreen.

Dinger holds out the stethoscope. "Here, Captain Krimheen, take a listen. His heart is good . . . I think I give one more heart-thing. What you think?"

Krimheen takes the instrument and bends low over Malloreen, ignoring that he has crumpled Shara. Dinger holds the pick-up to the patient's chest; Krimheen listens intently. Then he straightens up—Shara scrambling with him—and says as if to himself, "Is good." He looks down at Malloreen and says something more in Ziellan; an unmistakable softening of his features, almost a smile, is seen by all. Either this alien captain is deeply involved with his crew, or Malloreen means something special to him, Asch thinks.

As Krimheen turns to go back to his command post, he nearly trips over a small figure on the floor by his feet. It's Tomlo.

"No fight!" it pleads. "No fight. Is good peopre. No kill."

Krimheen addresses it sharply in Ziellan, but the little creature persists. "Tomlo unne'stan' fight!" it sobs. "Fight bad."

Zilla draws it away gently and returns to help Dinger administer another tab of digitalis to Malloreen. Malloreen gasps out what seems to be a question. They catch the word "Zhumanor."

Shara, from Krimheen's grip, suddenly speaks up. "No Zhumanor! We Yoomans."

Krimheen grunts angrily, feeling control of the confrontation slipping away. "Yoomanor—Zhumanor," he says. "You look same Zhuman, you talk same Zhuman, you smell same Zhuman, you have wa-teh same Zhuman—"

"No!" Shara interrupts him, twisting around. "Maybe we look Zhuman, talk Zhuman, maybe we have water in us—but we no *smell* same Zhuman! Zhumanor smell bad!" She looks up at her big captor with the hint of a mischievous smile.

"Talk finish!" Exasperated, Krimheen regains his armhold on her neck with a jolt that sends her lower jaw upward. There's an audible click of teeth.

"Now—" begins Krimheen, but breaks off as he sees the intensity with which the others are staring at the woman in his arm. He looks down, too, as a great shudder racks her from feet to shoulders. Her head droops sideways. "Uh-h-h," she sighs—a strange, mournful sound. Krimheen loosens his arm-grip. Unsupported, Shara crumples to the floor at his feet.

One last shudder convulses her, so that she lies supine. A trace of vomit bubbles from her mouth.

"Oh, my gods—you've killed her!" Dinger cries, and dives down on the floor by her, his head on her chest.

Torrane has drawn closer to Zilla, who is staring horrified. "Sh-she *dead?*" Torrane nods and opens his mouth to say more, when Captain Asch's voice cuts him off.

Under his shock and grief, Asch has been thinking hard. "There will be no explications," he says sharply, choosing the word with care. "This is a terrible happening. But Shara would want it to count for something, she knew the stakes are peace or an unspeakable war. . . . Captain Krimheen: I told you—I talk you—you no know Yoomans. I talk you, no do bad thing Shara, she die. Now you see Yoomans no Zhumanor? We help you sick friend"—Asch points to Malloreen, who is gazing at the scene with his large, uncomprehending eye. "Why you kill our friend?"

As he says this, the sight of the figure on the floor, and his own past tense for one who a moment before had been a living, irrepressibly merry girl, chokes him up. Through blurred eyes he sees that Krimheen looks a shade uncertain. Good. "Zilla," he asks, "you have word for *accident?* Thing that come when no want?"

Confusedly, sniffling, she checks her Human talkie-book. "Mis-stake? I think is mis-stake?"

"I no want kill . . . this Yooman," Krimheen says reluctantly.

"Right. And you no want kill us, I think? . . . Zilla, tell him this is what will come to us all if he do same he do. And then come war with Federation. Bad war. What he do now very big. He must think big. Tell him he must come to Federation with us, talk what mistake he do. Then will be no war—will come peace!"

"Good." Zilla takes a sniff of her $CO_2$ and addresses the big captain squarely, in resonant-sounding Ziellan phrases. He seems to listen, but at her repeated mention of the Federation, he suddenly bursts out:

"Feder-ation! Feder-ation! I no see Feder-ation, I no *coluf* Federation! I no know Feder-ation. I think you Feder-ation big *Magglegg!* I see four —three—Zhumanor, *na* Yoomanss. I think you want I go Zhumanor base. Feder-ation, I sick!"

Asch holds his temper with all his might. "No. Federation is big, is same like Allowateera. No make one more mis-stake! Federation make bad war, have big ships. But Federation no want war. Federation want make friends."

Krimheen seems to think this over, glancing down at where Dinger and Torrane sit guard beside Shara's composed body, glancing at Malloreen.

"What is *friends?*"

"I know," says Zillanoy. Asch silently thanks whoever made up the talking-books that the word is there for Zilla to explain. It is becoming unhappily clear to him that even if Krimheen assents to their plan, in the immediate influence of Shara's sudden death, his consent could come unstuck again at any moment. When his ship is here, say; and at every step of the way, he will have to be repersuaded all over again. Oh, if only the Federation— But don't think of it. It's up to him alone.

"Be friends," he goes on when Zilla has finished. "Friends is this: When we come here, you sick. You go die. Very easy, very quick we kill you, take ship. But do we catch you, kill you? Do we do bad things? No! Same friends, we do all good things. We work help you no die. Look Malloreen! We do same friends, we do same Federation. Now I want you come Federation, say hello, look we good people. You talk of Zieltan, make friends. That's all, no more! Oh, don't you see, you obdurate ape—we *must* be friends or there will come a terrible war! Long, long war, everybody die. Zieltan die. . . . We must trust one another—trust one another or die!"

Krimheen says nothing for a moment. Then he asks, "What this, *trust?*"

"*Trust* . . ." Asch has the feeling that deeper and deeper waters are swirling around him, while he is armed only with a leaden splinter. Vaguely he realizes that Krimheen now has his weapon pointed, as if absentmindedly, at his head. No matter. "*Trust* is—I know you talk true, you know I talk true. And I know you want do good things, you know I want do good things. . . . Look! I show you *trust:* If you say you go FedBase, we go in sleep-boxes. I *trust* you talk true. See?"

Krimheen is frowning hard. "You do . . . this? You go in sleep-boxes?"

Asch holds up a hand. "If—*if* you say you go to FedBase. We trust you talk true, no go to Zieltan. We go in boxes. What you say?"

Is he crazy? Asch wonders. To venture all on this alien mind? Well, if it fails, they can always use the damned little kill-teeth. He stares hard, trying to read Krimheen—but he can't; he knows only that the alien has turned on them once, after they had saved his life.

Krimheen stares back, steel-hard. Then he glances at Malloreen, and his face changes slightly, in what manner Asch can't tell.

"Fede—" Krimheen starts.

But what he is about to say is never known.

A cutting flash hits the view-ports, and their artificial gravity judders. All turn to look outside.

Floating an indeterminate distance away is a shiny metal sphere. A few antennalike devices protrude from it. As they stare at it, the callers in both ships crackle and boom.

Krimheen quickly turns his volume down, still staring at the strange vessel.

"Hello?" says a Federation voice. It sounds young and excited. "Ah, *Rift-Runner* there? Federation Experimental FTL craft XK-five calling *Rift-Runner*. They tell me you need a lift."

The voice becomes even more informal. "How about thirty-six hours round trip? I had breakfast at Base this morning. Ah, and who's your big friends?"

" 'FTL'!" mutters Dinger, quick on the uptake. "By the All! We've been away a long time. . . . Oh, Shara, Shara . . . Poor kid."

Before either of the astonished captains can reply, the voice gives a muffled squawk. "Hey—what's happening to me? I feel like I'm growing extra arms—and a tail?"

Captain Asch draws a deep relieved breath for the first time in a long while.

"I think," he says to Krimheen, "I think now you see our Federation!"

"And that was about it," FedBase Executive Jonne tells her visitor, who has been out of touch for many years.

"We ferried them here in three trips, after Krimheen's fuel ship had arrived and docked on and got their air-plant started again. Captain Krimheen woke up his second-in-command and instructed him to proceed here, emitting a signal so they could be rendezvoused en route. And after he'd had a good look at Nine hundred, he asked to go back to his ship so he could use their FTL communications to contact his fleet out east and get the attacks on Federation colonies called off.

"Of course it was horribly sad about Shara, dying like that so close to home. But you know, we discovered that Captain K. felt genuinely bad about it? At the services, he suddenly unpinned a big decoration from his chest and laid it on her hands. Such a good gesture—and suitable, too; her death certainly played a part in convincing him that we weren't Black Worlders, and averting war between his people and ours.

"Of course we turned ourselves inside out to give Krimheen a royal-type reception. And the hospital staff was ready with a big roll-bed for Malloreen. He got steadily better, such a nice young person. What an uncanny thing, that digitalis worked on his heart! But apparently the neuroelectrical aspect of their bodies is quite similar to ours. The rest is wildly different from anything on this side of the Rift. A wonderful mystery, life forming in gas and dust-clouds.

"Their reproductive system is another wonderful mystery, too. At first we thought we were in for trouble—the little Murnoo, Tomlo, dropped dead at the main entrance! But this seemed to be accepted as a form of their Ritual; they gathered 'round and sang a long song of Thanksgiving for peace, in which I may say we all joined.

"Their housing here was no problem, once the nutrition staff had learned to synthesize palatable food. Of course we had their quarters air-conditioned to the right CO two, and dry, with plenty of spare tanks. And we were working on a portable tank, until we found that they really were quite happy strolling 'round with their tumblers of dry ice. So we just assigned a courier to trail after them with a load of the stuff. We also assigned a nice girl as official translator—what a loss, Shara!—and she soon got on wonderfully with them both. Would you believe Captain K. turned out to have a keen sense of humor?

"It was his reception here that decided him to take a flying tour of the Fed via our FTL ship, while his warships proceeded straight out east. Zilla asked for Lieutenant Torrane to come along and help finish a Ziello-Human handbook they're working up. From what I hear, we may be having our first Ziello-Human romance. And the translator went along, too. I'm getting them back, though; for chauvinistic reasons I kind of want Nine hundred to keep its lead as a center of Ziello expertise. . . ."

Exec chuckles at her own pride and picks up the bottle of Eldorado VIII wine they have been sharing.

"Let me refill you. And have another of these—" She offers a plate of morpleases.

"The trade prospects look very good, don't they?" her visitor asks. "You say they don't have video technology. But they have, I gather, artificial gravity and FTL communication, which seems to be based on a different principle than our *c*-skip drive ships. . . . Of course, the *c*-skip costs an arm and a leg to operate; after the first glory period of damn-the-costs flying, Central is making it clear it has to be reserved for bona fide life-or-death emergencies. Unless the Ziello can cheapen it, they'll have to do the same thing."

"Of course. But the thing is, with both FTL transmission *and* transport, the chances of war by inadvertence go down exponentially. . . . My gods! What a blessing!"

Exec leans back and focuses her grave eyes on her visitor.

"Do you realize how close we came to that? If it hadn't been for a dozen tiny things—blind chances—we'd be at war with the Harmony right now. We were closer even than Captain Asch knew; he knew that Humans had committed atrocities on those Ziello allies, but he wasn't aware that Ziello ships were already blowing up Federation planets in Sector Three hundred. If nothing had happened to change our views of each other, we'd have blundered into full-scale war."

She sighs, sips her wine.

"The thing that impresses me—hells, *scares* my hair up—is the *pre-cariousness* of the whole great balance. If any one of a host of little things had gone differently—a rain shower not coming just when it did, say—we'd have had war.

"Only the whim of that alien girl to study the Black Worlders' language, and her return when she did, made everything that followed possible. It's as if the great issue rode, from moment to moment, on the tiny acts of individuals. Even that strange little being Tomlo carried the whole weight in its feathery paws when it bravely decided to call for help to the enemy, and let them in.

"Even poor Kathy's death played a part, by alerting Zilla to them. And Shara's putting in that fatal tooth, that made her die so easily, that gave Krimheen pause. We'll have to disabuse him about that one day, by the way. . . .

"And if Malloreen hadn't been who he was—Krimheen's sister's son, the only child in their family; sheer luck that he was on that ship. And sheer luck that a plant-derived chemical the Ziello couldn't possibly have worked on him. And sheer luck again that the FTL ship was ready—"

"But your moving stars and suns to get the use of it," her visitor puts in. "That wasn't exactly chance."

"Yes, I expect I was one of the tiny individuals for a moment . . . Oh, so many crucial little happenings tipped the enormous scales." She sighs again, more relaxed than she has been for many years, and smiles.

"And never forgetting the sheer indomitable will of Captain Asch, arguing over and over with a bull-headed, patriotic battleship commander with planet-breakers in his racks, and what he thought was the enemy in sight. . . . I drink to that, to a man who rose to the challenge of defining 'trust' in pidgin-Galactic—with a gun at his head!"

# At the Library _____

**I**t is some days later when the two Comeno students approach the pool where the chief librarian's deputy is testing some waterproof cassettes for aquatic clients.

"Oh, I'm so sorry," she says through the speaker in the pool wall, "Myr Blue is on detached duty this ten-day. He's doing an appraisal on a collection of antiques. If you'd care to leave a note for him, you'll find a recorder marked with his name at the end of the main counter. And his in-box is there."

They thank her and repair to the main front desk. The tall Comeno boy lays their sheaf of documents carefully in a bin marked "Moa Blue —Special." The recorder is beside it.

"You talk," the boy says. "You know I always freeze up."

"And I go too fast." She laughs. "All right, I'll try." She lifts the small mike. "Myr Blue? Myr Moa Blue? Greetings! This is from your two Comenor, Gilderlee and Rosavan. We've just brought back your third tale and we're so sorry you're away. But we can tell you, it certainly *was* a treat—both historically and personally. It gave me, that's Rosie, real cold shivers—my folks were on one of those colonies that were barely rescued from the Black Worlders in time! And historically it's magnificent—imagine that little ship, *Rift-Runner*, just bouncing in and landing in the middle of the whole great Harmony out to kill Humans. And everything being so complacent and confused that they bounced right out again! And we *loved* Zilla. And it was thrilling—actually hearing the splashing and shouts when the Human girl Kathy was dying, so many centuries ago. And the storm, and the poor Humans running—do you know, I took quite an aversion to Captain Krimheen after a bit. Although he was doing what he thought was best for his side; he was just so *stubborn,* wasn't he? Oh, dear, all this sounds so trivial, the truth is I'm vibrating like a school kid from the excitement, and I haven't settled down to serious thought about all the implications.

"Well, I won't burden you with more of these enthusiasms, but just join with Gildy in one great big final thank-you. We'll drop in to say hello one day soon if you wouldn't mind.

"And one thing more, if you wouldn't mind—you see, we have this kind of diplomatic problem as to the dedication of our joint paper. It's customary to dedicate to one's tutor, you know—but Gildy and I have different tutors, and we've both had special help from others, too. So we thought we'd solve the whole thing by treating them all in a paragraph, and making the official dedication to you, Myr-and-Doctor Moa Blue, for very special enlightenment. Would you mind? It would fix everything, and no one could object, and—and we'd just love to. Plus, it's true—you gave us help no one else could. And you didn't need to, you could have told us to go look things up ourselves. And then we wouldn't have found a thing. I do hope you'll say yes; we'll drop by for your answer after you're home again.

"Now here's Gildy to say thanks and good-bye, too—Gildy, go *on*— with love, Rosavan."